# The Lights of Alexandria

A Conjurer of Rhodes, Book 2

**Jack Massa**

Published by
Triskelion Books
www.triskelionbooks.com

The Lights of Alexandria
Copyright © 2019 by Jack Massa

ISBN 978-0-9976461-4-6

Print Edition published January, 2019

Cover design by Mirna Gilman, BooksGoSocial.

## Dedication

## to Jaime Henriquez

Sometimes it is Greek to me,
but not to him.

But, in addition [to large Greek and Jewish communities], Alexandria housed tens of thousands of Egyptians and people of innumerable other races. For it was an immensely cosmopolitan centre, the first and greatest universal city ... Alexandria was a place that beckoned to young and lively people of all races and creeds, to come and join its seething and infinitely varied activities.

— Michael Grant
*From Alexander to Cleopatra,*
*The Hellenistic World*

How can magical workings be explained? By sympathy, by the fact that in Nature there is an attraction of like things and an opposition of unlike things, and by the multitudes of forces that converge in all living beings.

The true magic is Love and Strife in the Universe. True magicians simply uncover these forces and turn them to their use.

—Plotinus
*The Enneads*
3rd Century CE

# The Story So Far

*As told in A Conjurer of Rhodes, Book 1, The Mazes of Magic.*

In the century following the time of Alexander the Great, a young Greek named Korax finds himself a slave in Egypt. Worse, his mind is beset with periods of madness and his memories confused and scattered.

Purchased by the High Priest Harnouphis, Korax is given an Egyptian name and transported to a great temple in the city of Memphis, on the Nile. He is put into service as a translator and scribe. But Harnouphis also has another plan: to tap the young Greek's extraordinary talent as a seer to advance his own ambitions.

As Korax's wits and memories return, he forges a plan of his own: to learn enough magic to escape from Egypt and return to his home island of Rhodes. A divine vision guides him—the Goddess Isis promising a chance at freedom if he is willing to serve the gods.

Initiated into the Egyptian Mysteries, Korax begins the slow process of learning the divine arts of magic. Harnouphis, meantime, has made alliance with the dark god Set. He plans to use Set's power to betray his fellow priests and make himself supreme ruler of the temple. Guided by Isis and then by Thoth, the god of magic, Korax foils the plot, kills Harnouphis, and flees north toward Alexandria.

## Fictional Characters (in order of Appearance)

Korax - A Greek, native of the island of Rhodes. Lately a temple slave and initiate of the Egyptian Mysteries. Traveling under the name Astrametheus.

Metiochus - Assistant headmaster at the Museum in Alexandria.

Miriam - A young Jewish woman and fledgling magician.

Zakur - Father to Miriam. A scholar and elder of the Jewish community.

Krateros- High Priest of Pan and leader of the society of magicians.

Drakas - Marshal of the Royal Guard. Loyal to Ptolemy.

Prodotus - Ambassador to the court of Ptolemy from the neighboring land of Cyrenaica.

Manetho - An Egyptian priest and magician.

Manolis - Ambassador from Carthage.

Kalyssa - Wife to Manolis. Priestess of Tanit and member of the society of magicians.

Peristeria - Priestess of Tyre and magician. Friend to Miriam and Kalyssa.

Leukon - Celtic warrior of the Trocmi people, a mercenary soldier.

## Historical Personages (appearing or mentioned)

Zenodotus of Ephesus - Head of the Library of Alexandria.

Timon of Phlius - Philosopher of the Skeptic school.

Philetas of Cos - Scholar and poet, author of epigrams.

Theocritus of Syracuse - Poet, author of idylls.

Callimachus of Cyrene - Poet, author of hymns and epigrams. Friend to the King.

Herodas of Cos - Poet, author of mimes.

Lycophron of Chalcis - Tragic poet, and grammarian.

Asclepiades of Samos - Poet, author of lyrics and epigrams.

Ptolemy II - Macedonian King of Egypt. Patron of the arts and sciences.

Arsinoe - Sister and Queen to Ptolemy.

Magus - Ptolemy's half-brother. King of Cyrenaica, to the east of Ptolemy's Egypt.

Antiochus, son of Seleucus - Greek king of western Asia. Ptolemy's rival.

Antigonus Gonatas - King of Macedonia. Also a rival.

Bilistiche - Noblewoman of Ptolemy's court. Owner of race horses.

Aristarchus of Samos - Astronomer and mathematician.

Ctesibius - Engineer and inventor of water clocks.

Archimedes of Syracuse - Mathematician, engineer, and inventor.

Herophilus - Physician and anatomist.

Polyeuktos of Athens - Sculptor.

Apollonius of Rhodes - Poet, author of epics.

# Chapter One

On a clear spring morning in the twelfth year of the reign of Ptolemy II, a young man sat on the jetty at Pharos Island gazing out to sea. Behind him the Great Harbor of Alexandria swarmed with trading ships from many ports. Along the harbor's curving rim stretched white quays and red-roofed warehouses. Adjacent to the docks, a straight causeway a mile long linked Pharos Island to the city. To the young man's right, an enormous three-tiered tower loomed against the cloudless blue sky—the wondrously tall Pharos Lighthouse.

But Korax kept his eyes fixed on the surging whitecaps. Out there beyond the horizon lay Rhodes. He could almost touch the island with his mind, almost see the temples, the noble houses on the hillside, the golden Colossus of Helios striding over all. Almost, but not quite. A yearning to return home stung his heart. He wondered again if he was making the right decision.

Three months in the town of Naukratis had effectively transformed him back from an Egyptian scribe to a Greek gentleman. Naukratis was an old trading city on the Delta, founded by Greek merchants centuries ago. Within its walls stood a gymnasium, baths, temples and guild halls dedicated to the Olympians. The money from the Mansion of Ptah had served Korax well. His chubby belly was gone, and lean new muscle armored his limbs and torso. He wore a linen *chiton*, dyed sea blue, a gray *chlamys* with a fashionable pattern of spirals and stars on its edges. He carried a short sword and a beaded satchel slung over his shoulder. His hair, grown in thick and black, was tied with a scarlet ribbon.

Plenty of silver still jangled in his purse. If he chose, he could go this morning and buy passage on a freighter bound for the

Aegean. Standing, he stared back across the harbor, letting that notion run through his thoughts.

*No. He was not ready.*

Some deep-seated instinct warned him against going home. More perplexing, the inner warning was wrapped in layers of fear. His memories of Rhodes were still incomplete, perhaps unreliable. He had grown up in a merchant family, studied at a fine academy, served his first summer as a naval cadet—all that seemed clear enough. But then, he believed, he had committed a foolish crime, a grave impiety. He had conjured the God Dionysus to help him win a singing contest and humiliate a group of bullies. Next day, those same young men had caught him in the street and—he did believe—beaten him to death. Only the witchcraft of his mother, Anticleia, had brought him back from the shore of the River Styx.

That was the last clear memory he possessed. His mind, he surmised, had been damaged in that passage out of the Underworld. For some time he had been mad. The tale of how he had ended up in Egypt, and a slave, was a torpid mass of darkness and confusion.

At times, he even wondered if *all* of his memories might be false, delusions spawned in his time of madness. Perhaps that was why he feared returning to Rhodes, feared learning that the identity he remembered had never existed.

*No. He refused to believe it.* He knew at the core of his soul that he was Korax, son of Leontes.

And yet, the idea of going home to prove it once and for all filled him with unreasoning panic.

More than once, he had discussed this painful dilemma with Thoth-Hermes. But his magical ally gave no helpful reply. Korax had stirred the scrying bowl, seeking to discover what had occurred in the months he could not remember. Had he indeed been kidnapped by Cretan pirates, as he suspected? But if so, why had a ransom never arrived to set him free? But all his attempts at scrying had yielded only dim pictures that dissolved before he could grasp their meaning.

On first arriving in Naukratis, Korax had written to the parents he remembered, saying he had won his freedom after two years of enslavement. Yesterday, on reaching Alexandria, he had dispatched a second letter—walking the docks until finding a ship's captain whose route would take him to Rhodos, capital city of Rhodes. In the note, Korax gave his father and mother the name of the inn where he was staying and begged them to write in reply. He informed them he planned to stay in Alexandria for a time, to study.

Of course, the peculiar nature of his intended studies was something he did not divulge. His father would never understand. And while his mother might comprehend his magical ambitions, she too would probably disapprove. Besides, it was better not to discuss such matters in a letter that could possibly go astray.

Korax's chest rose as he sucked in the tingling sea air. Across the water to the East, along the promontory known as the Lochias, spread the grand halls and gardens of Ptolemy's royal palace. Beyond those grounds stood the famous Museum and Library. The greatest scholars, philosophers, and poets in the world dwelled in Alexandria. Intellectual men and women of every civilized land flocked here to teach and learn. It was said that all the knowledge in the world had been gathered in this place.

Surely that must include knowledge of magic.

After much pondering and brooding, Korax had decided on this course: He would spend some months in Alexandria, seek to master the occult gifts given him by the gods. Perhaps, when he had realized his potential as a magician, he would feel ready to return to Rhodes. His strange and winding fate had brought him to this most wondrous of cities. There must be a purpose in that, an opportunity to be seized.

Or was he simply avoiding the problem, unwilling to face his bottomless fears? As a young man he had been so decisive, even reckless. Was it the frustrations of slavery or the slow, painstaking study of the Mysteries that had made him so reflective? Perhaps he was being overcautious ...

*Enough!* Korax thrust the painful enigma from his mind. He straightened his cloak and started back along the jetty, stepping carefully over the slick, black boulders.

He returned the way he had come that morning, through Pharos Town and across the causeway. The wide, smooth road was crowded now with traffic—merchants and porters leading donkey carts, pilgrims bound for the Temple of Poseidon, tourists come to visit the Lighthouse.

Seen from the causeway, the grand capital spread before him in a sweeping view of granite, alabaster, and marble. Alexander himself had founded the city, on a sandy peninsula at the northwest tip of the Delta. According to the legend, he had traced its layout in the sand, setting down the broad avenues at such an angle that the inhabitants would always enjoy the fresh breezes of the sea. From the beginning, the Greek capital had stood apart from the land it ruled. So it was known across the world as Alexandria *by* Egypt.

Reaching the mainland, Korax crossed the busy docks and passed through imposing, iron-ribbed gates. He ventured down the main avenue, the Street of the Soma, with its twin rows of sphinxes and shady colonnades. A half-mile's walk brought him to the center of the city, where the street crossed the famous Canopic Way.

Here, across the square from the gold-encrusted Tomb of Alexander, a new temple was rising amid the bustling of workmen and unending din of stone-cutters' chisels. Korax had learned that the temple would honor Arsinoe-Aphrodite, Ptolemy's sister-queen in her deified persona. Judging by the width of the stepped platform and the number of fluted pillars already partially raised, the finished shrine would approach the scale of the huge Greek temples of Ionia.

Korax turned east onto the Canopic Way, a road so wide that ten chariots could easily ride abreast. The steps and stoas of public buildings stood along the road, interspersed with rolling lawns, heroic bronze statues, and dappled groves.

The sun hovered near zenith when he reached the Museum. Monumental steps ascended to a high, Corinthian portico. On the entablature above, a painted frieze depicted Zeus with his nine daughters, the goddesses of all the arts. Korax admired the sculpture for a long moment before trotting nimbly up the steps.

Through paneled bronze doors he entered a *cella* built, as in a typical Greek temple, with columns along three sides. Statues of the Muses occupied niches along the walls. A throng of scholars and students milled about, some holding scrolls or writing tablets, others gesturing in animated conversation. Korax wove his way across the mosaic floor, tapping on shoulders and asking for directions. Soon he was pointed down a narrow staircase and found the offices of the schoolmaster.

A white-haired clerk squinted up at him from behind a writing table. Korax bowed and introduced himself.

"Greetings, sir. I am Astrametheus, a young man of good family from Hermopolis. I wish to enroll as a student." He drew three letters of introduction from his satchel and handed them to the clerk.

Since arriving at Naukratis, Korax had deemed it prudent to assume a new identity. The possibility remained that his name could be matched to that of a runaway slave. His experience preparing official documents made it simple to forge the necessary letters, just as his fluency in Egyptian and Greek made it easy to play the role of a young Greek gentleman from a town on the Upper Nile.

The old clerk scrutinized the letters, then rose and carried them off to an inner hallway. In a few minutes he returned beside another man, a balding scholar with wrinkled forehead, hooked nose, and trenchant eyes.

"Welcome, young Astrametheus," the scholar said with enthusiasm. "Welcome to the Temple of the Muses. I am Metiochus, assistant headmaster and priest to the divine sisters who inspire the mind."

"An honor, sir." Korax nodded with polite solemnity.

Metiochus held the letters in his hand. "I learn that you wish to study with us. You could not have found a better institution. The greatest scholars in the world call the Museum their home."

"Such is my understanding," Korax avowed.

Metiochus ushered him aside, while the old clerk returned to his duties.

"As you may know, all of our faculty are supported by royal stipend. You are free to attend their public lectures, as you are to read in the Library, all at no cost to you—by the generosity of their Divine Majesties. However, most men of rank and quality desire more personal instruction. For that, you may enroll as a student and have continual access to the company and discourse of our eminent scholars. This privilege is available for a modest annual tuition, plus room and board, should you choose to live in our communal halls, as most students do."

"Funds will not be a problem." Korax hefted his purse meaningfully. "I can pay coin in advance, or if you prefer, establish a letter of credit at the Royal Bank."

"Of course, of course." Metiochus waved the trifling matter aside. "We can arrange the details later. I see in your letters that you are keen to study both music and philosophy."

Korax nodded. "My interest in the former is broad. I look forward to hearing recitals of every form and period. My requirements in terms of philosophy however are specific—you might even think them eccentric. Before I commit to enrollment, I wish to learn about the different schools and methods taught here."

"Oh, you will not find us lacking on that score! King Ptolemy's largesse has attracted leading exponents of every school. But there's no need to rely on my poor descriptions. I will take you on a tour of the grounds, where we will doubtless encounter lectures in progress."

"An admirable suggestion," Korax agreed.

Taking Korax's arm with the familiar air of a gentleman with a protégé, Metiochus conducted him from the office. They walked down a corridor painted with musicians and nymphs in soft pastels.

"I believe you might be our first pupil from Hermopolis," the schoolmaster said. "I did not know there was much of a Greek population there."

"A small but growing community," Korax answered. "A number of officers, my father among them, settled as landowners by the grace of the king. Our gymnasium is respectable, though our supply of books is paltry I fear."

"Then you will relish your time in Alexandria, my young friend. It is the king's avowed purpose to collect at least one edition of every book ever written into his great Library."

They emerged into sparkling daylight on a vast, crescent-shaped colonnade. Below the steps spread terraced courts arrayed with fountains and flowerbeds. A little distance along the porch, a lecture was in progress. A gray-bearded teacher, tall and ascetic, discoursed to a circle of young men and women.

"He is Echedorus," Metiochus murmured. "Taught by Zeno himself at the Stoa of Athens."

From his school days in Rhodes, Korax recalled the Stoic doctrines. "They believe, do they not, that the Universe is the manifestation of a World Soul, a divine fiery breath that permeates all things?"

The assistant headmaster tilted back in surprise. "Eh, yes, that does describe their views regarding divinity."

"I see much to recommend it. However, I do not think their school offers the practical teachings I seek."

"Hmm." Metiochus evinced a tinge of disappointment. "Well, no matter. There are others to choose from."

They descended the steps and strolled into the vast court. Encountering other lectures in progress, they stopped each time to listen. Korax heard discourses from an Epicurean, an Aristotelian, and a Platonist. At each stop, after listening for a short time, he shook his head and prodded the schoolmaster to walk on.

"I have some familiarity with all of these philosophies," he said. "But I fear that none of them offer the metaphysical instruction I seek."

"For a young man from the provinces you seem exceptionally well-informed," Metiochus remarked with a frown. "I'm afraid our list of options grows short. We do have itinerant Cynics and Skeptics give lectures on occasion, but none in permanent residence. They tend to be disreputable, unwashed fellows. There was one who came through a couple of years ago, Timon of Phlius by name. While at the podium he grossly insulted the Museum and the faculty. He will not be invited back, I promise you."

"I do not think those lecturers would answer my needs in any case," Korax said. "I was hoping to learn the practices of the sage

Pythagoras, or perhaps applications of the wisdom of Empedocles, who first described the Four Elements and the opposing forces of Love and Strife that spur their eternal motion."

"Mysticism! Now you do sound provincial, young man. I'm afraid the philosophers you cite are not highly-regarded in modern times."

Korax knew this already. "And yet, I am assured the wisdom of all the world flourishes in Alexandria."

"Well, that is true enough." The scholar's reply held an edge of wariness.

"What is it you are not telling me?" Korax demanded. Into his voice crept the power of command taught him by Thoth: "My quest for this wisdom must be satisfied."

"Well ... There is another school," Metiochus stammered. "Or at least, a group of scholars, if that name can be applied. They are not at all affiliated with the Museum, you understand." He lowered his voice confidingly. "They are said to admit students of all races, and to teach an amalgam of curious rites. Not entirely reputable, to be sure. I could not, in good conscience, direct a young Greek gentleman to them."

"I understand your reservations. Yet I must insist. I am determined to find and interview these scholars."

"Well, they don't have an institution," Metiochus answered with exasperation. "I can only tell you that they are said to congregate sometimes at the Paneum."

# Chapter Two

The Paneum was a curious, tall, circular structure, resembling nothing so much as a gigantic pinecone. Neither Greek nor Egyptian in design, its architecture echoed certain hive-like mounds known in Ionia and the islands of the North Aegean—shrines dedicated to the worship of archaic gods. But the structure raised by the Ptolemies was far grander than those. A colossal mound of gray and white stones, it towered nearly eighty feet against the limpid Alexandrian sky.

Korax arrived there in mid-afternoon, having retraced his steps along the Canopic Way and trekked past the Tomb of Alexander. The grounds of the Paneum bordered on the winding streets of Rhakotis, the old Egyptian quarter. A rugged stone fence enclosed a park of sloping lawns dotted with stands of cypress and sycamore, tiny shrines, and grottos. At the center, a spiral ramp led up the outside of the giant mound, rising to the top where priests conducted the rites of Pan.

The summit afforded a spectacular view of the city and the sea, and had become an attraction for tourists and idlers. Wandering across the grounds, Korax passed many who fit that description, but spotted no one who seemed to have official connection with the temple. He entered a small columned pavilion near the base of the mound but found it empty save for a granite statue of Pan, laughing deviously over his pipes.

Pan, the shepherd's god, was a special patron of Ptolemy's Macedonian ancestors. The Paneum, with its artificial mountain wilderness, reflected that overt aspect of the god. But Korax understood that in philosophic circles Pan carried another, esoteric meaning. He embodied the concept of all the gods or, alternately, the God of All. It stood to reason that a society of scholars pursuing the Mysteries would choose his temple as their meeting place.

But how to find them? The grinning face of the god offered no clue.

Korax set a coin at the feet of the statue. He uttered a brief prayer, asking Pan for his blessing and guidance. Then he returned to the daylight.

Lacking another plan, he started to climb the spiraling path of the mound. From the base he could see that it circled seven times before reaching the summit. In places among the boulders, grass and shrubs clung to the steep slope, adding to the naturalistic effect. Korax half-expected a mountain goat to come romping down the trail.

He had completed the fourth circuit when he passed a narrow recess. Under a rock lintel, a small door of blackened bronze led inside the mound. Korax surmised the door must lead to a storage vault, perhaps used for groundskeepers' tools. But an inner prompting tugged him from the path. He stepped down into the recess and tried the door. After a firm shake of the handle, the latch gave and the door creaked open. Cool air flowed from the blackness within. Korax decided to investigate.

A short distance down the passage he faced a wall formed of the same rough boulders as the exterior. But a slender stairway opened to the right. More cool air drifted up the stairs, carrying a veiled scent of perfume or incense.

Korax felt his way along the wall, since the light from the open doorway was lost to him now. The steps curled down, then ended in a corridor with smooth masonry walls. The floor slanted gently upward as the passage turned, mirroring the outer curve of the mound. All was silent.

Korax groped along the tunnel for some time. Then a light appeared ahead, a blurred flickering of candle or lamp. As his vision improved, he strode forward confidently. The light came from a portal of smooth-cut stone. Korax rounded the corner and stopped.

He stood on a gallery that circled the inner core of the mound—an enormous hollow chamber. Spots of daylight shone at the distant pinnacle, enough for him to tell the vast dimensions.

A clay lamp burned on the floor in front of him, set before a balustrade that lined the gallery. On the rail of the balustrade was a cushion, and on the cushion sat a young woman, cross-legged, balanced precariously. Behind her was empty air, with the floor of the chamber far below.

Astonished, Korax examined the woman. Her eyes were closed and her back erect: she sat in trance or deep meditation. She wore pale blue robes and yellow slippers. Her complexion was dark; she seemed Phoenician or Babylonian perhaps. She had narrow shoulders and face, with a high forehead, pointed chin, and tiny mouth. She would not be called beautiful by Greek or Egyptian standards, yet Korax found her appearance compelling. Perhaps it was her pose of meditation, but he sensed intelligence, wisdom, power. Perhaps he sensed a kindred spirit.

Abruptly, her eyes opened. Her shoulders jerked, and for an instant Korax feared she would tumble backward and fall to her death. But her hands shot down and caught the rail. Next moment, she thrust herself off the cushion and landed softly on her feet.

"Who are you? How did you get in here?"

"I apologize. I did not mean to frighten you."

"I am not frightened."

But she took a step back as Korax approached. He peered over the balustrade, glimpsing ramps and galleries at many levels. The drop ended four stories below on a black, circular floor.

"Isn't it dangerous to practice your meditations on such a perch?"

"I know what I am doing." She seemed younger than Korax had thought at first. But now she took the offensive: "Tourists are not allowed in this place."

Korax leaned back, momentarily daunted by her intensity. He leveled his voice: "I am not a tourist, only a humble seeker of wisdom."

The young woman paused. Her eyes seemed to dilate, and she scrutinized him for a long moment. "Humble? I do not think so."

Korax grinned and gave a courteous bow. "Please forgive my abrupt appearance. I am Astrametheus, a son of good family from the town of Hermopolis."

"How did you get in here?"

"Through a door on the outer path. It was unlocked."

"So, is it the custom in Hermopolis for men of good family to invade sacred grounds uninvited?"

"No." Korax smiled again. "Not so far as I know. But I came in answer to an inner call. I've heard that a company of philosophers meets in this place, practitioners of the divine arts. I greatly wish to make their acquaintance."

"To what purpose?"

Korax spread his arms. "To join them perhaps. I have some learning and experience, which I wish to augment."

"Have you indeed? From Hermopolis?"

"Well ... several places. But what of you, young-woman-whose-name-I-do-not-know? Is it the mystic arts of Babylon that teach you to sit in trance over a yawning abyss?"

The corners of her mouth twitched, the start of a smile that she quickly suppressed. "I will take you to Krateros. He will decide if your request merits consideration."

She gathered up her lamp and cushion and indicated for him to follow. They walked along the gallery of the vast, quiet chamber.

"This is truly remarkable," Korax said. "I'll wager not one person in a hundred knows that this structure has a hollow core. It was built by the first Ptolemy, so I understand. Though I do not recall the architect's name."

"Are you planning to write a travel book?" the young woman asked. "Or are you just full of prattle by nature?"

Korax winced at the gibe. "I would much rather hear your story, if you would disclose it. But so far you've not even told me your name."

"I am Miriam, daughter of Zakur."

The names sounded Phoenician or Nabataean perhaps, which would fit with her looks. "And your nationality?" he prompted.

She gave a sidewise glance, disapproving his inquisitiveness. Still, she answered, "I was born in Alexandria. My father's people came from the region of Hebron. We are Jews."

"I see." An Aramaic-speaking people—Korax knew little about them. He seemed to recall they were monotheists, worshippers of some grim, shapeless god. Their priests supposedly possessed ancient texts of powerful magic.

Miriam preceded him down a series of ramps, which connected one gallery to the next. Soon they reached the lowest level, the floor of the great hollow space. Again Korax sniffed traces of incense, more definite now. Their shuffling footsteps on the paving stones made the only noise.

Passing through a portal, they traversed a corridor illuminated by filtered daylight. Before Korax could discern the source of the light, they stepped into an even brighter chamber. It was spacious and furnished with stools, tables, and shelves full of papyrus rolls. A statue of Pan grinned down from a niche in the far wall.

Two men of middle age sat conferring at a table spread with documents. One was dark, solemn, gray-bearded, with forehead and features resembling Miriam's. The other was Greek, likely a

Macedonian—large and broad-headed, with curly brown hair and prominent eyes. Both men frowned when they saw him.

"Miriam, why are you disturbing us?" the graybeard asked. "Who is this person?"

"I am sorry, father," Miriam replied. "This one appeared out of nowhere on the gallery above. He entered through an outer door on the spiral, which he says was unlocked."

"Oh. I was responsible for sealing the doors after the last ritual," Miriam's father commented thoughtfully. "Perhaps I forgot to do that."

The chamber was lit by several large windows in the shape of multi-pointed stars. Yet these windows did not open to the outside. Stepping over to examine one, Korax saw that it contained a large mirror, which reflected daylight from an angled shaft above.

"Most ingenious."

The large Macedonian had stood and was glowering. "Who are you? For what reason do you invade our sanctuary?"

"He says he is called Astrametheus, from Hermopolis," Miriam answered before Korax could speak, "though I'm not sure I believe it. He claims to be a student seeking instruction."

"I am Krateros, high priest of Pan," the large man said. "Is Astrametheus your true name?"

"Well, I have gone by other names." Korax strolled toward the table. "For the moment, Astrametheus is the most prudent to use. I will willingly divulge my other names to you in time, should I find this company trustworthy."

Zakur slapped the tabletop. "You presume too much, young man!"

Korax halted, taken aback by the elder's anger. His pose of bluff self-confidence was being perceived as arrogance and discourtesy. He cleared his throat and gave a formal bow. "Forgive me gentlemen. I presume nothing. I apologize for my unorthodox arrival in this holy place, as I have already apologized to the young lady. I am not in the habit of breaking into temples. But I am in the habit of heeding inner guidance, which has led me to this meeting."

"I see." Krateros appraised him. "Are you an initiate?"

"Yes, of the Egyptian rites."

"Indeed?" Zakur fixed Korax with a dubious, penetrating stare. "A Greek, scarcely past twenty, yet initiated by the Egyptians. You seem to possess an unusual history."

Korax returned the gaze, unabashed.

Krateros noticed the beaded satchel, and his eyes widened as though with an insight. "Perhaps you carry something of value."

Korax pulled the bag from his shoulder. "Perhaps if I share it with you, you will welcome me into your society."

Krateros lifted a palm. "That would be for the whole group to decide. All true-hearted candidates are welcome to apply for admission." His glance fell again on the satchel. "Of course, one who is already an initiate, and who brought with him gifts of knowledge—such a candidate might find a readier welcome."

Smiling, Korax opened the bag and removed a roll, a copy of one of the magical texts given to him by Amasis, the high priest who had befriended him in Memphis. He untied the ribbon and spread the papyrus on the table. Zakur and Krateros leaned to examine it. Miriam craned her neck to peer over Korax's shoulder.

"Most interesting," Krateros said.

"It looks authentic," Zakur grunted. "Can you read it, young man?"

"Of course. I studied for more than a year in the House of Life. I will not say in which temple."

"A man of mystery," Krateros commented, half-smiling. "You do intrigue me, sir. We have several in our circle who can read the hieroglyphs, and others of us are learning. Perhaps you know enough to act as tutor."

Korax glanced at Miriam. Her expression revealed a new respect, though none of her reserve had melted.

"I am not averse to sharing what I know," Korax said. "Of course, I would hope the arrangement would be mutual."

"That is the function and purpose of our society," Krateros declared. "We are a group of scholars from many nations. Our mission is to advance knowledge of the divine arts and unravel the secrets of Nature—for the good of all peoples. That is our charter from the king, whose blessing and patronage we enjoy."

"Then you are exactly the society I hoped to find," Korax said. "I will do all in my power to prove myself worthy of your company."

He extended his hand. Krateros grasped him firmly by the wrist. Korax then turned and offered his hand to Zakur, but the graybeard merely folded his arms in his sleeves and nodded.

"As I mentioned," Krateros was saying, "all honest candidates are welcome to seek admission. The application process involves a test, administered by our entire group. If you wish, I will arrange an examination to take place at one of our general meetings."

"I could ask no more," Korax replied. "And I will leave you this text, as a gift and sign of friendship."

"We accept it," Zakur answered, his stern expression softening a little. "Miriam, please show our visitor the way to the main portal. Then, if you would, please ascertain that all the outer doors are properly locked."

"I will, father."

"Thank you, esteemed gentlemen." Korax bowed his head. "May I ask when and where the next general meeting will occur?"

"We will summon you," Krateros said. He and Zakur had resumed their seats and were scrutinizing the papyrus.

"Very well. I am staying at a small inn, on the Street of Pomegranates, west of the causeway. It might be a little hard to find."

"No matter." Krateros gestured dismissively. "You will receive our summons. If you don't ... well, no further test will be necessary."

Retrieving her lamp, Miriam conducted Korax through the corridor and across the circular chamber. In the faint light, Korax discerned life-size statues set in hollows along the walls. Otherwise, the space was empty.

He ventured to make conversation. "I gather you are an initiate in this society, Miriam. How would you recommend I prepare myself for the test Krateros mentioned?"

"You don't really expect me to answer that, do you?"

Korax smiled, shaking his head. "I confess, I don't know what to expect of a girl who practices trance in a high and dangerous place. Is that one of the arts I will learn in your group?"

She paused, near a low rounded portal of white brick. "That practice is my own invention. And please don't mention it to anyone. My father would not approve."

"Aren't you afraid of falling?"

"Of course. Don't you see that is the point?"

They passed through the portal and descended a long, slanting tunnel. Korax, walking a step behind, pondered what she had said.

"You are a strange young man," Miriam remarked. "You claim to be an initiate of the Egyptian Mysteries—which I sense to be the truth. And yet you act so frivolous, lacking all solemnity."

"Do I strike you as such? Perhaps it is merely the difference in our cultures." When Miriam made no reply, Korax reflected: "To be honest, there are parts of myself I am still seeking to discover—or rediscover, for the truth is, some of my memories are lost to me."

She might have twitched a little at this disclosure, but did not ask him to explain.

Korax sighed. "Perhaps, as you say, I am a creature of contradictions. But the same might be said of you, a Jewish maiden studying mystical arts in the Temple of Pan."

"My people worship one God," she said. "But those of us who are privileged to study the deeper wisdom understand that God shows many aspects to Creation, and there are many ladders by which man, and woman too, may ascend to comprehension of divinity."

"Yes," Korax agreed. "You remind me of the Egyptian teachings: They describe various spheres that the soul must rise through to reach the source of the divine light, or again, many halls that must be passed for one to arrive at the Hall of Truth."

They had reached the end of the passage. Miriam threw a latch and pushed open a pivoting door. Bending low, they stepped through the opening. Korax saw they were in the pillared pavilion, behind the statue of Pan where he had left the coin.

Hesitantly, Miriam extended her hand. "I bid you good day, Astrametheus of Hermopolis. I hope we will meet again."

He touched her fingertips. "Korax is my true name, Korax of Rhodes."

# Chapter Three

While awaiting the summons of the magical society, Korax spent pleasant, relaxed days in Alexandria. He rose early in the mornings and left his inn. After crossing into the Royal Quarter, he stopped first at the School of Heracles, the city gymnasium. In a courtyard of the monumental building, he exercised with weights, twisting and stretching to the music of flutes. He practiced with a wrestling coach to increase his flexibility and strength. Out in the fields, he ran, threw the javelin, or trained with sword and buckler. He did not expect to need fighting skills in Alexandria, but a Greek gentleman did not neglect his arms training.

After a bath and a rubdown, he strolled across an extensive park dotted with fountains, clusters of flowering myrtle, and groves of sycamore. To his right, behind a stone fence stretched the Zoological Garden, where resided Ptolemy's collection of plants and animals from all parts of the known world.

Ahead stood the great Library. Built adjacent to the Museum, the Library had a matching, crescent-shaped colonnade of imposing grandeur. Along the columned porch and below in the terraced gardens were set innumerable nooks and benches for reading. Inside the many rooms was the immense collection of books.

Ptolemy the First had sent agents to all corners of the Greek world to purchase every text they could find. Continuing his father's program, the present Ptolemy had recruited scholars from foreign lands to translate the books of their native cultures. An army of scribes and clerks were employed to copy, arrange, and catalogue the vast collection.

Korax spent his afternoons wandering from room to room, perusing scrolls at random, reading whatever took his fancy—some science and philosophy, but mostly poetry and plays. What a pleasure it was to renew his acquaintance with Aristophanes, Sappho, Euripides. Korax could easily imagine spending the rest of his days entertaining himself in this palace of books.

One day, in the sunny garden beside a bubbling fountain, he was reading a collection of verse when a voice interrupted him.

"Astrametheus. Young Astrametheus, I recognize you."

Metiochus—the assistant headmaster from the Museum. Korax rose and greeted him politely. Metiochus sat down on the bench and gestured Korax to do likewise.

"I wondered what became of you. Did you discover the conclave of mystics you were seeking?"

"I am still exploring my options in that regard," Korax answered with some reticence.

"I see. Well, I hope you will come to your senses and reconsider the mainstream philosophy that we offer at the Museum. I swear before Zeus you will find no better education. In any case, I am pleased to see you well. May I inquire what you are reading?"

Korax showed him the papyrus roll: *New Epigrams* by Philetas of Cos.

"Well, you have excellent taste in poetry at least. One of our greatest contemporaries, to be sure."

Actually, Korax found the work a bit cool and affected. Still, he refrained from saying so. Not only would that be discourteous, it would mark him as ignorant in the eyes of the schoolmaster. Philetas had set the standard for the current crop of Alexandrian poets, had tutored many of them himself.

Metiochus set a hand on Korax's knee. "You know, Astrametheus, I feel a certain affection for you, despite your bizarre philosophical bent. Perhaps I can encourage your education by inviting you to a reading at the Salon of Calliope. It is four nights hence, by invitation only. Theocritus of Syracuse will be reading a new work. And it is rumored that Callimachus himself may favor us with a verse or two." Metiochus squeezed Korax's knee encouragingly. "Will you come, my young friend?"

While Korax had no interest in Metiochus' romantic advances, the man's friendship was not to be despised, and the invitation was certainly welcome. With a gentle smile, Korax placed the scholar's hand back into his own lap.

"I am delighted to accept your kind invitation."

While each of the nine Muses had a salon dedicated to her arts, the Salon of Calliope was deemed the most prestigious. On the evening of the next full moon, an eminent collection of scholars and courtiers gathered outside a banquet hall overlooking the courtyard of the Museum.

In the twilight, Korax arrived on the crescent portico, freshly bathed and perfumed, dressed in his gray chlamys and his best pleated chiton. He halted at the edge of the gathering, a little intimated by the size and finery of the chattering mob. As a young man of good family in Rhodos, Korax recalled a few occasions when he had mixed in intellectual company. But those days seemed more than a lifetime ago. Besides, the elite society of Rhodes was but a poor collection of candles compared to the starry firmament of Alexandria.

"There you are, my young Astrametheus. So glad you could attend." Metiochus clasped his arm with a proprietary grip. "Come, let me introduce you to my friends."

He ushered Korax toward the entrance of the hall, where a group of robed scholars stood talking. They were noble, mature men in their thirties or older. Several wore laurel crowns of gold or silver, emblems of their status as prize-winning poets. A few of the elder men were accompanied by protégés, trim youths with perfumed hair and kohl-shaded eyes who stood in the background, listening respectfully.

"Who is this young Ganymede then?" One of the crowned poets demanded, staring at Korax with drink-reddened eyes. "Metiochus, you lecherous stork! Another handsome student taken under your wing?"

"He is Astrametheus of Hermopolis," Metiochus replied with a blend of embarrassment and fastidious disapproval. "Permit me to introduce some of our esteemed faculty: Zenodotus of Ephesus, master of the Library; Theocritus of Syracuse, who will perform for us tonight; Herodas, himself a talented young poet; Lycophron of Chalcis, a most-learned man of letters ..."

Except for Herodas, Korax knew all of these famous men by reputation. As each extended a hand, he touched their fingertips, enchanted as though in a dream.

"...And this ill-mannered buffoon"—Metiochus gestured at the red-eyed, unkempt poet who had spoken earlier—"is Asclepiades, whose meager talent I fear he long ago extinguished through gross debauchery."

"Well said," Asclepiades exclaimed. "And sadly near the truth." He grabbed Korax by the wrist and shook vigorously.

"Gentlemen." Korax's voice was constricted. "I am truly honored, overwhelmed, to meet so many prodigious talents."

"Ha! His speech is as pretty as his eyes!" Asclepiades growled. "Tell me, are there many more like you in Hermopolis, young man?"

"Oh, I doubt that." Korax smiled diffidently.

"But where is Callimachus?" Metiochus asked. "He was here just a moment ago."

"He stepped inside, ostensibly to review his lines," Theocritus answered.

"He's in a snit as usual," Asclepiades said. "Perturbed because the king and queen sent their regrets."

"Oh, I had not known their majesties planned to attend," said Metiochus.

"It was supposed to be *a surprise,*" Asclepiades scoffed.

"Who else is here, from the court I mean?" Herodas stretched his neck to scan the crowd.

"Well, the king sent Drakas in his stead," Asclepiades muttered. "So all of us had best tether our tongues." He turned a mordant glance on Korax, who must have looked totally out of his depth. "Drakas is Marshal of the Royal Guard. All poets fear him. He's been known to torture authors who satirized the monarchy."

"I see Prodotus the Cyrenaican ambassador is here." Metiochus changed the subject.

"Naturally, since Callimachus let it be known he might perform," Asclepiades grumbled. "It would be impolitic for the ambassador to miss a reading by Cyrenaica's national bard."

"Who is that with him?" Theocritus inquired. "The tall Phoenician with the excessive ringlets in his beard?"

Zenodotus squinted in that direction. "That is Manolis, the new ambassador from Carthage."

"Really?" Asclepiades swung his head with sudden interest. "Is his wife with him? Yes, there she is, that exquisite creature with the neck of a swan and arms decked in bangles. They say she is a witch, you know, a priestess of Tanit."

Korax followed the collective gaze to observe the woman. She stood beside her distinguished husband, obviously years younger than he. Both wore rich garments of rose-pink and gold, folded and draped in the Phoenician fashion. At once, the woman sensed the scholars looking at her. She stared back across the terrace with a tranquil, enigmatic expression. Korax decided the attribution of witchery might not be an exaggeration.

"Come, O blessed companions of the Muse! Enter the Banquet of Calliope!" A red-caped herald had appeared on the threshold to proclaim the summons.

The convivial babble of the crowd never ceased as they filed into the hall. Perfumed cressets blazed along the walls, the light fluttering over lofty murals full of grand, heroic figures of myth. Garlands of myrtle and hyacinth festooned the tables and couches. From a corner, a trio of flute, lyre, and drum offered a lilting melody.

Attendants in green and gold tunics conducted the guests to their places. Metiochus and Korax were led to a couch near the rear of the hall. Korax sat at the edge, scrupulously keeping his distance from the older man. While Metiochus' amorous interest was plain, the schoolmaster was far too refined to press his attentions unless signaled that they would be welcome.

"There is Callimachus." Metiochus reclined on an elbow and pointed with his chin to the front of the chamber.

The famous poet, slender and impeccably groomed, stood on a low dais and watched the assembly with a grave, aloof air.

"I will introduce you to him later," Metiochus promised.

"Who is the soldier with him?" Korax asked.

He referred to a stout, white-haired Macedonian with a scarred face, clad in a silver corselet and scarlet cloak. The warrior sat in a broad chair of carved ebony, facing the audience with a surly demeanor.

"That is Drakas," Metiochus replied in a whisper. "He sits tonight in the place of the king."

When the guests were all settled, slaves entered with serving trays and ewers of mixed wine. In their wake floated the aromas of hot, spicy foods—peppered eel, roasted oysters, sesame cakes

JACK MASSA

baked with almonds and apricots. Korax eagerly tasted morsels
from a dish set before him. Immediately, he gulped chilled wine to
quench the fire in his mouth.

Metiochus chuckled. "The stylish cuisine of Alexandria might
take some getting used to, my young friend."

At the front of the chamber, Callimachus lifted his cup. He
waited in stern silence for the murmuring to grow still. Then he
spoke in loud, oracular tones. "Welcome all, to this night when we
celebrate Divine Eloquence, First Sister of the Parnassian Nine."

Deliberately, he tilted the cup and spilled his libation onto the
tiles.

The evening commenced with several preliminaries. A fat,
waggish poet named Dosiadas recited witty epigrams composed
around riddles and word-play. Two young men in heavy makeup,
students of the Museum, performed a comic mime accompanied
by flute and drum. Corinna, a matronly poetess, sang a hymn of
praise to the divine queen Arsinoe. Korax drank it all in with vivid
delight, realizing how sorely he had missed the exaltation of lyric
and song.

Soon Theocritus arose from his place in the front row. Tall and
handsome, the thirty-year-old Syracusean was already deemed a
leading light among the poets of Alexandria. Tonight he would
perform a new idyll, he announced, the tale of a formidable
woman who, fearing the loss of her lover, resorts to sorcery to win
him back.

Stroking the strings of a gilded lyre, Theocritus began. In a
high-pitched voice, he sang the words of his heroine, Simaetha by
name. Standing in her garden beneath the moon, she ordered her
servant to bring ingredients for casting a spell: laurel leaves and
pottery bowl, red wool for knotting, a witch's wheel. Each verse
concluded with a rhythmic refrain: "Bring to my arms my lover, O
magic wheel."

As the monologue unfolded the audience listened in rapt silence, enchanted more surely than Simaetha's errant lover. Theocritus told how the woman burned barley husks in a fire, then a wax figure of the man. She called upon Selene, goddess of the moon, and Hecate, queen of witches.

Gradually, Korax became aware of a prickling at the back of his neck, a warmth behind his forehead. The cresset-lights of the hall wavered, distant and dim.

Suddenly his gaze swung away from the poet. Two rows ahead, a black-haired woman was watching him—the wife of the Carthaginian ambassador, the priestess of Tanit. She nestled on a couch beside her husband, the dyed fabric of their garments overlaid. But her long neck was twisted and her face turned to Korax. Her brow lowered in puzzlement, and for a moment their eyes stayed fixed on each other.

*"Bring to my arms my lover, O magic wheel."*

The woman's eyes shifted away, and Korax blinked.

She had cast an idle glance over her shoulder, surveying the hall. Their eyes had met unintentionally for an instant, nothing more. Surely, it was only the poet's art that had made him imagine otherwise.

Still, from that moment, Korax found it difficult to concentrate on the performance. His eyes and his thoughts kept straying to the young wife of Carthage with her silver jewelry, tumbling black hair, and dark, mysterious eyes.

# Chapter Four

Theocritus completed his song, bowed deftly to the roars of acclaim, returned to his couch.

Callimachus waited until the cheers had subsided before standing to deliver the evening's finale. He launched into his poem without introduction. Like Theocritus, he performed with a lyre. But he only touched a note here and there as he recited.

His piece recounted a dream in which he was transported to Mount Helicon to converse with the Muses. There followed a series of disconnected episodes in which the goddesses instructed him on the proper forms and duties of a poet. The whole was packed with cunningly elaborate metaphors and abstruse mythical allusions. Korax understood about half of the lines. Plainly, most of the audience found the piece equally impenetrable.

Callimachus halted abruptly, seemingly in mid-verse. The banquet hall remained hushed for some moments, no one sure if the poet was finished. Deliberately, Callimachus stepped across the dais to resume his seat.

In the chair beside him, Marshal Drakas smacked his hands together with loud solemnity. Taking their cue, the rest of the audience erupted into applause.

"Astonishing, wasn't it?" Metiochus clapped energetically.

"Truly," Korax said, trying not to sound sarcastic.

"It will take some time to get close to him after such a performance," Metiochus declared. "But as promised, I will introduce you."

The audience of the salon rose from their couches. A few departed, but most lingered in the hall to converse about poetry and other erudite subjects. Korax followed Metiochus to the front, where the gathering was thickest as people waited for a chance to congratulate the performers. Zenodotus the chief librarian and Asclepiades the poet stood near the dais.

"My friends!" Asclepiades cried with drunken good humor. "And how did our young hero of Hermopolis enjoy the recital?"

"Wonderfully well," Korax replied. "I can honestly say I've never heard the like in Hermopolis."

"A nimble reply." Zenodotus eyed Korax with sly amusement.

Asclepiades had turned to greet two others who at that moment were passing by. Korax's lips parted as he faced the Carthaginian ambassador and his wife.

"Ambassador Manolis, so nice to see you!" Asclepiades cried. "Perhaps you remember me, Asclepiades, writer of scurrilous epigrams."

"Of course." Manolis gave a dignified nod. "I am happy to meet you again, master poet, and you also, Zenodotus. Allow me to present my wife, Kalyssa."

The lady bowed her head demurely. Standing before her, Korax wondered at his earlier perception of this slender young woman as a sorceress. Though undeniably beautiful, she now impressed him as nothing more than a shy young wife.

"Most enchanting." Asclepiades boldly seized her hand and kissed it. "A lady who has inspired many paeans to her beauty, I am sure."

Zenodotus cleared his throat. "And may I present Metiochus, Assistant Headmaster of the Museum, and his young friend, Astrametheus of Hermopolis."

The ambassador and his wife nodded cordially.

"Hermopolis," Manolis said. "A city of the Upper Nile, is it not?"

"Yes," Korax replied. "It stands midway between the great cities of Memphis and Thebes."

"And how long have you been in Alexandria, young man?" Kalyssa asked him.

Korax's glance darted to her. "I am sure my lack of refinement betrays me. I am but newly arrived from the province—and freshly dazzled by the beauties I find here."

Even as he finished speaking, he wondered if he had been too bold.

But it came to nothing, as a shadow of movement drew all eyes. Another man joined the circle: Marshal Drakas, his military cloak swaying from broad shoulders.

In some past battle a spear had torn Drakas' face, leaving a broad, pinched scar from jaw to forehead, his left eye shrunken and yellow. The horrible wound gave his face a gruesome yet oddly poignant and dignified appearance.

"Good evening, ambassador," Drakas said, showing a curt nod to the others. "I trust you found the performances enjoyable."

"Oh indeed, marshal, thank you," Manolis said. "Though of course my poor grasp of your language prevented me from comprehending all the nuances of the poetry."

"If you mean Callimachus, then have no worry," Asclepiades declared. "The rest of us don't understand him either."

Korax repressed a smirk, and saw a brief smile flicker on Kalyssa's lips. Everyone else looked solemn.

"Well, if it's language lessons you need, you've found the right company." Drakas nodded toward Zenodotus and Asclepiades.

"I regret that their majesties could not join us as planned," Manolis said. "It is not due to any trouble, I hope."

"No trouble," Drakas answered guardedly. "A conference with their financial advisors ran longer than expected, that is all. The king and queen are preparing for meetings next month with their governors and the high priests of Egypt."

"Oh, yes, the annual Synod," Manolis remarked. "But I fear there might be some cause for concern there. I have heard troubling rumors that the grain harvest will not be sufficient this year."

Drakas frowned. "I could not say, ambassador. That information is not within the scope of my duties."

"Oh, of course." Manolis shifted his glance downward.

"Perhaps Astrametheus can enlighten us about the harvest," Kalyssa said. "He just told us that he is newly arrived from his home city upriver."

All gazes turned on Korax: the ambassador and his wife with polite but pointed inquiry; Drakas with a belligerent, appraising scowl; the scholars surprised and nervous.

These past few months, Korax had thought little about his life in Memphis. But mention of the harvest brought the memories flowing back. He recalled the Egyptians' perpetual anxiety over the grain supply, their unceasing resentment of Ptolemy's heavy taxes. Sympathy for the people he had lived among for nearly two years caused him, against all caution, to speak his mind.

"There *is* serious concern about the harvest. Many fear unrest, even starvation. Most landowners hope that the king will be persuaded to lower the grain quota this year, to ensure there's enough food for the people."

A chill silence followed his remarks, and Korax immediately regretted speaking so bluntly. Straightforward utterance was not the norm in Alexandria.

"Well, we don't often discuss poetry and politics on the same evening," Metiochus noted with a feeble laugh.

"It is best for poets and their students to not discuss policy at all," Drakas declared, staring at Korax. "I am sure you will learn that quickly, as you appear to be an intelligent young man."

"Oh, but is that really true?" Ambassador Manolis inquired. "I had understood it was the Greek tradition for politicians to also be poets and philosophers. Am I once again mistaken?"

Another awkward silence ensued. Korax observed the three scholars gazing at the floor.

"Times change," Drakas said simply. "And now, I bid you all good evening." With a nod to the Carthaginians and a last, grim glance at Korax, the marshal turned and strode away.

"I fear my innocent questioning resulted in awkwardness." Manolis sighed. "I am still learning the etiquette of your court. I had believed the Macedonians to be a blunt, straightforward race. But that is not at all the case, is it?"

"No," Zenodotus agreed. "It is not."

# Chapter Five

Drakas walked along the curving colonnade, through the shadows of pillars and spaces of moonlight. Out of the sight of other men, he allowed a rolling limp to enter his stride. The limp was a remnant of his early career, like the scar on his face—gifts from Ares, the god of war.

Both trophies had come to him on the same fateful day, during the Wars of the Successors, when Alexander's generals fought for possession of his vast empire. Drakas had been a young captain, a commander of cavalry in the service of the Macedonian warlord Antigonus. At the high-water mark of his fortunes, ambitious to reunite the whole empire, Antigonus had invaded Ptolemy's stronghold in Egypt. Their armies clashed in the deserts of Gaza.

The invasion had been ill-fated from the start. Antigonus' supply ships were delayed by treacherous weather. Hungry and unpaid, his army soon lost morale. Many deserted to join Ptolemy, who offered the mercenaries not only food and coin, but land holdings in the Nile Valley. Then, having bled the enemy for weeks, Ptolemy launched a merciless attack, spearheaded by brigades of war elephants. Antigonus' infantry panicked and broke ranks.

But even then Drakas possessed a keen eye for an opponent's fatal weakness. From a hilltop position on the flank, he ordered his unit to charge. The unexpected attack, with the braying of trumpets and lances aimed at the elephants' eyes, reversed the panic. The elephants turned and trampled the Egyptian lines.

The reversal was temporary, of course. Ptolemy's forces soon regrouped and advanced again. By midday, Antigonus' army was in full retreat.

So Drakas learned afterward. He himself lay on the field, his leg broken, half his face torn. His life surely would have ended there, had not Ptolemy himself witnessed the reckless charge. The heroic enemy captain was carried to the king's own pavilion, his wounds tended by royal physicians. When Ptolemy returned to Alexandria a month later, Drakas traveled with him, now an officer of Ptolemy's royal guard, a "Friend of the King."

The king had many friends at court, of course. But Drakas eventually outmaneuvered or outlasted them all. His courage and ruthlessness made him more than a match for any soldier or minister. But it was his knack for reading motives, sensing flaws, and predicting actions that made him preeminent in the devious politics of the court—those qualities and pure loyalty. Unlike most other courtiers, Drakas knew no motive except to assure the well-being of the king. After all, he owed Ptolemy his life.

So Drakas had served the old monarch for twenty years. Then, for the last twelve, he had served Ptolemy's namesake and heir. No deed was too onerous, too dangerous, or too bloody that Drakas would not perform it unhesitatingly in service to the House of Ptolemy. That was his honor and his pride.

Now he marched across an expansive garden that gradually ascended seven levels. Beside him, an artificial stream flowed down through pools and waterfalls. Approaching the gates of the palace, Drakas once more concealed his limp. The sentries recognized him and stood a little straighter. Drakas surveyed them sternly through his one good eye as he passed.

Within the palace precinct, he crossed a series of tiled courtyards and magnificent, pillared halls. Broad stairways in between made his journey a continuing climb. This part of the palace ascended to the Lochias, the promontory that overlooked the Great Harbor. Innumerable cressets and lamps lit the palace grounds nearly as bright as day.

Reaching the summit at last, Drakas entered a sprawling enclosure with pylon gates like an Egyptian temple. Through an outer hall, he traversed a tall corridor lined with a whole company of his royal guard—sturdy spearmen in crested helmets and scarlet cloaks. They were stationed here more for show than because of any potential threat. Beyond this hall stood the throne rooms and royal apartments.

At the portal of an audience chamber, Drakas stopped and conferred with a steward. The council had ended a short time ago, he learned, though the queen remained inside with a few advisors. The king had already retired to his quarters.

Drakas found Ptolemy on the terrace of an exquisite chamber furnished in silks, ebony, and gold. A handful of servants and guardsmen hovered in the background.

The king had a weak, receding chin, his curly hair adorned with a gold diadem. His red and purple robes clung to a narrow figure with a soft, protruding belly. In Drakas' view, Ptolemy would have done well to spend a bit more time on arms training and less on luxuries and intellectual pastimes. The king stood feeding bits of pear to a pet monkey on his shoulder.

"Majesty."

"Hello, my friend." Ptolemy smiled at the marshal. "I hope your evening was not so tedious as mine."

"About as I expected," Drakas said. "As your highness is aware, modern poetry does not run to my tastes."

"Indeed, we all must bear our bitter duties." Ptolemy grinned at his chattering pet. "Who else attended? Anyone of note?"

Drakas glanced out over the sloping grounds and the Great Harbor below. Across the water, the Pharos Lighthouse sent its beacon out to sea.

"The Cyrenaican ambassador was there."

"Prodotus? Oh, yes, to hear Callimachus, of course."

"He was accompanied by the new envoy from Carthage, Manolis."

"Indeed?" The king pursed his lip. "Did those two seem particularly friendly?"

"That is hard to say."

"But worth noting, nonetheless," Ptolemy concurred. "Ah, here is wine."

A serving girl had appeared with a gold tray. Ptolemy handed the monkey to an attendant, who hastened forward to receive the pet. Another slave also stepped forward, a man in the short black tunic of a taster. At a sign from the king, the man poured wine into a gold goblet, swirled it a moment then immediately swallowed it down.

Ptolemy and Drakas watched the taster in silence for the space of thirty heartbeats. Finally, the two men glanced at each other and nodded simultaneously. The king took the goblet, and the taster retreated to the shadows. Ptolemy himself refilled the cup, then poured a second one for Drakas.

"A new vintage, from Crimisa," Ptolemy remarked.

"Then let me have some," a woman's voice interrupted. "Strong wine would be most welcome."

Drakas and everyone else bowed as the queen approached. Even Ptolemy inclined a little at the waist, as if by reflex. Arsinoe flowed across the terrace in a gown of white silk and a purple and gold *himation* draped on her shoulder.

"My darling." The queen leaned against Ptolemy, kissed him on the cheek, then took his goblet and drank. She handed him back an empty cup, smiling in satisfaction. Then she pressed against him once again and kissed his earlobe.

Drakas politely averted his gaze. Arsinoe had red-dyed hair and arresting blue eyes. In her mid-forties, seven years older than her brother, she had lost little of her renowned sensual beauty.

Like all of Alexandria, Drakas had been scandalized when Ptolemy announced he would divorce his wife to marry his own sister. Propaganda about the tradition of sibling marriage among the pharaohs—not to mention that of Zeus and Hera—had done nothing to quell his disquiet. Still, it was the king's choice and he accepted it. If necessary, he would die to protect Arsinoe without a moment's hesitation. Of course, if it served the king, he would just as readily put his sword through her body. Given Arsinoe's colorful history, it might come to that someday.

Leaning on the king's shoulder, she peered at him now with a disarming smile. "Good evening, marshal."

"Majesty." He bowed again. "You've worked late this evening."

"Indeed, our meetings were laborious." She addressed her brother: "I went over the reports from the Fayum again. Even with that grain taken into account, I am convinced we will need to reduce expenses by approximately one-sixth."

Ptolemy winced and reached for the ewer. "We've extended our kingdom from Upper Egypt to the shores of Asia," he declared morosely as he poured, "yet now we cannot maintain the forces necessary to hold it."

"It is only for one year," Arsinoe replied soothingly.

Ptolemy grunted. "In one year we could lose Lower Syria. In one year, Antigonus Gonatas could win back the whole Aegean!"

"Neither event is likely," Arsinoe assured him. "Any losses we suffer will be temporary. Remember the lessons of our father: patience and, above all, keep our own kingdom secure."

Over the rim of his cup, Drakas watched her with admiration. Arsinoe had inherited the cunning and iron determination of the old king—qualities her brother had received in somewhat smaller measure.

Ptolemy fretted. "So, I must reduce the taxes."

The queen gripped his arm with both hands. "Listen, dear brother: Egypt is a great cow whose milk gives us nourishment. But if we milk her too much, she'll run dry. What good will it do us to build up the navy if our armies are occupied putting down rebellions on our own soil?"

The king looked sullen. "What do you think, Drakas? Must I lower the grain quotas of Egypt so our *cow* will not run dry?"

"I think the queen gives wise counsel, as ever," Drakas answered automatically. His expression grew pensive, and his good eye blinked.

"What is it?" Arsinoe prompted. "Speak frankly, good Drakas."

"Nothing of importance. I was just thinking, I heard this matter discussed earlier, at the salon."

"What?" Ptolemy cried. "They were not debating our policies at the banquet of the Muse I hope!"

"No, majesty," the marshal said. "Only some student spoke out of turn, a protégé of one of the schoolmasters. He's recently arrived from the provinces. He said all the landholders of Egypt hope the king will lower the quotas this year. They fear starvation among the populace."

"You see?" Arsinoe lifted her eyebrows. "Even the Muse counsels us to this wisdom."

"Oh, excellent," the king grumbled. "Now we're listening to youths from the provinces. Perhaps we should dismiss all our ministers and hire provincial students in their places!"

# Chapter Six

H is head full of poetry, Korax made his way home through the lamp-lit streets of Alexandria. The full moon rode high, ringed by a circle of bright colors in the misty sea air.

The Street of Pomegranates angled through a modest neighborhood south of the causeway, between the docks and the old Egyptian quarter. Tradesmen, merchants, and students from various nations inhabited the warren. Korax had rented a comfortable room in a hostel called the Seven Seeds Inn.

He passed through the downstairs common room—empty at this hour except for a few late drinkers. The landlord called out to him from behind the counter, offering to sell him a cup of wine. Korax politely declined. Instead he took a candle and climbed the narrow stairs to his chamber.

Once inside, he pushed open the shutters to let in the moonlight. He stripped off his garments and lay down on the bed beside the casement. In a pleasant, dreamy mood he gazed up into the night sky.

Soon he drifted into a sleep or a half-sleep. He found himself in a vast, murky cavern. The dense sea air mingled with the fragrance of exotic blooms. From a distance, he perceived the crashing of waves. Then the steady sound began to carry voices, whispering a name.

"Astrametheus." "Astrametheus of Hermopolis."

He sat up in bed, feeling a presence, as though unseen spirits floated in the air. He stood and paced across the room, his heart thumping. He pondered for a few moments, then knelt and pulled a basket from under his bed. He took out his wax statue of Thoth and set it on a table. From the candle he fired a lump of black incense and set it in a censor. He sat down naked in front of the statue and took long, even breaths.

"Hermes, god of magic, I call you to this place."

"My young friend of Rhodes. It is some time since we have spoken."

"I need your counsel."

The voice in his brain sparkled with mockery. "Do you only call on the gods when you need assistance?"

Korax's neck stiffened. "I made many sacrifices at your shrine in Naukratis."

"Indeed you did, and they were most welcome." Hermes seemed to be laughing at him.

"I have promised to serve the gods," Korax said. "Is there some duty I must answer?"

"Not at the moment."

"Then I ask again for your counsel. This dream I had, if it was a dream. What is its meaning?"

"Surely you can guess. It is the society of magicians. They have sent you their summons."

"I thought so. They call me to the Temple of Pan tomorrow?"

"No. They call you there now."

The mist had cleared from the sky, leaving the moon a golden shield hung on a tapestry of stars. Korax hurried through the dim, deserted streets. He had dressed in a chiton and sandals, wrapped the gray chlamys over his shoulder. He had considered bringing the beaded satchel, but decided not. Instead he had slung on his sword-belt. The streets of Alexandria were patrolled by a watch, but at this late hour, in this part of the town, robbers might be lurking.

As he neared the grounds of the Paneum, he saw that the iron gates stood shut and guarded by two sentries. The men wore black hooded cloaks and carried truncheons.

"Reveal your name and business," one of the guards ordered.

"I am Astrametheus of Hermopolis. I believe I have been summoned."

The man nodded. "Surrender your weapon to me."

Korax removed his sword-belt and handed it to the sentry. The other man pushed the gate open.

Passing inside the wall, Korax was confronted by a figure dressed in a loose white robe and holding a lamp. The person's face was concealed by a cowl and a mask of hammered gold. From the size and slender shape, Korax guessed it was a woman. She raised a finger to the lips of the mask, commanding him to silence. Then she gestured with the lamp for him to follow.

At first, Korax wondered if his guide might be Miriam. But after a few steps, he concluded not. This person moved with a sinuous confidence, unlike the rather stiff adolescent stride he recalled in the young Jewish woman. Beneath the hem of her robe, small feet appeared, bare on the grass. Korax glimpsed the sparkle of a toe-ring.

They entered the pavilion of Pan and moved through the shadows. Behind the statue of the god, the secret door stood ajar. The guide motioned Korax to enter first. Bent at the waist, he felt his way down the passage. Soon the height increased and he could walk upright. Faint illumination appeared ahead.

The tunnel ended in the great circular chamber at the interior of the stone mound. Moonlight glinted through slanted vents in the distant pinnacle. At the center of the black floor burned a ring of lanterns.

A solemn voice issued from the area of light: "Let the candidate come forward."

Korax and his guide stepped noiselessly across the chamber. As they approached, he spied perhaps forty persons seated on cushions, each behind a flickering lamp. Twelve of the company sat in an inner circle, the others in a second circle outside the first. All of the figures wore white robes with hoods and gold masks with the same blank, enigmatic expression. A dense cloud of incense floated in the air.

Korax was led to a seat in the center of the concentric circles. His guide repeated her earlier gesture, warning him to silence, then withdrew to take a place at the outer circle. Korax stared at the masks and waited.

For a long time all was quiet.

Korax's spine grew tense and achy. A tingling crept over the skin of his arms. He took deep breaths to quell his emotion, but the smoky incense made him lightheaded. He could feel the minds behind the blank visages, probing him.

Needles seemed to prickle his nerves. The prickling grew sharper, till tiny worms of flame were crawling all through his body. His limbs trembled. He forced himself to keep still, to stare resolutely.

Abruptly a jolt shuddered through him and the fire vanished. His whole being was enveloped in an aura of peace and relief. A tall person rose from the inner circle. When he spoke, Korax thought he recognized the voice of Krateros.

"My brothers and sisters of the Paths of the Mysteries, this candidate seeks admission to our Society. What is your judgment of his worthiness?"

"He is most worthy," said a woman's voice from the outer circle. "He has talent and a brilliant mind."

"Brilliant yes, but inconstant," said a deep male voice with an Egyptian accent. "He lacks clarity and depth."

"He is young," answered another. "He only needs cultivation."

"He knows Thoth-Hermes. I sense the god's influence."

"Yes, I felt it too. A peculiar paradox: His knowledge is shallow, yet his experience is profound."

"He is courageous."

"But also willful and proud."

"Once he was arrogant, but his soul has been tempered by suffering."

"He feels the pain of others and knows compassion—rare in one so young."

"I sense that his spirit is lost. He is not sure what he wants."

"Surely that is true of us all to some degree."

"Still, it worries me that his heart is frivolous."

Knots tightened and re-tightened in Korax's belly. Their perceptions sliced him apart, he thought, with the cool efficiency of a chef filleting a fish.

"His ability is undeniable, but does he have sufficient dedication?"

"He has promised to serve the gods. That is a worthy ideal."

"Yes, and he holds to that strongly."

A hush settled over the enormous chamber. Korax waited nervously, straining to keep still. Finally, the man he believed was Krateros spoke again.

"I thank you all for your assessments. By their tenor, I believe we are agreed to offer this young man membership in our Society. Is there anyone who disagrees?"

Silence.

"So let it be done."

The masked figures stood all at once. They picked up their lamps and filed after Krateros, who had turned and was pacing across the floor. Korax clambered to his feet, his knees unsteady. His guide appeared beside him and indicated he should follow. They took their place at the rear of the line.

A chant began, rolling in low powerful tones through the long procession. The sound vibrated inside Korax's head: three lines in some archaic tongue; three more, in another language he did not know; then a third verse in Egyptian:

Light rushes forth
In rays manifesting
From the mind of the One

At the edge of the chamber, the procession moved up a curving ramp. It mounted to the first gallery and turned a complete circuit. The chanting never altered as the company filed up the next ramp and around the second gallery.

In all, the magicians ascended seven ramps and circled seven galleries. Each circuit grew shorter, as the walls of the enormous space curved inward toward the summit. At the top of the seventh ramp, Korax followed his guide into a narrow cleft of rock. At one point, the way grew so narrow he had to turn sideways to squeeze through. The chant had ceased, and for an alarming moment he feared he had lost the company. Then he emerged to find his guide awaiting him at the base of a winding stair. They climbed together and walked out onto the roof of the Paneum.

The moon now floated in the west. Stars glinted in the blue vault, seeming to reflect the countless lights of Alexandria that twinkled far below.

The company had formed a single circle within the round parapet. Korax was led to the center, where Krateros, still masked, stood before a plain stone altar. On the stone sat two gold vessels: a bowl full of wine and a platter piled high with cakes.

"Here at the summit of the Temple of Pan," Krateros said, "we honor and worship all gods and goddesses. Young stranger, known to us as Astrametheus, I bid you welcome."

"Welcome." The word echoed around the circle.

The priest lifted the bowl and handed it to Korax.

"I give you wine, the blood of the god who eternally dies and is reborn: Osiris, Adonis, Dionysus. May his sacrifice renew the strength of your blood."

As Korax tilted the bowl to his lips, the voices repeated the divine names.

"Osiris. Adonis. Dionysus.

Krateros held the gold plate. "I give you bread, the gift of the goddess who eternally sustains all life: Isis, Astarte, Demeter. May the fruits of her body replenish your spirit."

All in the circle chanted: "Isis. Astarte. Demeter."

Korax took a morsel and ate it.

Krateros said: "All gods are one. All goddesses are one. All life is one. This is the Mystery of Pan."

The priest's hands came up and lifted away his mask. "Now, Astrametheus, it is my privilege to welcome you to our company, the Society of Alexandrian Pan. And it is your privilege, as our newest member, to serve the wine to your fellow magicians. May this sacred meal sustain us all in our quest for the Hidden Knowledge, the True and Highest Wisdom."

"So be it," the voices of the circle intoned.

Exultant, Korax lifted up the wine bowl. His guide came forward and picked up the platter of cakes.

Around the circle, the other magicians had all removed their masks. One by one they stepped forward to partake of the ritual meal. Korax gazed into their faces.

"Welcome, Astrametheus. I am Alcyoneus of Thessaly," said a wiry, black-eyed Greek.

"Haremhab of Thebes."—A stout Egyptian with shaven head.

"Manetho, Priest of Ra in his Mansion at On."—Another Egyptian, solemn and stern.

"Peristeria of Tyre. I welcome you, young man."—A portly, middle-aged Phoenician woman with eyelids shaded blue and ringlets dyed with henna.

"Zakur of Jerusalem." His voice was deep and gruff. "Welcome, young man."

"Miriam of Alexandria. Welcome, my friend." Korax grinned at her, and Miriam's eyes revealed a hint of pleasure.

The greetings continued: men and women from Babylon, Syria, Persia, India, Nubia, Cyprus, Macedonia, Italia, and Greece. Korax gazed into their eyes, measured their spirits, their power. From some he felt skepticism or judgment held in abeyance. In most he sensed hidden aspects, elements of themselves that they shielded. But in no one did he sense animosity or ill will.

Finally the last of the company had met him and partaken of the meal. Krateros took the bowl and poured out the rest of the wine as a libation. The white-robed company milled about in groups, conversing. Korax turned to his guide, and realized she alone had not yet uncovered her face.

"Kind lady who guided me so well," he said, "is there a ritual reason you still wear your mask?"

Her shoulders quivered as though in a laugh. She spun on her heels and walked away. Korax followed her to the edge of the circular roof, where she leaned her back against the parapet.

"Surely now you are mocking me," he said. "There can be no reason for you not to show your face ... unless I have offended in some way. If so, it was through ignorance, not intention."

This time her laugh was audible. Her hands clasped in front of the mask, the fingers adorned with silver rings.

"I will show you my face, but there's a price. Tell me your true name. It is not Astrametheus, I feel sure."

"Ah," Korax nodded. Recalling how deftly the magicians had probed his mind in the chamber below, he saw no further point in concealing his identity. "Korax is my true name. Korax of Rhodes."

"Korax? A pleasure." A wave of her hand swept the mask away. "I am Kalyssa of Carthage."

Korax stared in delighted surprise, his thoughts fleeing back to the idyll of Theocritus. "I saw you looking at me, during the performance."

She giggled heartily. "Yes, I thought perhaps I recognized a fellow practitioner. So imagine my surprise when I came here tonight and was asked to guide a candidate—and it turned out to be you. I could hardly contain my laughter. Since I am a new member myself, such a loss of self-control would have reflected on me very poorly."

"Oh, be careful of this one, my young friend!" Peristeria, the elder Phoenician woman, embraced Kalyssa and kissed her on the cheek. "She is a cunning sorceress. I think you will be no match for her."

"I am not so sure of that." Miriam stepped near and wrapped her arm around Peristeria's waist. "Astrametheus is himself full of guile. I think it is Kalyssa who might be overmatched!"

The three white-robed women laughed merrily, their arms entwined with mutual affection. Bemused, Korax decided his wisest course was to smile affably and say nothing.

"I know his true name," Kalyssa announced mischievously. "And it is *not* Astrametheus."

"Well," Peristeria chuckled. "If Kalyssa knows it, I'm sure all of us will know it soon."

Korax glanced at Miriam, who lowered her eyes with a secretive smile and said nothing.

# Chapter Seven

Korax returned to the Temple of Pan the next day. With his initiation complete, he was eager to resume serious study of the magical arts, hoping to at last find his way past the confusion and indecision that had plagued him since arriving in Alexandria.

By arrangement, Krateros met him on the steps of the columned pavilion. Eyeing the beaded satchel on Korax's shoulder, the high priest extended a cordial welcome. First, he conducted Korax on a tour of the grounds. Around the giant mound, in various grottos and outbuildings, stood nine secret doors. Each led to a tunnel that gave access to the inner chamber. Krateros showed Korax the hidden latches and bolts to open each portal. The shrine had been built during the reign of the first Ptolemy and designed in part as a staging place for the Mysteries of Samothrace. Later, those rites had been moved to the new Temple of Serapis in the Egyptian quarter. At present, the vast and intricate Paneum was used mainly by Krateros and his Society.

"We are an informal conclave of scholars," Krateros said. "We have no code of laws and no hierarchy. We are far more interested in acquiring knowledge than ranks or titles. Some of us are deemed elders, by virtue of our learning and experience. But all of us recognize that we are merely students of the Mysteries. Anyone of the Society with particular knowledge may play the role of teacher at a given time. You, for instance, will presumably instruct us in the Egyptian writing."

"I am happy to teach what I know." Korax answered, a hesitation creeping into his voice. "But really, I have much more to learn than teach. As someone noted last night, I've had a few profound experiences but my knowledge is meager."

They crossed the floor of the interior, having entered from a winding passageway. Korax followed Krateros through a portal and down a corridor. Daylight, directed through the ingenious system of shafts and mirrors, lent a ghostly illumination.

They turned a corner and walked into a high, narrow hall. Stellate skylights in the ceiling lit the chamber nearly as brightly as the day.

"Our main library," Krateros said. "I will show you the nexus of our work."

Korax gaped as he scanned the walls, lined with shelves and nooks stuffed with scrolls. Ladders built with tiny iron wheels made it possible to reach the books at any height. The library was unoccupied, the air tinged with the dry tang of papyrus.

Krateros retrieved a roll and spread it out on a long table. The papyrus presented a diagram of ten circles, arranged in an oblong pattern and linked by straight lines. Numerous words and symbols were inscribed within the circles and along the interconnections. The annotations had been done over time, by different hands, in various alphabets.

"Have you seen anything like this in your studies?"

Korax shook his head. In the House of Life he had come across many elaborate glyphs, but nothing resembling this design.

"I am not surprised," Krateros answered, wide-eyed. "It is derived from the joined visionary insights of our members. We call it the Tree of Creation. It is a map of the Cosmos and also of the human soul—for the dynamic structure of the one mirrors the other." Krateros traced a part of the diagram with his finger. "It shows the tenfold emanations of the Divine Will, which eternally creates and sustains the Universe. We conceive of this Will as both a Word, whose sound vibrates perpetually, and a Light rushing forth from the mind of the Prime Mover."

JACK MASSA

Here was an idea Korax could relate to his own learning. "That dual understanding is also a foundation of the Egyptian teachings."

Krateros nodded, his face alight. "As you can see, each circle of emanation is associated with numerous names and powers, as are the rays that connect the circles. Our group's work is an ongoing search for these correspondences. By understanding the sympathies between manifested forms, we begin to unlock the creative forces of the Cosmos."

"Such correspondences are also known to the Egyptians," Korax said. "Each sphere has its daemons, spirits, and gods. Also associated numbers, sounds, colors ..."

"Yes," Krateros whispered. "Each nation has its own variations. Yet, the essentials of all the traditions correspond. That is one of the wonders we have learned. Here in Alexandria, for the first time in history, practitioners from many lands have gathered to share and compare their wisdom. It is the perfect time and place to be a magician!"

Korax smiled, momentarily caught up in the high priest's excitement. But as his eyes returned to the Tree of Creation, a troubling thought loomed, appalling in its intensity.

"With so much knowledge, known and unknown. How can one ever hope to attain true proficiency in these arts?"

"Ha!" Krateros laughed. "That is the challenge, isn't it?"

"A challenge for fools."

Both men were startled by Zakur, who had approached their table unnoticed. The black-robed Hebrew nodded grimly at Korax, then took a seat on the bench opposite.

"My friend Zakur and I hold differing opinions on the subject," Krateros explained with an unruffled air. "I deem all wisdom worthy of study. I feel it is the calling of the magician to know as much as possible."

"While I shun even the title 'magician,'" Zakur said. "In my view, the purpose of the Mysteries is not to tickle man's vanity with magic. It is purely and simply to seek union with the Godhead. I liken the divine arts to this mound under which we sit. If the goal is to reach the summit, should a man not seek the most direct route? Or should he meander endlessly, scrutinizing every stone?"

Zakur's vehemence left Korax a little numb. Gravely, he pondered the man's argument.

Krateros yawned and stretched. "As I mentioned, you will find many opinions in our Society. Each member must choose his own path through the maze—or up the mound, as Zakur would have it." He waved at the book-lined walls. "All the knowledge we have collected is at your disposal."

Korax rolled his eyes over the immense collection. "That is gratifying, to be sure. But I had hoped to find guidance and instruction."

"Yes, yes, of course," Krateros answered. "There are many study groups you might join. Our Society includes astrologers from Babylon, a mage from Persia, a haruspex from Etruria. Or you might wish to start with the group led by Zakur and myself. Our subject is magical languages and the conjuring of spirits. It would give you a solid introduction to the complexities of the Tree."

"That would be helpful." Korax felt a little relieved, though his uncertainty lingered. "I am grateful to you both."

"So be it," Zakur said. "Now, I believe you were going to share some Egyptian texts with us."

"Yes, willingly."

Korax opened his satchel. He had made copies of most of the texts he had carried with him from Memphis. There was only one exception: a particularly arcane work that an inner prompting had told him to hold in reserve.

For the next half-hour, he read the Egyptian spells and incantations to Krateros and Zakur. They conversed about the hieroglyphs and the magical powers inherent in the symbols. At first, both of the elders seemed enthralled. But gradually Zakur became quiet and withdrawn. Finally, he prodded Krateros' elbow.

"These texts are fascinating, to be sure. But we do have other business to discuss. Perhaps we should adjourn to your study and allow Astrametheus to peruse the library."

"Oh? Yes, very well." The high priest of Pan scratched his curly head. "Examine the library at your leisure, Astrametheus." He and Zakur gathered up the Egyptian rolls. "I will have someone catalog these and shelve them. We will talk again."

The two men departed, leaving Korax alone in the airy, silent hall. For a time he sat motionless, his eyes roaming over the imposing stacks. An aching hopelessness settled in his heart, as though he were once again entering what the priests of Memphis called the Mazes of Magic—a dark, endless labyrinth from which he might never emerge.

He had not anticipated such a feeling. Indeed, he had expected the same elation he recalled from the day of his initiation into the House of Life. But then he had been naïve, unaware of the exhausting labors demanded of a magician. And he had been motivated by a burning purpose, to regain his freedom.

*What was his purpose now?* A voice in the circle last night had said that his spirit was lost; he did not know what he wanted. Perhaps this was due to the fact that his memories were still not fully restored. If he was not entirely sure of his identity, how could he know what he truly wanted?

Korax shook himself free of this gloomy introspection. Curiosity impelled him to rise and examine the library.

He found to his pleasure that most of the texts were either written in Greek or had been translated. The books ranged from the most elementary to the most abstruse. He found treatises on mathematics, astronomy, and alchemy; illustrated studies of herb lore and potions; rituals and prayers to the gods of India, Persia, Scythia; explanations of the runic alphabets of the Germanic and Celtic peoples.

Korax was leaning high on a ladder, studying a Babylonian star chart, when a voice surprised him and he nearly lost his balance.

"Krateros said I might find you still here," Miriam cried. "Oh, I am sorry! I did not mean to startle you."

Gripping the shelf, Korax glanced down at her and laughed. He lowered himself agilely to the floor.

"They were talking about you," Miriam said, "Krateros and my father. I hear you are going to join our study group."

"Yes. Krateros invited me. So you are also a member?"

"It is one of the groups I work with."

"Really? What are the others?"

Her secretive smile appeared and quickly vanished. Her gaze shifted to the wall of books. "What do you think of our library?"

"Astonishing ... And a little overwhelming. To be honest, it makes me question whether I can ever learn enough."

"Oh? You surprise me. This is not the blithe, self-assured Korax I know."

He laughed dully, shaking his head. "I am certainly not so blithe and self-assured as I wish to appear."

Surprised by his confession, Miriam's voice grew soft. "But you don't have to learn everything. Only enough to follow your path."

Korax shrugged, feeling hopeless again. "You have perceived my problem exactly—discerning my path."

Her face expressed a gentle empathy. "You remember Peristeria, the priestess? After reading you in the circle last night,

JACK MASSA

she believes you have great talent as a seer. Would you like to try an experiment? A little test of your abilities?"

Korax grinned, nodded in acquiescence.

"Good!"

Miriam led him out of the library and up the ramp to the second gallery. Halfway around the circle, they entered a small alcove with stone benches and a basin full of water. Miriam took two cushions and tossed them on the floor. From a shelf she took a silver bowl and dipped it in the water.

"Have you used a scrying bowl before?"

"Many times," Korax said.

Miriam set the bowl on the floor, then sat cross-legged on one of the cushions. Korax settled himself across from her.

"I will send images into the water with my mind," she said. "You then tell me what you see."

Korax shut his eyes and stilled himself. When his spirit had quieted, he looked into the bowl and let the impressions flow into his mind.

"I see a cat, a gray one ... Now he has taken on human shape. He is Bast, the Egyptian god of cats."

"Oh, well done." Miriam's eyes glistened. "Now you cast an image, and I will try."

Korax obeyed. Several moments passed.

"I see a city." Miriam stared with hollow eyes. "A fine Greek city on a hill. There is a giant there, a golden giant standing near the harbor. He is enormous!"

"It is Rhodos," Korax said. "My home."

"You miss it very much."

Tears welled in his eyes. Korax deliberately pressed down the surge of grief.

"I think you will return some day," Miriam said quietly. Then she brightened: "We have an affinity, you and I. I sense that, by working together, we can help each other's powers grow. If you are willing?"

"Oh, yes. I am willing."

They stared at one another in silence. The constriction around Korax's heart seemed to dissolve. Without thinking, he reached over and squeezed her hand.

His touch broke the spell. Miriam shifted and pulled her hand free. She stood, her face flushed and tense.

"I must go now. My father will be looking for me."

She poured the water back into the basin and replaced the bowl on the shelf.

"I will see you at the study group," she said and hurried away.

# Chapter Eight

The constellations of summer wheeled slowly into the southern sky. Long, scorching days baked the deserts of Egypt. But in Alexandria, steady winds from the sea kept the atmosphere balmy and pleasant.

Korax was living a dual life—as a dabbler in music and poetry at the Museum and as a serious student of the Mysteries.

Metiochus the schoolmaster soon lost interest in him, since Korax failed to return the man's romantic advances. But Korax continued to read in the Library. He listened to public lectures and attended seminars given by poets. He purchased an expensive lyre and regained his familiarity with the instrument. He began to sing at parties and recitals and soon attracted the notice of the literary elite, for they always valued talented young players. The maudlin, shaggy Asclepiades in particular befriended Korax and invited him to salons and banquets. Korax enjoyed the poet's rowdy spirit and mordant honesty. Asclepiades in turn appreciated Korax's youth, quick wit, and excellent singing voice.

His excursions into the scintillating world of the Museum gave Korax welcome relief from his metaphysical work. He was finding the pursuit of the magical arts increasingly tedious and frustrating.

Once each fortnight, he met with the study group, sometimes at the Paneum, sometimes at the house of Zakur in the Jewish Quarter. The members gathered around a large table spread with papyrus rolls. Speaking in varied accents, they would expound on the texts they were reading, discuss principles, compare the teachings of their different traditions. Each magician would leave with an assignment, a new incantation to write or an approved conjuring to perform. At the next meeting, the members reported their results back to the group.

Korax performed his solitary work in his room at the Seven Seeds Inn. He drew a circle on the floor with charcoal, burned incense and scented candles, traced sigils in the air with dagger and wand. He uttered the syllables of magical formulas, breathed deeply, and waited.

Often the effects were imperceptible, the experiments failures. But sometimes a being would appear in his mind, a daemon or spirit, a visitor from one of the vast multitude of realms in the living Cosmos. Then Korax would test the creature, ask questions, record the responses.

Through this deliberate creation of rites, and practice to test their effects, the group intended to develop a corpus of magical knowledge, a mapping of all the hidden correspondences in the Universe. The concept sounded intriguing. But in practice it devolved into an exercise in abstractions, an endless pursuit of knowledge for its own sake.

As to the uses of magic, practical application, such matters were almost never discussed. Korax gathered that some of the elders, at least, put their knowledge to use—for spiritual transformation, even to wield power on the earthly plane. But they never shared the secrets of those workings, or, if they did, it was only with a trusted colleague or apprentice. Each magician was expected to find his own spiritual path. More and more, Korax felt exactly as he had when studying at the House of Life, a wanderer lost in a maze.

Most of the work was done in Greek, but Korax also tutored some of the group in the Egyptian writing and the spells he had brought out of Memphis. At the same time, he and a few others learned the rudiments of the Hebrew alphabet from Zakur. Suspecting that the Hebrew books contained occult power, Korax tried to get Miriam to teach him the language in more depth. But Miriam always declined.

Unaccountably, she had resumed her initial attitude of reserve. She no longer spoke of their working as a pair to increase their abilities. Korax thought he must have offended her that day in the alcove by taking her hand. But when he tried to apologize, she brushed the matter aside as though the incident never happened.

As for Kalyssa, Korax had not seen her since the night of his initiation, and he often wondered why. She did not frequent the Paneum or even attend the general meetings held every month under the full moon.

At those gatherings, the magicians all dressed in white robes and gold masks. After discussing general business and meditating together, they would perform the rites of Pan, chanting as they marched around the seven inner galleries, rising in a slow spiral to the distant ceiling. Emerging onto the roof at last, the company shared the sacred meal to honor all the gods and goddesses.

Korax never missed the monthly gatherings. They were the only time that the Society seemed at all like a community, when Korax the magician did not feel so utterly alone.

A winged creature hovered in his mind, with blue skin and yellow hair blown by a perpetual wind.

"Fair and lovely spirit," Korax whispered. "Tell me your name."

"I am Nomarabek, the Lion of the Air."

"Tell me of your realm."

"It is the sky beneath the Moon. It is home to ten thousand voices. The wind sighs in its belly."

*Lovely poetry*, Korax thought. But he had heard much like it before. He put down his stylus and tablet.

"What can you tell me of Rhodes?"

"That island is your home."

"Yes. What is happening there, with my family? Have they received the letters I sent?"

"I cannot tell."

"You mean you cannot see?"

"I cannot tell you."

"But why?" His voice rose in frustration. "Why are these matters hidden from me?"

"I cannot tell you."

Korax growled and thrust himself to his feet. With curt words he dismissed the daemon, then drew a banishing pentagram in the air. Restlessly, he paced the circumference of his magic circle. After a time, he sat down again at the center. He fired a fresh lump of incense and prayed for Hermes to appear.

"Korax of Rhodes, I am here at your summons."

"Swift Herald of the Gods, I thank you. I am troubled and need your advice. For all my scrying and conjuring, I still can learn nothing of Rhodes or my family. No replies have come from my parents, though adequate time has now elapsed."

"What do you suppose is the reason?"

"I do not know ..." Since arriving in Alexandria, he had dispatched three letters on three different ships. Delivery of messages over the sea was a haphazard business, but surely one of those posts should have reached his mother and father.

"More than two years have passed," he whispered grimly. "Perhaps they both are dead."

"Not a possibility you wish to consider. But there is also another."

"Yes," Korax muttered. The deepest doubt of all, the fear he continually tried to deny. "That all my memories are false. That I am not the Korax of Rhodes I remember. That I will *never* regain my past."

"That is indeed your fear."

But he recalled so much: his father, white-haired Leontes, his much-younger mother, Anticleia, small and dark with somber eyes. More: an uncle, aunts, cousins; family banquets and business disputes; sailing on freighters in his teens, visiting the ports of the Aegean, learning the winds and currents; reading in the library of his school; sweating below decks in a galley, his hands blistered from the oars that summer when he trained with the navy.

"Where could all those memories have come from, if they are not real?"

"I can assure you they are real," Hermes said. "You *are* that Korax of Rhodes you remember."

"Then what is the answer?" he cried with exasperation. "Why can I not remember how I came to Egypt? Why can I not see Rhodes now with my scrying?"

"Some things are hidden by Fate," Hermes said, "whom men call the Goddess Tyche. As your poets tell you, in the affairs of mortals, she is supreme. And she is fickle. Sometimes, the best a mortal can do is wait for her to reveal her secrets."

Korax smacked the floor in irritation. "But how can I live with the uncertainty? Perhaps I should just go to Rhodes and face whatever awaits me there."

"You are free to do that, or to stay."

Korax opened his eyes and stared at the dim, empty room. He had desired freedom for so long. Now freedom itself was a burden. He peered into his heart, seeking guidance. The answer came forcefully: Before he could return to Rhodes, he must gain better mastery of his magic.

"I will stay for now," he said. "I will continue my studies."

Hermes agreed. "That is the path the gods favor for you. There is much you can discover here. But it requires you to show patience."

"Patience again." Korax laughed bitterly. The same word the Goddess Isis had chided him with in Memphis, insisting he must endure the life of a slave. *Why must the gods always counsel him to patience?*

"Because you are a foolish, impatient mortal," Hermes answered the unspoken question. "Now, I suggest you write another letter to your parents, since it is possible the others did not reach them. Then I suggest you return to your studies, since this is the path you have chosen. Finally, I recommend that you give thanks to the gods and enjoy your time in Alexandria. Your life here is really most pleasant."

The rites of Pan had just ended. The white-clad members of the Society chatted on the circular roof. Korax spotted the Phoenician priestess Peristeria, standing alone by the parapet. He had heard it mentioned that Kalyssa was her pupil. He approached politely.

"Good evening, lady. Perhaps you remember me, Astrametheus of Hermopolis?"

A droll expression appeared on her painted face. "Oh, indeed, young man. I remember you well."

"I am curious about your study group, the methods that you teach."

"Yes. But mainly you are curious about my friend Kalyssa."

Korax tilted back, chagrinned. "You read me too well."

"It is not hard," the priestess said with a laugh.

"It's only that I have not seen her in so long. I wonder if she is still a member. I hope she is not unwell."

"She is quite well." Peristeria stretched her arms overhead. "And of course she is still a member. She does not often come to the general meetings. As an ambassador's wife, she has many obligations."

"Of course."

"Would you like to see her again?"

Her frankness unnerved him. Still, he grinned. "I confess that I would."

"We've only been waiting for you to ask. Miriam does not feel you are a good choice for our circle, but I think that's because you make her shy. Our group is mostly women, but it is not for women exclusively. I believe men have much to add, if they are the right kind of men." She reached out a finger and traced something on his forehead. "Are you interested, Korax?"

Her speaking his true name was somehow not surprising. "What forms of art do you practice?"

"Well," Peristeria chuckled. "We don't spend time reading and theorizing. Our rites are most ancient. Our road to the gods is through our senses and feelings."

"Interesting. And you say Miriam is a member?"

"Oh, yes. I think you will see a completely different side of Miriam in our group."

"I have no doubt," Korax said. "I am intrigued."

"I thought you would be."

# Chapter Nine

**B**eyond the Jewish Quarter and the Gate of the Sun, the Canopic Way became a broad thoroughfare through the suburb of Eleusis. Here, past the sprawling hippodrome and temples to various deities, stood mansions of wealthy Alexandrians built among shady groves and pleasure gardens. Peristeria owned a relatively modest villa on the seaward side. The house, of brick and pink plaster, sat on the crest of a low hill planted with cypress and acacia trees.

Korax arrived in the evening, somewhat later than he planned. He had walked the entire distance from his inn. Peristeria had recommended that he hire a carriage, but Korax needed to preserve his funds. Life in Alexandria was expensive. Since his purchase of the costly lyre, his purse had become distressingly light.

The orb of the moon had already risen over the road. From within the walled enclosure, Korax heard the distinct throbbing of drums. He crossed the front garden and pounded on the stout wooden door. The gatekeeper, a muscular fellow with a shaven head, opened it a crack and scrutinized him warily. Korax identified himself and inquired if this was the residence of the high priestess Peristeria. The man pulled the door open and motioned him inside.

Korax followed the drumming across a flowered courtyard and into an airy hall. A serving maid took his chlamys and sword. She signed for him to sit on the edge of a marble fountain. While she removed his sandals, Korax noticed the carving on the fountain wall—a wild daemon with beard and brows of curling leaves. The face reminded him of a Thracian god known to his mother.

The woman washed his feet and anointed them with perfume. She handed him a white chiton of fine linen and a wreath of jasmine for his head. When Korax had changed into this apparel, she led him down a corridor painted with frescoes of satyrs and nymphs. The insistent drumming sounded from a portal ahead. The servant bowed and parted the beaded curtain.

He crossed into a wide rectangular chamber. Ionic columns surrounded a central, sunken floor with an opening in the roof above. A copper brazier burned in the middle, unleashing flames and clouds of perfumed smoke. Near the brazier stood a graceful carving of three goddesses, their backs to one another, their forearms intertwined. Bouquets of roses and chrysanthemums covered the altar at their feet.

The members of Peristeria's group were already present—Korax counted nine women and four men. Some he recognized from the Paneum, but others were new to him. All wore the light chitons and garlands of jasmine. They beat on hand drums or shook tambourines. Some waved their arms and danced with agile movements. Others reclined on cushions arranged on the steps around the sunken floor. Korax spotted Miriam, seated in a corner, eyeing him solemnly.

A jolly Peristeria appeared and clasped his arm. "My young friend, I am so glad to see you. I feared you might have changed your mind."

"Please pardon my late arrival," Korax said.

"No apologies are needed. You have missed nothing. Come."

Peristeria led him to a serving table set with a krater. Lithe figures of maenads and flute players encircled the bowl, painted glossy black on an orange background. The priestess dipped a shallow wine cup and presented it to him.

"Drink the nectar of Astarte and be blessed."

Korax swallowed the curious, amber-colored wine. It tasted sweet and sharp on the tongue, lingered and burned in the back of his throat. He began to feel intoxicated at once. Peristeria refilled his cup.

"Again."

Korax eyed the drink dubiously, but at her nod of encouragement he swallowed it down. Hugging his arm to her breast, Peristeria led him to a cushion a few steps away.

"Rest, my dear. The disorientation soon will pass."

Korax frowned, confused by her words. He lifted his face to ask her something, but she was already across the room. He realized belatedly that the wine must contain a powerful drug. He squinted at the fire, gauging its effect on his wits.

A young woman slid down onto the cushion beside him, bracelets jingling on her arms: Kalyssa.

"My friend, Korax! I am so pleased you decided to join us at last."

He gazed at her stupidly. "I only just learned that I was invited."

She arched her thin eyebrows. "How slow-witted of you!"

"Truly."

He stared at her face, flushed from dancing. Her eyelids shone green with malachite pigment; her lips glistened with rouge. He smelled her perfume and a wild arousal pulsed through his body. Under the chiton, his phallus hardened.

Kalyssa stood with the ease of a serpent uncoiling. She tugged on his arm. "You must dance."

"No, no," Korax replied. "I have no skill at dancing."

"Yes, yes," she laughed. "It is part of the rite. You must let the Graces move your limbs."

Despite his weak protests, she dragged him up. Under his bare feet the floor felt cool and soft—smooth green tiles scattered with rose petals.

Everyone was dancing now, even Miriam. Korax glimpsed her on the far side of the circle, gliding gracefully, swaying her hips. Their eyes met for an instant, then hers flitted away.

Kalyssa led him around the altar, stepping nimbly to the drumbeat. Awkwardly at first, Korax mimicked her movements. Soon the rhythm of the drums and the drug in his veins loosened his inhibitions. He stepped in time with the others, flailing his arms, pivoting on the balls of his feet. Someone handed him a tambourine, and he struck it in a fit of joy.

Round and round the magicians danced. Peristeria uttered a trilling, wordless cry. Other women repeated the sound, like the ululating call of some weird marsh bird under the moon. Korax looked up through the opening in the roof and saw stars spinning.

He never knew how long he danced. Some time later, he rested on the steps, sweating and exhausted. Kalyssa sat beside him, holding his hand, her ringed fingers twined in his. Once again, she had become his guide.

Peristeria stood before the altar and lifted her hands high. She pronounced an invocation in some unknown barbaric tongue. The members of the circle answered, chanting in hollow voices. Korax did not know the words, but he mouthed the syllables with all the others.

The fire sputtered and leapt higher. Korax blinked and stared. A being had appeared inside the writhing flames, a figure of gleaming gold. He stood a cubit high, a kind of satyr, in shape half-human and half-ram.

"Al Om Neb Kum Saan!" Peristeria intoned.

The other magicians echoed her words.

Beneath curving ram's horns, the daemon in the fire gazed about with curiosity. His lips parted, but Korax seemed to hear the voice in his head, not through his ears.

"The war in Asia now to end. Lower Syria under Egypt's banner. The purple cities find peace and prosper."

Kalyssa whispered in his ear. "Do you see the creature, Korax?"

"Oh, yes."

"You may ask him a question then."

"No need. He has already spoken his prophecy."

Korax awoke sprawled on a cushion. Full daylight shone through the outer peristyle. Several of the company still slept in the chamber, alone or cuddled in pairs. Wisps of smoke curled from the dying embers in the brazier.

He wandered outside and found the latrine. Back in the house, a servant directed him to a shaded veranda. Peristeria and a few of her guests were enjoying a breakfast of almond cakes and fruit. The smell of the sea drifted up through the garden. A bare-breasted young woman blew languid notes on a flute.

Peristeria greeted him warmly and introduced him to her companions. Korax knew one of the elder men from the Paneum, a Babylonian wizard. The others were strangers, dark-eyed women from Syria and the east.

Korax sat down on a stool and sipped a cup of water. The priestess asked him his impressions of their ritual. Her eyes widened when he described his vision and what the daemon in the flames had told him.

"You continue to surprise me. Anyone who can see the spirit is free to ask for a prophecy. But the answer you received unbidden was to the question I asked. The purple cities are Sidon and Tyre. The daemon foretells that the war there will end."

Korax nodded vacantly, his thoughts adrift. Perhaps the drug had not fully worn off.

"Your talent is appreciated. I hope you will consider joining us again," Peristeria said. "That is, if you did not find the evening disagreeable."

"Hmm? No, on the contrary, I quite enjoyed myself."

"I am glad. But you are wondering about Kalyssa. She went walking on the beach. I believe, if you go there now, you will meet her."

Korax smiled and set down his cup. He took his leave of the company and descended the steps into the garden. A winding footpath led him down the hill to a beach of black shingle.

The sun burned orange in the warm, humid air. Waves churned on the pebbles, like the slow breathing of a huge, invisible goddess. Korax spotted two women treading along the shoreline in the distance.

Walking toward them, he recognized Kalyssa and Miriam. They stopped and watched him approach. Korax spied faint smiles on their lips.

"He looks quite fit," Miriam remarked.

Kalyssa's smile widened. "We were wondering if you would have a headache."

"No indeed." Korax lifted his shoulders. "I am well."

Miriam thrust out her hand, palm up. "I have been unfriendly to you, for silly reasons—reasons I myself do not fully understand. Please forgive me."

Abashed, Korax touched her fingers. "Of course. I want us to be friends."

"And so we are. I am happy that you joined our circle. I hope you will return." Miriam hugged Kalyssa, and the two women kissed on the cheek.

"I will go and pack my things," Miriam said, eyeing them both with a brief, mysterious smile.

"I will follow shortly, my dear," Kalyssa answered.

She and Korax watched the young woman walk off toward the villa.

"I did not know you and Miriam were such close friends," Korax said. He had often wished for a chance to speak alone with Kalyssa. Now the moment felt deeply awkward.

"Yes. She is a dear child. She is like my little sister. And Peristeria is like an aunt to us both."

Her glance shifted back up the beach. Miriam, walking steadily, was now well beyond hearing them.

"She is fond of you, you know," Kalyssa murmured, "perhaps even infatuated. You must be careful of her feelings."

Korax reflected. He felt a protective affection for Miriam, as he did for his young cousins in Rhodos. "I understand. I would not harm her."

Kalyssa began to stroll. "You are a compassionate young man, and gifted. You can even dance a little."

"The weakest of my talents, surely," Korax grunted.

"Did you find our rite worthwhile?"

He contemplated the question. "I can conjure spirits with less effort using the techniques of Krateros. Yet, Peristeria's arts hold their own fascination."

He gave her a meaningful, ardent gaze. Noting the look, Kalyssa merely wrapped her garment closer and said nothing.

After a few more steps, Korax asked, "Your husband is not a member of the Society?"

She chuckled at the idea. "No, indeed. He is no magician."

"Yet he does not mind your participation?"

"Why should he?"

"Well, it takes you away from his house at night, even overnight."

She shook her head. "Ours is not a love match but an alliance between families. We respect each other and observe our social duties. Beyond that, we have separate lives."

"I see." Korax's voice lifted hopefully. "And he is not concerned about scandal?"

She laughed cynically. "My dear friend, this is Alexandria. A married lady is not considered fashionable unless she has a lover or two."

Impetuously, Korax gripped her arm. "Does that include you, dear lady? Are you fashionable in that way?"

She paused a moment, weighing the temptation. Then a teasing smile lit her face. "What an impertinent question! And certainly not one I should answer."

She walked on toward the house. "My carriage will be waiting. Do you have a carriage or do you need transport?"

Korax trudged glumly after her. "A ride would be most welcome."

She squeezed his arm. "Fine, we will all ride back together. What a pleasant time we shall have: you and I and Miriam."

# Chapter Ten

On the floor of the king's council chamber was a vast colored mosaic, a detailed map of the world. It stretched from India to Iberia and the far islands of Albion, from Nubia and Ethiopia to the Celtic and Scythian outlands—all surrounded by the great River Ocean.

With the voice of General Phradmon droning in his ears, Ptolemy stared down at the map, mentally tracing the boundaries of his realm. He could scarcely believe his good fortune.

The war for Lower Syria was over, after six years of bloody, indecisive campaigning. King Antiochus had been forced to make peace, his attentions distracted by rebellions in the east and an incursion of Celtic barbarians into Anatolia. Phradmon had returned in triumph, carrying the signed treaties. Now he reported on the disposition of troops along the new borders, the towns he had garrisoned.

The chamber was built to resemble the assembly halls of the old Greek cities. Tiers of marble seats rose on four sides around the mosaic floor. High ministers and retainers sat nearest to the king, subordinates and scribes grouped behind them. A host of attendants and guardsmen stood around the fringes. Only the king and queen had chairs, cushioned thrones of Indian rosewood, intricately-carved and gilded.

Ptolemy wore a ceremonial breastplate of chased gold, the red and purple cloak of kingship, the diadem on his head. Today his realm spread farther than his father's had ever done. All of Egypt was his, and now Syria north to Byblos. Cyprus was firmly in his grasp, and most of Crete paid him taxes. A chain of protectorates and alliances secured him the Aegean. The coastal cities of Asia paid him tribute as far as the Hellespont.

JACK MASSA

Yet Ptolemy did not feel secure.

Paradoxically, the news from Syria had incited worry, a slithering fear in his belly. Ptolemy studied the world map as if seeking the cause.

In Macedonia, Antigonus Gonatas had recently regained the throne. Many discounted him as a serious threat, viewing his position as far too precarious. But Ptolemy's stomach said otherwise. Grandson of the first Antigonus, son of Demetrius the Besieger, Gonatas seemed to share his family's remarkable resiliency. And, unlike Ptolemy, Gonatas was a seasoned warrior, adored by his troops.

Still, Ptolemy's fleet commanded the Aegean. And Arsinoe had planted a network of agents in all the major cities of Greece, surreptitiously stirring the populace against their Macedonian overlord. Hopefully, all that would keep Gonatas bottled up for many years.

Ptolemy's gaze traveled eastward, across Anatolia. The third great kingdom to emerge from Alexander's empire was that of Seleucus, now ruled by his son Antiochus. But that realm was vast and disconnected. Originally it stretched all the way to India, but already the eastern provinces had broken away. Now Antiochus had the Celts to contend with on his western flank....

"We thank you for your report, General Phradron," Arsinoe was saying. "We are satisfied with your diligent efforts. I know the king wishes to reward you personally."

"What? Oh, yes. Well done, general." Ptolemy slipped a gold ring from his finger.

The burly officer stepped up to receive the trinket, bowed stiffly to the king. Backing away, he bowed even more deeply to Arsinoe. "I accept this royal gift in honor of all the brave men of arms who serve your glorious kingdom, both on land and sea."

"Thank you, good friend." Ptolemy waved to silence him.

The council turned next to civilian administration of the new territories. The king's Chancellor, a subtle, white-haired official named Eupolis, called for reports from several of his ministers.

Soon Ptolemy slipped back into his gloomy preoccupation. His glance wandered over the map to Egypt. By all reports, the Nile was rising nicely, with still a month to go before it crested. Last year's feeble flood appeared to have been an aberration. Next spring, he could raise the taxes again. Then work could resume on opening the great canal from the Nile to the Red Sea. Completion of that project would swell the import of luxury goods from the east—and add much gold to the king's coffers.

Ptolemy's eyes shifted left, along the north coast of Africa. Cyrenaica—now there was a festering problem. The province had grown from a colony founded by Dorian Greeks. Ptolemy's father had annexed the territory, with its capital Cyrene, soon after Alexander's death. The obdurate Cyrenaicans had been troublesome ever since.

The first Ptolemy had installed his son Magus—the present king's half-brother—as viceroy in Cyrene. That solution had worked reasonably well for two and a half decades. But three years ago Magus, now in his fifties, had rebelled and proclaimed himself king. With the family's typical audacity, he marched on Alexandria. Only a revolt of desert tribes, hastily arranged and financed by Ptolemy's treasury, forced him to turn back.

Ptolemy wanted to crush Magus then, withdrawing all the armies from Syria if necessary. But Arsinoe insisted on a political settlement. Too costly to storm Cyrene, she said. Let Magus keep his little kingdom of sand. Buy him off with an alliance. She'd been wise to keep the forces in Syria, of course, as events had now proven.

Or ... perhaps she was saving Magus, to use as a lever against him?

Ptolemy turned to his queen, resplendent in her glittering ruby necklace and gold-threaded himation. Her eyes shifted to him, darted back to the minister giving the report. As usual in council, she was the one asking the questions, her mind like a scythe, sweeping to the essentials, leaving no pertinent fact unexposed.

*Was Arsinoe still a threat?* By agreeing to marry her, to make her queen and co-regent, he had satisfied her, surely. He always deferred to her on policy decisions. She was worshipped as co-pharaoh, her own cartouche carved on all the temples of Egypt, not to mention the giant temple he was raising for her cult in Alexandria. Surely all of that was enough to satiate even her ambition.

*Or was it?*

He must never underestimate her, a lesson her previous royal husbands had failed to learn. Sometimes, he almost believed she was a goddess—just as desirable, as fickle, as dangerous. No matter how much he depended on her political genius, no matter how deeply he relished their perverse marriage, he could never fully trust her.

Mournfully, Ptolemy scanned the sea of faces in the council hall. Who was there that a king could fully trust? His gaze drifted inevitably to the grisly countenance of old Drakas.

"Trust no one," his father had said, when nearing death. "But distrust Drakas last of all."

Not far from the Museum stood the Royal Odeion, a semicircular theater with tiered seats for five thousand. This evening the gorgeous, high-roofed hall was thronged with Alexandria's elite. In celebration of their victory in the war, the king and queen had commissioned new works from the city's great poets.

Kalyssa sat in the fourth row, dressed in silk and silver. To those who noticed her in the dense and noisy crowd, she appeared pretty and insignificant, an ornamental companion to her distinguished husband. Kalyssa played the role of the immature, guileless wife with practiced ease. But behind her sheer veil, her eyes roved the audience, her receptive mind judging looks and attitudes, measuring expressions, pondering hidden motives.

For Kalyssa, observing the powerful of Alexandria was more than idle amusement—much more. She had been chosen to wed Manolis and accompany him on this mission because of her talent as a sorceress and seer. Her role was to read mental currents, suggest courses of action, ferret out potential allies and foes. The rulers of Carthage had impressed upon Manolis and his wife the importance of this assignment. But it was the priestesses of Tanit who had forecast that its success or failure might ultimately determine Carthage's fate.

Turning her mind from that fearful prophecy, Kalyssa surveyed the courtiers—whose rank and importance was indicated by their proximity to the curtained royal box. Closest to that place sat Chancellor Eupolis with his white hair and voluptuous young Macedonian wife. Next to them sat Zenodotus, the chief librarian and royal tutor. And of course the omnipresent, gloomy Drakas posted himself near the throne.

Arrayed on either side sat the usual gathering of retainers, high ministers, diplomats, scholars, and officials. For the most part, Kalyssa studied the women who accompanied these men. She could usually tell a man's mood and fortunes most easily by observing the demeanor of his woman—those who had women. Men who favored their own sex were typically more difficult to read.

A flourish of brass trumpets sounded at the grand portal next to the orchestra. Everyone stood, anticipating the arrival of the royal family. The theater swelled to the music of flutes and drums. A trio of boys pranced through the portal, dressed in chitons sewn with flowers and scattering petals over the floor. Ptolemy and Arsinoe appeared arm-in-arm, arrayed as the sibling gods in lavish garments of glossy white. Behind them, in measured procession, walked the king's adolescent children—young Ptolemy, Lysimachus, Berenice. Born to Ptolemy's former wife, the children had been adopted by Arsinoe as her own.

Shouts of acclaim and applause filled the hall, echoing off the roof. Standing beside Kalyssa, Manolis clapped tepidly. He considered these boisterous displays rather vulgar.

Watching the monarchs, Kalyssa searched her mind for impressions. The king seemed ebullient tonight, grinning as he waved to the crowd. Ptolemy always enjoyed his entertainments. For all his intelligence and shrewdness, the king was essentially a shallow man.

Arsinoe was another type altogether. That woman's soul had cavernous depths. As ever, the queen appeared gracious and poised as she surveyed the adoring audience. But beneath that gleaming armor, Kalyssa sensed a perpetual tangle of seething emotions—wariness, ambition, fathomless dread. Kalyssa felt simultaneously fascinated and repelled by the queen.

When the royal family was seated, attendants raced up and down the steps, extinguishing half of the scented cressets. Others sidled along the edge of the orchestra, lighting lamps at the foot of the stage.

Another trumpet call signaled the start of the recital. The poet Callimachus, slender and austere, walked out on stage. He spoke in verse, accompanied by the plucking of harp strings from the orchestra. He invoked the Muses and the glorious sibling gods, then introduced the first performance.

For the most part, the poets sang their own compositions. Some played lyres. Others were supported by musicians or choruses who stood in the orchestra. Generally, the works were hymns or paeans, praising the House of Ptolemy in lofty, monotonous terms.

An amusing departure from this trend was a comic mime written by Asclepiades. His piece lampooned the enemies of the royal house. Costumed actors portrayed these rivals as various ignoble beasts, strutting and braying across the stage. The masked chorus routed each in turn simply by singing Ptolemy's name. The king seemed to particularly enjoy the depiction of Antigonus Gonatas as a bearded, bow-legged goat.

An idyll by Theocritus returned the evening to form. The handsome Syracusean seemed intent on surpassing all precedent in glorifying the king. In his clear, high voice, he sang of the far-flung realms that owed Ptolemy allegiance, and lavishly extolled the king's power, wealth, and benevolence.

Callimachus, of course, had the finale. With his usual convoluted style, his hymn expressed adoration of Ptolemy and Arsinoe as the divine siblings. Callimachus seemed completely undisturbed that his poem retraced familiar ground. Some of his lines even sounded like direct copies from earlier pieces. Kalyssa contemplated this performance with puzzlement. She found Callimachus difficult to read—unlike other poets, who tended to be expressive, even flamboyant in exposing their inner selves. She knew Callimachus had been raised as a royal page, a boyhood companion of Ptolemy. A scholar rather than a soldier, he yet held the rank of retainer, "Friend of the King." But by some accounts, it was Arsinoe who bestowed particular favor on Callimachus. His rise to preeminent status at the Museum had occurred following her ascension to the throne. Odder still, Callimachus was a native of Cyrene, and Prodotus, the Cyrenaican ambassador, seemed to view him as a sort of conduit to the royal inner circle. Most scholars warily shunned involvement in politics. Kalyssa wondered if Callimachus might not be an exception.

Following the recital, a reception took place in the grand courtyard outside the Odeion. The fashionable crowd lingered among the fountains and galleries. Many waited in line for a chance to congratulate the poets or be received by the king and queen.

Kalyssa and Manolis chatted in a cluster of courtiers and diplomats. Kalyssa was wishing the tedious evening over when she spotted a figure looming at the edge of the gathering. One of the chorus singers, still wearing his robe and mask, had stopped deliberately to face her. He raised an index finger to the mouth of his mask. Then he turned and noiselessly slipped into the crowd.

The sign of silence suggested a member of the Society of Alexandrian Pan. But what did it mean? Why would a magician flash the secret sign in this public place? Her membership in the Society was another facet of her mission, another possible path to knowledge and the power to shape events. Whatever the meaning of the signal, she dared not ignore it.

"Pardon me for a moment," she said to Manolis. "I've seen someone I must greet."

Perplexed, she wound her way across the courtyard, keeping the masked figure in sight. He paused repeatedly, making sure she could follow. Past the fringes of the crowd, he climbed the low steps of the portico and waited in the shadows. Possessed by a touch of alarm, Kalyssa approached the man.

"Have we met, sir? Or are you some rogue who tries to lure women with mysterious signs?"

"Are you the kind of woman who follows such rogues?"

She laughed, recognizing the voice. "I suppose that would depend on the rogue."

Korax lifted his mask away. "I wondered if you would have the nerve to follow."

She glanced back across the courtyard. Manolis would miss her soon. Still, she lingered, her spirits buoyed. "I am surprised to see you here and in such costume. I knew you were a friend of poets, but not a performer."

"I'm not as artful as most," Korax confessed. "But my voice is sweet enough to get by, so they tell me. Did you enjoy Asclepiades' mime?"

"Oh, yes!" She laughed to recall it. "A highlight of the evening. Do you write poetry of your own as well?"

The question brought a pensive response: "I did once, long ago. These days I play the lyre and sing the words of others. It's not entirely for pleasure. The Museum pays a small stipend for each performance and, to be frank, my funds are low."

Her brow lowered as his meaning sank in. "You don't have money? But I thought your family was wealthy."

"They are." Korax shrugged. "But I am far from home, and the coin I brought to Alexandria is almost gone."

Kalyssa placed a firm hand on his shoulder. "My friend, we must remedy this problem. People with our talents should never lack for money."

# Chapter Eleven

Thi is really thrilling," Miriam cried.

Korax had to agree. He sat in the grandstand with Miriam and Kalyssa, watching the first race of the day. Behind him, the granite seats were crowded with spectators, a colorful, clamoring mob from all strata of society. They watched as five chariots rushed around the oblong track of the hippodrome.

The excitement swelled to a roar as the chariots careered around the final turn. The red team, driven by Triballus of Antioch, held off the others and dashed first across the finish line.

"We won! We won!" Miriam shouted. "How much money did we earn?"

The three friends had arrived in the morning, riding out from the city in a carriage hired by Kalyssa. She had paid for their entry at the gate. More importantly, she had used her prestige as an ambassador's wife to gain them access to the paddock area, where the teams were being walked and harnessed. Korax and the two women leaned on a fence, mentally probing the minds of horses and drivers. Comparing impressions, they reached a consensus on which team they thought would win each race. Then they went out to the courtyard and placed their bets. Kalyssa fronted the funds for the experiment—450 drachmas wagered over nine races.

"With odds of three to one," Korax said, "We are now 150 ahead."

"But this is easy!" Miriam laughed with glee. "Oh, but don't tell my father," she added for perhaps the seventh time. "I am certain he would disapprove."

"This day will definitely be our secret," Kalyssa said, wrapping an arm around each of them.

In the second race their team failed, making a slow start and never catching the leaders. But after that, their luck ran pure. When the eighth race of the day ended, they had picked a remarkable six winners.

Their exultant celebrations did not escape the notice of other spectators. A small crowd gathered around them, expanding after each win. Seasoned gamblers inquired about their picks and compared their own wagers. Others, with no betting interest, cheered with them, enjoying the vicarious thrill of their victories.

During the wait before the final race, the group was approached by a tall, elegant woman in a dress of pale silk and an embroidered himation. Her earrings and intricate necklace sparkled with garnets and gold. Four bodyguards wedged through the crowd to open her way.

"Kalyssa, is that you? I thought I recognized you, my dear."

"Bilistiche!" Kalyssa seemed a bit disconcerted as she kissed the woman's rouged cheeks. "So lovely to see you. These are my friends, Astrametheus of Hermopolis and Miriam, daughter of Zakur the Jew."

Bilistiche gave them a disinterested nod. She spoke to Kalyssa, as though the others were beneath her notice. "Quite an unusual trio you make. Is the ambassador not with you?"

"No. My husband is not a devotee of sport."

"Indeed? You on the other hand appear to be quite the expert. Word of your winning streak has flitted all over the stadium."

Kalyssa lowered her glance, hesitant to reply.

"It's true." Korax inserted himself into the gap. "We're having quite a lucky outing."

Bilistiche eyed him mistrustfully. "Six winners out of eight. I invest in horses, my friend, and I would call that *astonishingly* lucky."

Korax merely shrugged with feigned innocence.

"Perhaps one day you will share your secrets with me," Bilistiche said.

"Perhaps." Korax smiled archly. "One never can predict."

"Who is she?" Miriam demanded when Bilistiche and her entourage had departed. "And why is she so rude?"

"I apologize for her manners," Kalyssa answered. "She is one of a number of unattached noblewomen who decorate the court. Some say she's a distant cousin to the Ptolemies, though others dispute that. But it is widely agreed she is a mistress of the king."

Bilistiche's insulting behavior was forgotten as the last race of the day commenced. Korax and his friends leaped to their feet as their team nudged into the lead on the third circuit. They screamed with jubilation as the chariot held off a late challenge and hurtled across the finish line.

As the crowd dispersed, the friends hurried down to the gate to collect their winnings for the day—seven races out of nine.

The interior of their carriage shook with gleeful laughter as they rode back to the city. Their first stop was the house of Zakur in the Jewish Quarter. As the driver opened the door, Kalyssa reached into her bag and counted out seven silver drachmas. She pressed the coins into Miriam's palm.

"Here, my friend, a little money to spend in remembrance of our adventures."

"Oh, thank you!" Miriam said. "And thank you for bringing me along. I've never had so much fun. But remember, not a word to my father."

"We promise!" Korax and Kalyssa declared simultaneously.

All three of them laughed as Miriam climbed down from the carriage.

"I can't remember when I've had a better time either," Kalyssa confessed when the vehicle was moving again. "I spend so much time playing the diplomat's wife, pretending to be less than I am.

It is such a pleasure to have friends I can be myself with and not pretend."

"It is the happiest day I've had in Alexandria," Korax agreed, "in fact, in many years."

They rode in silence for a time, the cushioned benches rocking beneath them. Soon the carriage approached the gates of the palace complex where they would part. Kalyssa opened the money sack and counted out 450 drachmas, her original investment. Then she set the heavy bag in Korax's lap.

"This is for you."

"What?" Korax was astonished. "You're giving me all the winnings?"

"Of course. Didn't you realize? The whole purpose of today was to finance your stay in Alexandria."

He weighed the sack in his hand: enough coin to support him for a year or more.

The carriage jolted to a stop.

"But how can I repay you?"

Kalyssa placed her small hand on his wrist. "By continuing your studies. By continuing to be my friend."

In his delight, Korax had to suppress the urge to embrace her.

The driver swung open the door.

"When can I see you again?" he asked.

Kalyssa considered. "Perhaps you will honor me by agreeing to dine some evening with the ambassador and myself."

"Of course. It would be my pleasure."

"Bring a guest with you then, someone of culture who can offer diverting conversation."

"Roasted pheasant, baked shellfish, fig pastries ..." As ambassador Manolis spoke, a troupe of attractive youths and girls carried in serving trays heaped with the delicacies. "I endeavored to compose a menu representative of my country, but not overly exotic for your tastes. I hope I have succeeded."

"Most admirably," Asclepiades exclaimed. "My appetite is whetted."

But the poet stared not at the dishes, but at the legs of the pretty slaves who carried them. Korax's eyes swerved nervously to Kalyssa. Across the narrow dining room, on a couch set beside her husband's, she returned the glance with faint disquiet.

When Korax approached Asclepiades, the rowdy poet had leapt at the invitation—relishing the chance to dine with the ambassador of Carthage and his lovely wife. On reflection, Korax wondered if he ought to have chosen a more subdued companion.

During the banquet, a Phoenician woman played the harp with placid strokes. A warm breeze floated in from the portico. The ambassador resided in apartments on the palace grounds east of the Lochias, his gardens overlooking the sea.

Between mincing mouthfuls, Manolis remarked on the recent performances at the Odeion. The conversation revolved onto the various poets of Alexandria, their forms and musical styles.

But, after consuming many tumblers of wine, Asclepiades grew maudlin and surly. "The sorry truth, ambassador, is that our poetry is in decline. We Greeks have not produced a great drama since Euripides nor a decent epic since Homer. The best we moderns can scratch out are short lyrics, but even there we do not approach the centuries-old glories of Alkaios or Sappho. We are dwarves in the shadows of titans." He flourished a greasy hand for emphasis. "In our miserable inadequacy, we dissect the great authors of old, write books about their books. Then other parasites creep behind and write books about our books. It is poetical incest—Oh, please forget I used that word, it's not a subject we ever mention in Alexandria."

"What an unhappy picture you paint," Manolis observed. "Do you concur, Astrametheus?"

Korax lightly set down his cup. "My opinion is only that of a student, of course. But I do not see the picture as quite so bleak. I believe many great poets are writing today, Asclepiades among them. Certainly the idylls of Theocritus move the soul."

"Indeed," Manolis chuckled. "I still shudder to recall that one about the sorceress."

Korax eyed Kalyssa, whose gaze flicked away discreetly.

"Perhaps Astrametheus will favor us with a song," she said. "He's brought his lyre, as I asked."

"Yes, please," Manolis encouraged, "if we might so importune."

"Oh, his voice is honey." Asclepiades lifted his cup for a slave to refill. "He could wring tears from the eyes of a statue. Play something classic, my boy. None of our modern excrement."

Korax picked up his lyre. As he plucked notes and tightened pegs, he considered what to play. With the instrument tuned, he began—a lyric of Sappho, one of his favorite love songs. In it, the great poetess described a wedding feast where she sat watching the bride. She expressed her secret, burning passion for the girl, who henceforth belonged irrevocably to her husband. As he sang the words of hopeless longing, Korax could not help but stare at Kalyssa. By the end of the song, he saw with satisfaction that her breathing was shallow, her skin flushed.

"Marvelous!" Asclepiades proclaimed. "Now that is true poetry. I vow we are gnats by comparison. Gnats!"

Kalyssa excused herself to go and take some air in the garden. Manolis cordially offered his guests more wine. The Phoenician harpist resumed her playing.

But soon the conversation dwindled. Asclepiades had become too drunk for coherent discourse, and Korax's thoughts kept straying after Kalyssa. Presently, the ambassador stifled a yawn. Pleading extreme fatigue, he announced he must retire. He insisted his guests stay and enjoy themselves. He instructed the slaves to attend them.

When Manolis had gone, Asclepiades called for more wine. He seized the slender girl who served him and tried to wrestle her down onto his couch, swearing he would write an immortal poem to her beauty. In the struggle, wine splashed over his arms and face. The girl skipped away, giggling.

Korax took the opportunity to escape outside. He found Kalyssa on the terrace, leaning her elbows on a vine-covered rail. As he drew near, her eyes stayed fixed on the young moon, hung like a sickle over the sea.

"You should not try to seduce me," she said. "I would count it a favor if you did not."

"But why?" Korax demanded. "You plainly feel attraction to me, and I am on fire for you"

She peered at him searchingly, then turned back to the moon. "I save my fire for my magic."

Korax leaned forlornly beside her. "You mean as a priestess of Tanit you must remain chaste?"

She answered after a pause: "That depends on what you seek from the working."

"And what do you seek, Kalyssa?"

"Power, " she answered defiantly, "as great as I can draw."

"Why?"

"To accomplish great things. I have glimpsed the power of the gods, Korax. I would use it to serve my people, my city." She sighed, the passion draining away, leaving a frail note of sadness. "But I'm afraid I lack the talent and probably always will."

Her heart was so noble, Korax thought, her aspirations so fine. That is what magic should be for—to make a difference for good in the world. And on the greatest possible scale.

"What do you seek from magic, Korax?"

"I don't know. I suppose I believe it is my gift. I must follow where it leads, just as Asclepiades and Theocritus must write poetry—simply to be who they are."

"But where does it lead you?"

"Where indeed? That is a question that often torments me."

He stared out to where the moonlight shimmered on the water. He wasn't even sure why he stayed in Alexandria. His magical studies seemed an endless, pointless meandering. But if he had a purpose like Kalyssa's, and could draw down that kind of power ... A thought slipped into his mind, of a certain scroll given him by Amasis in Memphis—the most profound of all the texts, the one Korax had never shared with the Society.

"There might be a way," he said. "I mean to achieve a higher kind of power."

Her eyes opened wide, as though his words had spawned a living presence, a creature she could touch.

"Perhaps you should follow that way, Korax. You have extraordinary talent—all of us see it. If anyone in our circle can achieve that kind of magic, it is you."

In the morning, ambassador Manolis rose from his bed in a sour mood. He pulled on a dressing gown, dabbed perfume in his beard, and ambled off to look for his wife. After a fruitless search of her chambers, he was directed by a maidservant to the garden. He found Kalyssa seated beneath an arbor, amid plots of herbs and flowering vines—plants she had imported from Carthage and Phoenicia and tended with her own hands.

"A word with you, Kalyssa."

"Of course, husband."

She did not look up, preoccupied with a spread of seeds on the bench beside her. The oracle seeds left no room for him to sit down, and she gave no sign of sweeping them up. Annoyed, Manolis paced across the path and sat on the bench opposite. He cleared his throat emphatically.

"I do not object to your following your own interests, or socializing with whomever you wish. But I feel it is an imposition when you require me to spend an entire evening with—shall we say—uncongenial company."

"I am sorry. The evening did not turn out as I expected."

"Indeed." Manolis scratched beneath his thick, curled beard. "Do you know that loutish poet slept all night in the dining room? He's gone now, thankfully. I assume the young one is also."

"Yes, he is gone."

"I trust you will be reasonably discreet."

She frowned, confused. "Oh ... I am not sleeping with him, Manolis."

The ambassador shrugged. His gaze followed hers, back to the oracle spread. After a pause, he continued in a dispirited voice.

"Since we are on the subject of your activities, I have been wishing you might be of more help to me, Kalyssa. With the end of the war, this is a crucial time for us. We need to be gaining the favor of the king and queen, pressing them for an alliance. So far, my progress has been miniscule, at best."

She eyed him coolly. "You are too impatient, husband. Egypt's favor must be cultivated over time. And as for my activities, rest assured: my will is fixed on our mission as firmly as your own."

She moved a hand to indicate the oracle seeds. "I know you view my arts as ineffectual. But I am beginning to see how they might yield results most advantageous to our cause."

# Chapter Twelve

The star-shaped windows in Krateros' study gleamed with reflected daylight. Korax stood at a table beneath one of the stars, a papyrus in his hand. Deliberately, he untied the red ribbon and unfurled the roll.

*The Five Towers of Nectanebo*
*Or The Book of Merging His Soul with the God*

Korax wasn't sure why he had withheld this single text from the Society. But his recent talk with Kalyssa had solidified in his heart the sense that his current studies were insufficient, that he should be attempting much more.

He stared at the inscription Amasis had penned above the title:

Read this one last of all, grandson. Attempt this path only when you have mastered all magical skills and are mighty in the spirit of Maat.

Till now, Korax had only skimmed the text, dissuaded by its complexity and the Egyptian master's warning. Now he sat down and read it through. The roll was written partly in hieratic, partly in the ancient glyphs. It described a technique for merging with a god—not merely calling one down and conversing, not borrowing a bit of mystic energy temporarily, but permanently absorbing a measure of the god's power. Five successive ceremonies were described, which must be performed over a period of years. Before attempting to scale each of the *Five Towers*, the magician had to prepare through extremely intricate and demanding rites.

"Hello, my friend." Krateros walked in from the corridor. "What brings you to my office today?"

Korax bowed respectfully. "I wanted to ask your opinion of this, an Egyptian text."

The tall Macedonian bent over and scrutinized the roll. "Where did you get it?"

Korax waved the question aside with a cryptic expression. Krateros frowned and returned his attention to the papyrus. As he studied it, his prominent eyes bulged.

"Exceedingly interesting. My command of Egyptian is modest, of course. I will ask Manetho to translate it."

"I will make you a copy," Korax assured him. "Mostly, I wanted your opinion of the main idea."

"Extremely profound—if I understand it correctly." He pointed to the inscription at the top. "This writing was obviously added at a later date. Some master warns his—grandson, is the word?"

"Yes."

"... Warns him against these workings until he is well-versed in magic and full of wisdom."

"I know," Korax said. "Understandable, given the purpose of the rites. Some of the books in your library mention such accomplishments, but they provide only hints and riddles."

"Or speak of legendary mages who have done such work," Krateros confirmed. "You are correct. Some of the Society—Manetho among them—claim to have dabbled along these lines. Frankly I have doubts about their claims, or at least their degree of success."

"Then you doubt such workings are possible?"

"Possible? Certainly, they are. Why not?" Krateros glanced soberly at the book. "Dangerous too. To absorb a god is not a trifling thing—hence the master's admonition concerning Maat. Without meticulous care and mental balancing ... well, obliteration of the mind could easily result, don't you think?"

Korax nodded absently. The danger was certain, but the temptation enormous.

Krateros unrolled the papyrus further to scan latter portions of the text. "These preparations are extremely difficult and time-consuming."

"So you would expect," Korax pointed out, "for rites that invoke such colossal power."

Krateros turned to him with open mouth. "Are you intent on pursuing this work, Astrametheus?"

Korax gazed down at the scroll and wondered.

"Hermes, god of magicians, please honor me with your presence."

"My young friend of Rhodes. What would you of me?"

"It is in my mind to undertake a new course of magic."

"So?"

"I seek your advice on the wisdom of this endeavor."

"Why do you wish to ascend the Five Towers?"

"To expand my abilities, to fulfill the potential the gods have given me."

"Those are noble aims. But they are not the only reason. What else does your heart desire?"

Korax could not conceal the answer, from the god or himself. "Kalyssa."

"She has desires of her own. They may not fit with yours."

"I know. I cannot force her to love me. And I would not bewitch her into it. But there is sympathy between our hearts already. If I can draw great power and pledge it to her service, I can win her love. I am sure of it."

"Hmm. The ascent is treacherous. You are young and inexperienced. A magician who is not highly adept might become irretrievably lost."

"I have surmised as much."

"So, you will risk madness to win this woman?"

Korax tightened his lips. That was indeed the risk he was considering. But the desire, the love he felt for Kalyssa ... "Some say love is a form of madness. Perhaps I am already mad."

"A madman does not question the wisdom of his path."

"You are right. Yet I still ask: Do you see this direction as unwise?"

"If I said yes, it would not matter. You have already decided."

The carriage jostled along the Canopic Way toward the house of Peristeria. Beyond the open curtains, the estates and villas of Eleusis crept slowly past, their roofs and treetops flushed in the golden light of late afternoon.

"You seem preoccupied today," Miriam said to Korax. "What is on your mind?"

Resting on an elbow, he gazed blankly at the two women. They sat together on the opposite seat, among perfumed draperies and cushions—Miriam in her modest robes, Kalyssa with her silk gown and bare arms adorned with bangles.

"Did you hear me?" Miriam pressed.

"Yes. You are correct. I am preoccupied."

"By what?"

Korax sat up with a sigh. "I might as well tell you both now. This will be my last visit to Peristeria's circle for a while." He reached into the satchel at his feet. "I have decided to attempt a new course of studies. They will consume all my attention."

He fished out a papyrus and handed it to Miriam. "This is a Greek rendering of the text I will be working from."

Miriam extended the roll and held it in the daylight by the open curtains. Her eyes sped over the text. "This is recondite indeed! You seek to merge your soul with a god?"

"Yes."

Miriam kept reading. "Are you sure this is wise?"

Korax's stare was locked on Kalyssa. He saw a thrill in her eyes, and it ignited his heart.

"I will need assistance at certain times," he said. "A wise friend or two whom I can trust."

"I will assist you," Kalyssa declared, her gaze unwavering.

"Of course," Miriam muttered doubtfully. "We both will help."

# Chapter Thirteen

Winter came to Alexandria, bringing nights of fog and gray, cloudy days. Along the harbors, empty ships rode at anchor or were dragged into shipyards for refurbishing. Steady winds from the north blew brisk and cool, sometimes pulling in rain from the sea.

Korax passed the days and nights submerged in study. He no longer visited the Museum or frequented salons and recitals. His face was absent from the groups led by Krateros and Peristeria. Many days, he neglected even to exercise at the gymnasium. Instead, he worked continuously in the library of the Paneum or in his room at the inn, preparing to scale the first of the Five Towers.

The book actually presented the main rituals only in skeletal form. It prescribed initial rites of purification and intricate, detailed preparations. But it required the magician to write the formulas and invocations for himself, based on the aspirations of his soul.

First, he must choose the god he would merge with. After due reflection and emptying of his mind as instructed by the text, the answer came to Korax: Helios, the all-seeing, all-knowing god of the sun, the patron of Rhodes. Once made, the choice seemed obvious—although, in his heart, Korax never knew if he chose the god or the god chose him.

Each sunrise found him meditating on the lawn of the Paneum. Each evening he contemplated the sunset from the top of the lofty mound. He envisioned the sun-disk blazing at the center of his body—brilliant, all-powerful, eternal.

Often Kalyssa and Miriam would meditate with him, sharing the visualization, amplifying its force. Joining together in this work strengthened the friendship shared by the three of them.

None of them spoke of this, yet all were aware. Their commitment to this magic forged a bond, a profound spiritual connection.

Kalyssa hunted up the herbs and pure resins Korax would need. She assisted in the magical rites to harvest and prepare the plants. Miriam helped by reading aloud the invocations Korax wrote, while he settled his mind into trance and absorbed the words at a deep inner level.

Midwinter approached, increasing the feeling of urgency. The Rituals of Nectanebo could only be performed at one of the four cardinal points of the year, the days of solstice and equinox. Korax hastened to be ready to climb the First Tower at the winter solstice, the most auspicious day of all, the moment of the Sun's rebirth.

The rite required a high place for summoning the god and an inner chamber for receiving him. Krateros provided a cell off one of the upper galleries of the Paneum's interior. The high priest looked forward eagerly to hearing the results of what he considered a most interesting experiment.

Korax acquired an Egyptian staff and carved the top into the figure of a falcon. He purchased a full-sleeved white gown of the finest linen and a band of black silk to cover his eyes. He ate only modest portions of bread and fruit, drank only pure water. As the days grew short, he focused his being more and more on the dazzling image of the sun.

On the day before the solstice, in the late afternoon, he bathed in a pool on the grounds of the Paneum. He donned the fresh white garment and took up the falcon staff. Barefoot, he crossed the clearing and followed the path that wound through the deep shade of poplar trees. At the edge of the grove, he met Kalyssa.

"I wanted to give you my blessing." She squeezed his hand. "And bid you safe journey."

Korax delighted in the love that flowed from her touch.

"Miriam regrets she could not be here," Kalyssa said. "She will bring you the meal tomorrow at noon."

He tightened his grip on her hand. "Miriam is a dear friend, and her talent has been a great help. But you are my muse in this work. I adore you as a poet adores his goddess."

Her breath caught, and her dark eyes glistened. "I only hope I am not sending you into too much peril."

"We both know the dangers. But our preparations have been thorough, and I am not afraid. Kalyssa, if I fail, have no regrets. But if I succeed, whatever power I may draw from the god I will pledge to your service. I promise."

She hugged him impetuously, and Korax reveled in the embrace. After some moments, it was he who asserted his will to separate from her. With a blithe smile, he turned and strode away.

He crossed the temple grounds and entered the mound through one of the secret tunnels. He walked to the center of the vast, empty chamber. There, he traced pentagrams in the air with a dagger and banished all extraneous impulses from his mind. Then, carrying the staff, he climbed the long path up the seven galleries.

In a chilly sunset, he stepped out onto the roof. The last of the day's tourists had already departed. Posting himself beside the altar of Pan, Korax began his chant. In a low, deliberate voice, he uttered the complex formulas he had written to summon the Lord of the Sun.

When the chant was complete, he tied the black silk over his eyes and sat down in the grass. He waited, visualizing the sun blazing in the place below his heart.

The book prescribed an all-night vigil. Korax sat erect through the long, sightless hours. A restless, clammy wind blew in the night. Loneliness crept into his heart, stirring doubts, then fears.

Persistently, Korax forced his thoughts back to the image of the inner sun.

At last, a brightening behind his eyelids told him dawn was breaking. He removed the blindfold and clambered stiffly to his feet. He set a fire in a bronze brazier and burned rose oil and frankincense. Uttering the proper charms, he fed bits of herb one by one into the flames: rue, sage, dill, heliotrope.

Closing his eyes, he breathed in the vapors. He lifted the falcon staff and repeated the long chant of summons to the Sun.

Soon, in his mind's-eye, the god's messenger appeared. A white falcon swooped down out of heaven. With a cry, it dropped a stone at his feet, then wheeled and flew away into the east. Korax opened his eyes and searched the ground. He discovered a smooth rock, a fragment of limestone. Had it been there before? It did not matter. It was the stone, or so he told himself. He picked it up, caressed its smoothness with his thumb.

He left the brazier burning and descended from the high place. Rounding the seventh gallery, he came to his cell, an unadorned chamber six paces square. Inside was an altar, a low table, and cushions. The altar was set with twelve white candles in holders of gold.

Korax took an iron stylus and scratched words and symbols on the soft white stone. After working for a long time, he slipped the stone into a leather pouch and placed it around his neck as an amulet. He lit the candles on the altar, then sat down with his back to the wall of the cell. Staring at the altar and the table, he waited for the next sign from the god.

The table lay empty. It needed food and drink. Dimly, he recalled that Miriam was supposed to bring the sacred meal. After some time, he noticed that the food and drink had appeared: bowls, a basket, a gold cup.

Korax's eyes swerved in his head. They discovered Miriam, standing in the doorway. White radiance shone around her and through her, her form like a vessel of glass. Korax tilted his head in wonder. The whiteness glimmered everywhere.

"Korax? Are you well?" Miriam's voice was a hollow buzzing in his skull.

He tried to speak, but his mouth was numb. He gazed at the candlelights on the altar—yellow stars coruscating in the clouds of whiteness. When his eyes traveled back to the doorway, Miriam was gone.

Korax gazed around the chamber, the radiant brilliance everywhere. The god was close now; he could feel it. He struggled to his feet, leaning on the falcon staff. For the third time he uttered the long chant of summons with all of its magical formulas. He finished by speaking these words:

Come to me, Helios,
God of the Rhodians, Lord of the Blazing Sun,
King, god, master.
I summon thee, god of gods,
Mighty One,
Lord of eternal light, limitless, undefiled.
Indescribable and ageless.
Sol Sosulle Phyte Moath.

I, Korax, son of Rhodes,
Lift my eyes to behold your presence,
Lift my soul to embrace your majesty
Lift my will to absorb your power.
Sol Sosulle Phyte Moath.

From this day thou art inseparable from me,
Thy power is mine,
Thy knowledge is my knowledge,
Thy life is my life.
Sol Sosulle Phyte Moath.

He repeated the words again and again, until the world around him vibrated with the sound. The vibrations intensified, shaking the stone walls asunder. It seemed the sun had come to earth. A light beyond description reached down its arms and took him in.

Kalyssa arrived at the Paneum early in the evening. Entering through the main passageway, she found Miriam waiting anxiously at the portal. The girl's clay lamp cast the only, tiny light in the vast stone chamber.

"I'm so glad you're here," Miriam said breathlessly.

They grasped hands, exchanged kisses. Kalyssa lifted her face toward the high galleries.

"Any word from him?"

Miriam shook her head, her thin shoulders tense. "I haven't been up there since noon when I brought the food. He was ... disengaged from his body."

"It should be over by now," Kalyssa declared. "I'm going up to see."

Miriam still gripped Kalyssa's hand. "Do you want me to come with you?"

"Do you want to?"

"Well, it might be better if only one of us goes. To be honest, it disturbed me to see him like that. Besides, I ought to go home. My father doesn't like my being out after dark."

"My carriage will take you," Kalyssa said. "I left instructions."

"I hope you will be safe."

"Of course. Korax would not harm me."

"If he *is* still Korax."

Kalyssa pondered that idea with a frown. She drew a sign of protection in the air then laid her hand on Miriam's shoulder. "Go, dear one. I will be fine."

Kalyssa lit a lamp wick from Miriam's lamp. She watched her friend disappear down the dark tunnel, then set her shoulders and walked across the chamber. Above her head, the galleries curved inward in their high concentric circles.

She ascended to Korax's cell on the seventh gallery. The chamber stood empty, the candles burned out, the food gone from the table. In the air, Kalyssa sensed a vast immanent force, like the tingling before a thunderstorm.

She circled the gallery and found the doorway to the roof ajar. She squeezed up the narrow passage and emerged under the stars.

Korax stood with feet spread wide atop the altar of Pan, staring down at Alexandria. His back was to her, the falcon staff in his hand. His pose made her think of a king surveying his realm—or a god.

She hesitated, an abysmal terror opening inside her. *What had he become?*

Abruptly, he pivoted and jumped to the ground. He watched her, unsurprised by her presence. In his dark glittering eyes, Kalyssa sensed enormous vitality.

"Korax?" Her voice faltered despite her effort of will. "Are you all right?"

He smiled fondly, bringing her a flicker of relief. The Korax she knew was in there still.

"Did you ... Did it work?"

Korax raised the staff and thrust its point into the ground, leaving it upright. His smile spread into a wild grin. "He is here. His power is in me."

Kalyssa crossed the space between them, seized both of his hands. "And you are all right? You are certain?"

"Yes."

"Oh, I am so glad." She embraced him, trembling in a mad torrent of emotions. He was Korax still. He was not hurt. And he carried such energy! She could feel the heat emanating from his body, warming her to the bones.

She leaned her head back, gazing in wonderment. "What will you do with all this power?"

"I told you. It is yours to command."

"But, nothing for yourself?"

His eyes glowed like an owl's. "There is only one thing I want, Kalyssa. One thing in all the world."

Rapture swelled in her breast. His love was such that he would risk everything for her, scale the heights of heaven, steal the fire of the sun just to lay it at her feet. Such a love was more than she had ever imagined. It kindled an undeniable response in her soul.

"I want you too. O my dear, I want you too."

She pressed her mouth to his. All her doubts and hesitations were gone, burned to nothing by this one thing they both wanted, this brilliant, blinding love.

They sank to the grass together, interrupting their kissing only enough to pull off their garments. She lay beneath him, clutching him with arms and legs. His body on her naked skin felt deliciously hot, like the sun in summer. Then he moved inside her, filling her with his heat. She cried out in a release of joy, the stars flashing far away, the divine sun pressing her down with its blazing need.

When the act was finished he lay atop her, the unquenchable heat still on his skin, though now he shuddered like a weeping child.

"My love, my love," she murmured in his ear. "My joy ... Mine forever ...Forever."

# Chapter Fourteen

The circle of faces stared at Korax with solemn intensity: Krateros, Alcyoneus, Zakur, Miriam, Manetho, and the other magicians of the study group. By concentrating just a little, Korax could read their thoughts. He could practically smell their emotions.

The group sat around a table in an upstairs room at the house of Zakur. Tonight Kalyssa also attended. Wrapped in a himation the color of the night-sky, she sat close to Korax's elbow. Since the night of the solstice, the two had been nearly inseparable.

"Thank you for submitting your account." Krateros set down the papyrus that he had just finished reading aloud. "You've done an admirable job of describing the preparations and the stages of the working. However, I am disappointed that you disclose nothing about what actually occurred at the culmination of the rite."

Korax answered with a blank expression: "For some experiences there are no words."

In his mind, he observed the diverse feelings swirling and clashing around the table: skepticism, curiosity, jealousy, anger.

"Not a very helpful reply," Manetho declared. "And hardly in the spirit of our Society." The bald Egyptian evinced a hostile distrust and, below that, a layer of envy. Manetho had read texts similar to the Five Towers, but had never dared pursue such work. He considered Korax a callow upstart.

"I cannot describe the indescribable," Korax said. "But I can tell you, as I wrote in my document, that I consider the working a success."

"Then you have truly absorbed the power of the sun god," Krateros said with the inflection of a barrister querying a legal point. His feelings were not hostile but neutral. As always, Krateros' overriding drive was pure hunger for knowledge.

"Yes," Korax replied, "a fraction of his power. This was only the first of the Five Towers. Its intent is to open the jar and pour in a few drops of the elixir. Subsequent rites gradually fill the vessel."

"But how do you know you were successful?" Zakur probed. "How are you different now?"

Zakur's interest was mixed with wariness. At a deep level, he felt these workings were unwise, perhaps even blasphemous. Korax glanced at Miriam, seated stiffly beside her father. In part, she reflected Zakur's mistrust. But her feelings roiled with deep contradictions.

Korax attempted to answer the question. "My mental vision is vastly improved. I can sense the thoughts and feelings of others more clearly and easily than before. And if I wish to see a distant place or person, I can generally call the vision readily to mind."

That last part was true, with a single exception. He still could not glimpse anything about his family or Rhodes. Curiously, that inability no longer troubled him quite so much.

"So, increased percipience and farsight." Krateros scribbled notes. "Anything else?"

Under the table, Korax pressed his knee against Kalyssa's thigh. "In one case, I was able to manifest my desire on the outer plane simply by wishing it."

Scanning the faces around the room, he saw an even wider range of attitudes: excitement, admiration, envy, outrage.

"This is a higher order of magic," he explained. "I intend to make it my chief occupation henceforth."

Miriam gazed at him with worry. Manetho glowered. Krateros and a few others were diligently writing.

Zakur cleared his throat. "I urge you to caution, young man. A thirsty man may drink too much and too quickly and drown."

Korax found it irksome for the rigid, narrow-minded Zakur to lecture him so. Still, out of respect for Miriam, he answered courteously.

"I value your opinion, revered sir. But I feel strongly guided to this work. After all, I am only doing what you yourself have often preached—choosing the most direct path up the mountain."

A statue of Hermes, long and dynamic of form, stood in a running pose at the top of the fountain. Beneath his winged feet, water cascaded into a circular pool.

Korax and Kalyssa sat on the pool's rim, their hips and thighs touching. Across from them on a garden chair sat Manolis, dressed in a flowing robe and a gold medallion of office. A table was positioned in front of his knees. Manolis unrolled a large papyrus, a map of all the lands surrounding the Middle Sea.

"My wife informs me you are a skillful seer and might be able to help us with your arts," the ambassador said. "Frankly, my past experience with soothsayers has been unremarkable at best. Still, I am eager to explore any route that might help my diplomatic mission."

"I will aid you any way I can," Korax replied, "for Kalyssa's sake."

In response, she smiled lovingly and pressed herself against his arm.

Manolis gave a small grimace at the blatant display of affection. He motioned toward the map. "How familiar are you with the lands and cities shown?"

The map's legend was written in Phoenician characters, in the Punic language of Carthage. Nevertheless, Korax jabbed his finger at various spots and rapidly spoke the Greek names of the cities:

"Alexandria, Sidon, Antioch, Rhodos, Ephesus, Pergammon, Pella, Athens, Sparta, Syracuse, Carthage, Cyrene."

"Very good," Manolis remarked. "But we must add one other to your list." He fingered a spot midway up the Italic peninsula. "Rome. It is a rising and dangerous power. In just a few generations it has grown from an insignificant river town to a state that now controls most of Italy. It has already conquered the Etruscan cities, which were allies of Carthage. It has annexed most of the old Greek colonies of the south. Presently, there are three great cities of the west: Carthage, Rome, and Syracuse. But Syracuse is weak, torn by factionalism. Eventually it will fall and all of Sicilia with it. Then only two powers will remain, Carthage and the voracious Romans. The statesmen and priestesses of my city all agree in this forecast: that war with Rome is inevitable. Naturally, we seek allies before the gathering storm. Egypt would be a perfect choice."

Korax studied the map. "I would expect that of the three cities, Egypt's natural ally would be Syracuse, since both are ruled by Greeks."

"Young man, that is exactly what Carthage would wish. We would encourage King Ptolemy to intervene in Syracuse, to prop up the current government or establish a client ruler. Either way, a Syracuse bolstered by Egypt would form a buffer between Carthage and Rome. My government has secretly suggested this course to the king and queen, so far with no result. Their position is neutrality in the west. They wish to maintain good trade relations with all three states."

"That is our dilemma," Kalyssa said quietly to Korax. "My heart tells me that you, with your seer's vision, may discern a course that will lead us to success."

Manolis added: "Ideally, we wish to secure a firm military alliance between Carthage and Alexandria and a pledge of intervention in Sicilia. But at the very least, we must ensure Egypt's continued neutrality, that Ptolemy makes no alliance with Rome."

"I understand," Korax said. "I will tell you what I see."

He swiveled and sat cross-legged, so he could stare into the pool. He focused on the bubbling tumult at the base of the cascade and allowed images to flow into his mind.

He envisioned the outlines of the map, only now it was not a map but the actual world spread below him. He viewed the lands and glimmering seas as Helios viewed them each day in his journey. Over the face of the shining world, he perceived armies and fleets swarming in continuous motion. The immense procession of history moved before his mind's eye, one state after another rising to prominence, only to collapse or dwindle away ...

*Too much.* The vision was too complex and ponderous to be of use. Korax shook himself and reset his shoulders. He concentrated, anxious to avoid disappointing Kalyssa.

"Well?" Manolis demanded.

"Hush," Kalyssa's voice urged. "We must wait for the answer, as from an oracle."

Korax turned his mind to the king and queen. All of Alexandria knew that it was the queen, Arsinoe, who held the true scepter of power. But when he peered into her soul, Korax discerned an abrupt twisting of fate, a calamitous fall. With an inner shudder, he switched his attention to the king. Ptolemy's destiny appeared much brighter. Though a man of modest abilities and little depth, he seemed blessed with extraordinary good fortune.

*The king held the key*, Korax decided. With slow application, his will could be swayed.

Korax blinked and turned to face Manolis. "I see the possibility of fostering the alliance that you seek. You must apply steady persuasion to the king."

Manolis' eyebrows lifted with surprise. "Not Arsinoe?"

"She is too strong to be influenced," Korax responded. "But it does not matter." He paused to look again, then nodded with certainty. "The king can be won over, in time. Ptolemy is a man who visits favors on his friends. His friendship must be won with patience and persistence. Carthage must woo him, as a suitor does a rich widow."

Kalyssa smiled triumphantly. But Manolis tugged his beard in frustration.

"Can you offer any hints about *how* to woo this widow?"

Korax glanced back into the shimmering waterfall. After a moment, he replied with a cheerful smile. "Yes, I suggest you develop mutual interests."

"No so fast, my dears," Peristeria pleaded as she trudged heavily though the sand. "I cannot walk as quickly as you."

Kalyssa and Miriam turned, smiling sheepishly as they waited for the portly elder to catch up.

"Forgive us, priestess," they both said.

Peristeria panted, perspiring in her voluminous robes. The young women had encouraged her to accompany them on their jaunt along the beach. Peristeria certainly needed the exercise. She had been gaining weight lately—almost unavoidable at her time of life. But more important to her was the chance to converse with her two young friends. They were among her most gifted pupils, and she treasured them dearly.

Miriam and Kalyssa had become very close. During last night's ritual, they had spent almost the entire evening side-by-side. Lately, Peristeria had often observed them holding hands, sometimes in earnest conversation, sometimes giggling like two

THE LIGHTS OF ALEXANDRIA

young cousins. She also knew the subject of most of their chatter—a certain young Greek.

"So how is the work going with my friend Korax?" she inquired.

The two girls eyed each other and smiled coyly.

"Very well," Kalyssa said. "His ritual at the solstice was a great success. Now he is helping me with my mission for Carthage."

"Is he indeed?"

"It's not only that," Miriam interjected. "She is in love with him. They are very much in love with each other."

"It is true, priestess," Kalyssa admitted, her color rising. "I've never been in love before. I want to be with him constantly."

"Oh, such love is wonderful," Peristeria reminisced. "Especially a first love."

She glanced at Miriam, searching for her response. On the surface, the girl seemed happy for Kalyssa. But Miriam had a depth of soul that was often hard to delve.

"There's even more," Kalyssa was saying. "When we were preparing for Korax's ritual, the three of us began meditating together. We've found that in concert we're able to raise astonishing energies. I think all three of us are growing much more powerful."

"Yes." Miriam gazed far out to sea. "I think so too."

But a note of equivocation in Miriam's voice left Peristeria uneasy. The high priestess sought out the young woman later that morning, before the carriage arrived to take her and Kalyssa back to the city. Miriam sat on a balustrade, studying a text penned in Greek.

"I'd like a word before you leave," Peristeria said. "As your priestess, I'm a little concerned about you."

Miriam set aside the papyrus anxiously. "Did I do something wrong in the ritual?"

"Oh, no, my dear child, of course not. I was just thinking about you and Kalyssa and Korax. I can see you are sincerely happy that your two friends are in love."

"Of course I am."

"But I also noticed, early on, that you had feelings for the young man yourself."

"No," Miriam declared. "You misread me. That would never have worked. Even if Korax had affections for me, my father could never have accepted my marrying someone outside our tribe. And I could never have gone against his wishes."

Peristeria's compassionate expression did not change.

Miriam shifted uncomfortably. "I suppose I might have felt some attraction to Korax at the beginning. But, after working with him and Kalyssa, I've realized that what really attracted me was something much deeper. There is a spiritual bond when the three of us meditate. It opens our souls to divine love. That is what we share, priestess, divine love."

"That is sublime, my child. Such love is the most perfect experience our souls are capable of. It is a supreme gift of the Goddess."

Miriam nodded, her face enraptured.

"Only I am concerned," the elder persisted, "because I do not wish to see you hurt. You must understand that opening your heart in such a way also opens it to the potential for disappointment and pain. Most who learn that sad lesson do so only at the price of great suffering."

Miriam pondered, her mouth turned down. "I will reflect on this wisdom, high priestess."

# Chapter Fifteen

A gigantic, ungainly creature with sloping back and towering neck gazed down from behind the tall fence. The stele set before the enclosure identified the speckled giant as a 'giraffe', a herbivore from the distant grasslands of the south. Its musky smell was overpowering.

"How perfectly hideous," Manolis declared with wrinkled nose.

Kalyssa responded with a patient expression. Arm-in-arm, the couple strolled along the meandering path of the Zoological Garden. They had passed the morning viewing exotic beasts in pens and colorful birds in sheltered cages. Mostly, the ambassador had borne the trial stoically. But now his impatience and irritation began to spill over.

"I do hope this excursion will be productive as your consort promised, Kalyssa. I fear I will be quite cranky if it proves a waste of time."

"There is your answer." Kalyssa pointed with her chin. "I believe that is King Ptolemy approaching."

A colorful party had appeared ahead on the tree-lined path: two tall men, richly dressed, a fabulously-attired young woman, a collection of attendants and bodyguards.

"So it is, by the blessings of Bel!" Manolis straightened his shoulders.

"Remember," Kalyssa prompted, "we must be casual, not overly eager."

The ambassador's manner had changed to one of smooth efficiency. "My dear wife, remember who I am. Your friend's prognosticating talent may have brought us this chance, but from here *my* arts will take over."

As the royal party neared, Kalyssa recognized the courtiers. The woman was Bilistiche, in a lavender gown and sandals tied with scarlet ribbons. The king's male companion was the stern Callimachus, wearing his gold-leafed poet's crown. When the king had come within a few yards, Manolis and Kalyssa backed off the path and bowed low.

"Ambassador Manolis, madam, my greetings," said the king. "I am delighted to see members of the court enjoying the wonders of my Garden."

"Oh, it is our pleasure, majesty." Manolis straightened. "We are most fascinated by your wonderful collection."

"You know Callimachus and Lady Bilistiche of course." Ptolemy made a vapid wave at his companions. While everyone bowed to each other, the king continued: "I did not realize you were interested in natural philosophy, ambassador."

"Well ..." Manolis made a modest gesture. "My culture's achievements are so insignificant compared to your own. But yes, I am personally intrigued by all the sciences."

"Really?" Ptolemy seemed pleased. "Come stroll with us awhile."

Manolis fell into step beside the king. Behind them, a huge, bare-chested slave carried a fringed parasol.

"Which of my animals do you find most appealing?" Ptolemy inquired.

"Oh, there are so many rare creatures. The giraffe, for example, a wondrous beast."

"Yes, he's one of my favorites too." The king grinned fondly. "So tall. You know, Manolis, there is a lecture upcoming at the Salon of Urania that might interest you. Aristarchus of Samos will elucidate the animals represented by various constellations. Do your interests extend to star-gazing?"

"Oh, indeed, your majesty. I would be thrilled to receive an invitation."

"Done. You and your charming wife must sit near us, so we can chat ..."

Kalyssa meanwhile walked several paces behind, the beautiful Bilistiche at her elbow.

"How surprising to meet you in the Gardens," Bilistiche remarked, "and in the presence of your husband too."

"I'm not sure what you mean," Kalyssa answered.

"Come, come, my dear. Lately you've been accompanied exclusively by that young man with the piercing eyes—What is his name?—the musician or magician or whatever he is." She laughed lightly. "No one is quite sure. I do remember though that he is an expert judge of horse flesh."

"Oh, you mean Astrametheus," Kalyssa replied innocently. "He is a student. He is tutoring Manolis and myself in the Greek language, improving our appreciation of your poetry and other arts."

"I am sure he is. Yet how odd that he is never seen in the ambassador's company, only in yours."

"Well," Kalyssa smiled girlishly. "My husband is so busy with diplomacy and ... everything. You understand. In fact, we are thinking of inviting Astrametheus to live in our quarters, so he might more readily tutor us both."

"How pleasant!" Bilistiche exclaimed. "That sounds like a very convenient arrangement."

In this amiable manner, the party continued its tour, visiting the enclosures of ostriches, leopards, and dog-faced baboons.

None of them took notice of a figure seated far away, beneath an olive tree at the edge of the Garden. With the hood of his mantle pulled over his head, Korax watched the leisurely perambulation of the king's party and read their unfolding thoughts. He mused with satisfaction, as he noiselessly fingered the strings of his lyre.

Miriam set a cushion on the rail of the balustrade. With utmost caution, she hoisted herself into place, hands gripping the rail, feet tucked near her hips. At her back was empty air, and the floor of the Paneum four stories down.

She stretched her spine, took deep breaths to quiet the fear. Finally, when she had found her balance and pushed the fear down to a level she could manage, she let go of the rail and rested her hands in her lap.

No book or elder had taught her this strange and dangerous practice. She'd discovered it on her own and always kept it secret. Its roots lay in her childhood, when she loved to climb on arbors and perch in tree limbs. When her mother first taught her to meditate—to empty her mind and contemplate inner divinity—it seemed natural to sit on a bench or sometimes on a terrace rail overlooking the garden.

Her mother died when Miriam was eleven. After that, her father started bringing her to the Paneum. There she had ample time by herself, while Zakur read in the library or discussed philosophy with his fellow scholars. Miriam adored the inner chamber with its lifelike statues and long circling galleries. Sometimes she would set out a cushion and lie in the middle of the floor, staring at the distant ceiling as if gazing up into heaven.

One day, near her fourteenth birthday, she went to meditate on the first gallery. The instant she set her cushion on the floor, an inner voice prompted her to place it on the rail instead. Miriam recognized the voice as an angel.

In the books of her people, angels carried messages from God. Sometimes they brought gifts, often trials. But ignoring an angel was never wise. Miriam went numb with terror. She pointed out that the suggestion was insane. The voice replied that fear was natural, but that only by conquering her fears would she ever attain the freedom that she longed for in her soul. Trembling, her breathing ragged, Miriam picked up the cushion and set it on the rail.

From that day on, angels visited her often. They taught her wisdom, how to open the channels of her spirit, and her magical abilities grew. Gradually, she moved her seat farther along the balustrade, rising from one gallery to the next.

Recently, for a time, she had quit the practice. That happened after she, Korax, and Kalyssa became close and started meditating together. In their friendship, Miriam found acceptance and pleasure. In their joint meditations she discovered much more, a mysterious bond that opened her spirit to divinity.

But lately that bond had been strained. The ritual at the solstice had changed Korax. Miriam found his new power both intriguing and repugnant. Her angels warned her that his magical path was dangerous. Of course, there also was the fact that her two friends had begun sleeping together. All of these changes left Miriam feeling alienated and perplexed. So she had returned to her high place, seeking to re-establish her inner balance.

But even now, as she attempted to still her mind, Korax and Kalyssa hovered in her thoughts like creatures of smoke. They were here at the Paneum today. She could sense their presence.

Her balance faltered. Her eyes popped open, and she grabbed the rail.

Best discontinue the practice for today, she decided.

With a sigh, she lowered herself from the balustrade. She carried her lamp down to the floor of the Paneum and left it in a niche. She passed through one of the hidden tunnels and wandered over the sloping lawns.

On the lower grounds of the temple enclosure grew groves of poplar trees. In a small clearing beside a fountain, Korax and Kalyssa sat on the grass, knees and hands touching. They opened their eyes and looked at Miriam.

"Hello, dear one." Kalyssa held out her hand. "Join us."

The tender greeting opened Miriam's heart. Affection and sadness together spilled out as she stepped across the clearing. They shifted to make a place for her. She sat down and clasped their hands. The three young magicians shut their eyes and entered meditation together.

The familiar, blissful harmony settled over Miriam, melting her barriers and her sense of estrangement. A current of mystic force arose, flowing from hand to hand. In her mind the current gleamed, spinning faster and faster—the divine power of love and strife that moves the Universe.

A rumbling issued from Korax's throat, a wordless chant whose source was not himself but the twirling ring of force. Soon all three of them were chanting, the sound rolling around their circle, rolling and building till it broke over them like a crashing wave, and the three friends flopped on their backs. They sprawled on the grass, staring at the sky, exhausted, panting, laughing, still holding hands.

Eventually, Miriam sat up, wiping her eyes. She turned her head and gave a whimper of shock. Her father stood at the edge of the clearing, watching sternly.

"Daughter, it is time to go home now."

On the long walk through the streets of Alexandria, Zakur did not speak. Miriam sensed his temper, simmering like a soup. She waited apprehensively for the pot to boil over.

From the start, her father had harbored reservations about her joining Peristeria's circle, and later her friendship with Kalyssa. He knew of her affection for Korax and regarded it with unspoken disapproval. His attitude had hardened after Korax embarked on the new magical path. But today was the first time Zakur had actually seen his daughter engaged in working magic with her friends. Somehow, Miriam felt as if he'd caught her naked at an orgy.

Father and daughter walked along the Canopic Way, past the Museum and the Royal Theater and through the gates of the Jewish Quarter. Here the character of the city changed abruptly. Narrow streets intersected twisting lanes lined with shop fronts and awnings. Unadorned buildings stood behind walled enclosures, all windows and courtyards facing away from the streets.

Zakur earned a prosperous living as an arbiter, an elder who facilitated business and political relations between the Jewish and pagan communities. The sight of gentiles visiting his house was common, though the respected elder's interest in occult studies was less well known.

Zakur pounded on the heavy outer door of his house. He pushed it open brusquely as soon as the servant came and lifted the latch. After entering the tiled courtyard, Zakur sent the servant away, then faced Miriam.

"Daughter, we must speak about your behavior. I am sorely disturbed."

She clenched her lips and waited.

Her father spread his arms in exasperation. "You stare at me with defiance! This is exactly my concern."

Wincing, Miriam lowered her eyes. "What have I done wrong?"

Zakur hesitated, as though he could scarcely count all her infractions. "It is unseemly for a Jewish maid to behave like a pagan. I have watched your activities for some time in growing consternation. Till now I have held my peace, because I do not like to interfere in your life. But what I saw today confirmed my worst suspicions."

She shook her head in bewilderment. "I do not see what I have done wrong."

"Then I suggest you spend less time studying magical texts and more time reading our scriptures—especially the Prophets."

She answered in a frosty voice. "I know the books you mean, father. I am not a harlot. My dress is modest. I do not paint my face."

"You speak as though you wish you could!"

Miriam clasped her hands in frustration and stared at the tiles on the ground. She quivered, holding back tears.

Zakur rolled his eyes toward heaven. "Miriam, the magic these people are doing … It is wrong. It is beyond what should be done. And it is perilous."

"I know," she sobbed. "But I am not doing the ceremonies. Only Korax is. And they are my friends."

"They are tainting you. Why can you not find friends among your own people?"

"You know why. There are none my age who share our studies."

"Ah!" Zakur turned and paced away. With a weary groan, he sank onto a bench near the stairway that led to the upper floor.

"I know it is difficult for you. To live as a Jew among gentiles is not easy. But believe me, those who do not hold to our traditions lose their identity. They try to live as Greeks, but they are not truly accepted by either community. They are nothing!"

"I don't believe that," Miriam said. "I don't believe I must deny myself all freedom just because I am a Jew."

Zakur dropped his jaw in dismay. "This is what comes from educating young women! What a mistake I made in allowing you to read philosophy."

"You made no such mistake," Miriam answered bitterly. "Mother taught me to read. If it were up to you, I'd never have learned. I'd be the illiterate wife of some fat merchant or drunken soldier. I'd have no life except cooking his meals and warming his bed."

"And whose bed do you desire to be warming, daughter?"

The remark struck Miriam speechless with rage. After a moment, she whirled and ran up the stairs to her room. She slammed the door so hard Zakur's shoulders jumped.

# Chapter Sixteen

On a moonless night, the Salon of Urania convened on the broad terrace of the Pharos Lighthouse. Neither lamps nor torches illuminated the spacious patio, located more than halfway up the tower, high above the sea. By order of the king, even the great beacon fire at the pinnacle had been extinguished—to allow unimpeded viewing of the stars.

Manolis and Kalyssa lounged together on a dining couch close to Ptolemy's sumptuous divan. They sampled sweets and expensive wines while the king regaled them with his knowledge of the heavens. Queen Arsinoe was noticeably absent, though several of Ptolemy's purported mistresses occupied couches close by.

When the sky had sufficiently darkened, Zenodotus the chief librarian rose before the audience and poured a libation to the muse. He then introduced the evening's lecturer, Aristarchus of Samos. The astronomer appeared, beaming, and made proper obeisance to the king. He spoke in couplets and accompanied himself on the lyre. He pointed out one constellation after another and recited illustrative tales about each.

Aristarchus had just begun his discourse on the Great Bear when Kalyssa experienced a tingling on the lower part of her spine. Instinctively, she looked over her shoulder.

On the second terrace far above, near the summit of the lighthouse, a cloaked figure stared down at her. From this distance and in the dark, her eyes could perceive no features, could barely see the person at all.

But Kalyssa knew who it was. Her love was watching over her, weaving his magic to aid her heart's desires.

On the upper parapet, Korax peered down and knew she had spotted him. A secret smile stretched his lips. His hands were moving, wrists twirling, long deft fingers bending and pointing. With his mind he spun out power, tugging the invisible flow of events, nudging them in favor of Manolis and Kalyssa, pushing aside obstacles to help them make inroads with the king.

Korax applied himself to this work unceasingly, until the lecture ended, torches were lit, and the audience began filing into the tower. Even after the salon had dispersed and the lower terrace was empty, he lingered.

Leaning on the high rampart, he gazed out over the dim and trackless sea. Somewhere in that immeasurable darkness lay an island called Rhodes. He had not thought about his home for some time. He had given up writing letters to his family, as none of them were ever answered. He had even stopped trying to envision the reasons why. Somehow, it hardly mattered anymore.

He turned and stared down across the harbor at the thousand lamps of Alexandria. This was his home now, this wondrous city full of riches and wisdom. Here he had found his magical path, a lofty purpose that stirred his deepest aspirations. And here he had found his love, such a passion as inspired poets to their most brilliant creations.

Korax walked to the far end of the terrace. From within the tower came the noises of men and hoisting machines. The lighthouse crew was lifting fuel and working to relight the beacon. But that would take some time. For now, there was only starlight. Korax rested his forearms on the smooth parapet and gazed dreamily down at the city.

Kalyssa found him there a short time later. He turned to see her running toward him from the shadowy doorway, the fabric of her himation flowing in the wind. She reached him, breathless, having climbed the spiral ramp inside the tower. Her arms slipped under his cloak, and she hugged him tightly.

"I left Manolis at the carriage and told him to go on. I just had to be with you. Thank you, my darling, for all your help. I do believe we are winning the king's friendship."

She lifted her face to him, flushed with excitement. They kissed tenderly.

Holding each other close, they stared down at Alexandria, its multitude of lights like so many jewels spilled across a carpet.

"I am so happy," Kalyssa breathed. "Everything is perfect."

Her words pricked a superstitious fear in his Greek soul. It was unwise to speak that way, a tempting of Fate.

Sometimes, at the peak of summer, a sudden chill enters the night breeze, a hint that the year is turning and winter will come. So Korax now sensed that the perfection of this moment held the seed of its own demise. Clinging to Kalyssa, smelling her perfume, he strained with all his will to make the moment last.

Sometimes in her meditations Miriam would slip into a trance. Then her angels would speak, in clear and powerful voices, or she would see visions, like dreams only more palpable and real.

This time, she envisioned a shiny corridor in some fabulous palace. Scented candles flickered, in holders carved like graceful hands of alabaster. Miriam walked slowly, dressed in a white camisia, a sheer nightdress like a pagan girl might wear. The flimsy fabric tickled her skin.

She stepped into a moonlit chamber. Curtains drifted in a mild breeze before an open balcony. In the silvery light she saw Korax and Kalyssa, seated among pillows on a multicolored rug. They smiled and held out their hands. Miriam approached, filled with affection for her friends.

But midway across the room she halted. Korax and Kalyssa sat naked, their lovely bodies poised and unashamed as statues. Chilled, Miriam looked down at herself and recognized with horror that her own garment had disappeared.

*She gave a violent start and lost her balance.* She clutched for the rail but caught nothing. Falling, she saw the roof of the Paneum receding between her feet. Her body pitched over, and the black floor hurtled up.

Miriam opened her eyes, gasping in terror. A gray cat gazed up at her with golden eyes and meowed plaintively.

She was in her bedroom, not the Paneum.

Whimpering with relief, she picked up the cat and hugged it tightly to her chest. She rocked back and forth, moaning quietly, until the cat grew impatient and struggled to escape. Releasing him, Miriam lay down on her side. She pressed her arms into her stomach and wept, stricken by loneliness and remorse.

There was only one remedy. And she knew she could delay it no longer.

Eventually, she sat up and rubbed the tears from her cheeks. She took a candle and placed it in the center of the floor. She fetched her ceremonial dagger from its hiding place. With it, she traced a circle of imagined fire in the air.

She stood at the middle of the circle, above the candle, and quieted her thoughts. Then she brought to her mind the great angels of the four directions. She drew their sigils in the air and called them softly by name:

"Raphael ... Michael ... Gabriel ...Uriel."

The cat lay at the foot of her bed, watching intently, its long tail shifting and curling in the air.

Surrounded by the protecting angels, Miriam thrust out her arms and summoned all her power.

"In the names of the Angels of the Quarters, and in the Name of the Great God that no man or woman may utter, I banish you, Korax and Kalyssa, from my heart and from my spirit. I bid you peace and go in peace. But I sunder the bond that is between us, now and forever ..."

She envisioned their bond as a stream of blue light, rushing out from her heart, past the confines of her circle. With a sweep of the dagger she cut the light three times.

"It is cut. It is broken. It is gone."

In her mind, Miriam watched the torn ribbons of light fade to nothing. She dismissed the angels and dissolved the circle. She snuffed the candle and hid away her dagger.

Exhausted, she lifted the covers and crawled into bed. The cat walked up to lie near her shoulder. Miriam reached out and gently stroked his fur.

For the first time in many nights, she slept a deep and peaceful sleep.

# Chapter Seventeen

The third Ptolemaeia took place that summer. The festival commemorated the deification of the first Ptolemy and his queen, Berenice. In imitation of the Olympiad, it was held every four years, a spectacular celebration combining arts and athletic competitions with grandiose observances of the state religion.

This year, victorious in Syria and with their widespread kingdom relatively at peace, Ptolemy and Arsinoe planned the grandest of all spectacles to honor their deified parents. The queen, in particular, seemed determined to impress the world with the wealth and far-reaching might of her Egypt.

The opening parade was staged on Midsummer morning under a flawless sky. The procession began at the huge Temple of Serapis and traversed the length of the Canopic Way. The population of Alexandria lined the avenue to watch.

In the forefront marched three thousand of the royal guard, the elite of Egypt's armies. The warriors stepped smartly, the clatter of greaves and shields matching a steady drumbeat. Sunlight sparkled on their crested helmets and polished cuirasses. It gleamed on the murderous points of their eighteen-foot-long Macedonian pikes.

Leading the column, Marshal Drakas rode on a muscular white stallion. The old cavalryman's hip pained him whenever he sat on horseback, but of course he showed no sign of that. Instead, his grim eyes swept the crowds, verifying that sentries and city watchmen were deployed in sufficient numbers to handle any outbreak of trouble.

Behind the guard rode an enormous baggage train devised to represent all the riches of the kingdom. Prized Egyptian oxen pulled carts packed with grain, oil, flowers, and fruits. The high priests of the land, in town for the Synod, rode in fabulous litter chairs, preceded by acolytes swinging censers and ringing gongs. Behind the clerics, Egyptian dancers and musicians rode in open coaches, playing harps and cymbals and waving to the crowds.

But the spectacle showed beyond doubt that Egypt was only the beginning of the Ptolemies' holdings. Representing Greece and the Aegean came mule carts packed with the finest wools, pottery, olive oil, and wine. Scores of Nabataean camels trod along, weighed down with frankincense and myrrh. Captives in the costumes of Persia, Bactria, and India rode in treasure wagons brimming with spices, rare woods, and gold. Tribute-bearers from Ethiopia carried dozens of ivory tusks.

Zakur stood at a spot along the parade route with a delegation of Jewish elders—bearded men in dark garb, stiff and solemn. Zakur watched the spectacle with a mixture of feelings: impressed by the magnificent display of wealth, thankful to his God that he lived under the protection of so mighty a king, yet simultaneously appalled by the shameless ostentation.

*Well,* he reflected, *keeping the proper balance was never easy.* At least his daughter no longer seemed so beguiled by the gentile culture. Miriam had ceased her troubling association with the pagan magicians. These days she seldom ventured from the Jewish Quarter, except on occasion to visit the library at the Paneum.

A blare of trumpets roused Zakur from his musing. The royal family approached.

Ahead rushed a flurry of boys and girls, scattering rose petals from silver baskets. Next appeared the monarchs' children—young Ptolemy, Lysimachus, and Berenice—standing with attendants in an open carriage drawn by twelve white horses.

Another gang of flower-bearers ran ahead of the king and queen, who were conveyed in a sumptuous chariot of ivory and gold. The sibling gods wore spotless white robes and simple gold diadems. Royal agents planted in the crowd shouted hurrahs, rousing everyone to worshipful acclamation.

Behind the monarchs came the accoutrements of their divinity. A sacred Nile boat topped with a huge crescent moon represented Arsinoe as Isis. A shimmering wagon adorned with naked nymphs and boys dressed as Eros portrayed her as Aphrodite. Long-haired Thracian priests carried pinecone wands ahead of a mule cart. The cart, spilling over with vines and blossoms, conveyed an enormous gold krater of wine. About the cart danced actors dressed as satyrs, maenads, minotaurs, and griffons. Behind this panoply, a host of brawny men painted green and clad in leafy garments dragged an enormous gilded phallus on wheels. All these devices were meant to depict the king's divine aspects—Osiris, Serapis, and Dionysus, the very lords of life.

The priests and priestesses of every temple in the city marched next. Among them walked Krateros, bedecked in robes of green and brown in his role as high priest of Pan. The rugged Macedonian held a silver shepherd's crook as his staff of office and grinned at the cheering throngs. Krateros enjoyed a good festival as well as any man. But today he especially looked forward to the opportunity to mingle with visitors from so many lands.

Not far from Krateros marched Zenodotus, the chief librarian and high priest to the Muses. He wore a gold laurel crown and carried a bronze scroll. His attitude was stately and serene. Rituals and processions counted among the ceremonial duties that he bore with patience. Left to his own desires, he would as soon have passed the time with his books.

Behind the religious officials streamed an endless parade of poets, actors, musicians, and athletes. They came from every corner of the Greek world to participate in the Ptolemaic Games.

Riding in a silver-chased chariot, the great Callimachus led the contingent of poets. He stood with tilted head, aloof and expressionless, though inwardly his spirit smoldered. Among the many things Callimachus detested, two he regarded as the worst of all evils: the common crowd and ostentatious display. Today's procession was therefore, to him, the most odious duty imaginable.

To the rear of his chariot marched happier men, including the stout Asclepiades. He bounded along in a jolly temper, looking forward to a month's worth of performances that he knew would include revivals of many classics. Of course, the banquets and drinking parties would also be delightful.

The procession reached its climax in the stadium at the southeast of the city. An enormous pavilion had been erected in the infield. Columns eighty feet high supported a striped awning of scarlet and white. A portico around the pavilion was lined with painted statues by the greatest sculptors in the world. Within the tent, one hundred and fifty couches were arranged for the king and queen's most favored guests.

The Lady Bilistiche reposed on one couch, her lovely figure adorned with garnets, lapis, and gold. Her attentive eyes surveyed the banquet arrangements, noticing who was seated where. She scrutinized the jewelry and apparel of the noblemen and women—especially the women. Bilistiche stretched languidly on the leopard pelt that covered her couch. She wondered how much longer before the king and queen arrived. Already the day had grown tedious.

Elsewhere in the pavilion, Manolis and Kalyssa reclined on cushions close together, though their thoughts were far apart. Their proximity to the royal divan suggested the ambassador's rising status, due to his warming friendship with the king. As servants scurried back and forth, Manolis eyed his fellow courtiers. For a time, he secretly watched Gaius Dominicus, the vulgar and energetic envoy from Rome, positioned at the far edge of the pavilion. But soon Manolis turned his mind to pleasanter subjects, rehearsing some amusing comments to offer later when he conversed with the king.

Kalyssa gazed across the infield to the thronged stadium seats. She knew she should be watching the members of the court, but her thoughts kept drifting back to Korax. With a tender smile, she wondered where he sat in the sprawling, motley crowd.

Banks of trumpets announced the arrival of the royal party. Everyone in the stadium stood. A chorus stationed in the infield sang a rousing hymn.

Far away, at the topmost row of seats, Korax stood watching. As his eyes scanned the procession, he listened with his mind, striving to pierce below the surface, to recognize the hidden meaning of events. He had lived in Alexandria over a year now and considered the city his home. Still, as he peered down into the stadium, he wondered where his fate was taking him. What role had the gods determined he should play in this vast and baffling pageant?

# Chapter Eighteen

Korax edged down a dark passageway, totally blind. He was trying to find his way by inner sight or the scent of the humid air. But now his groping fingers met rough stone—another dead end. Desperately, he pivoted and retraced his steps. He cursed himself for leaving the torch behind at the base of the stairs. *Time was running out.* He must find the chamber of the black pool soon or Baufre would die ...

Korax reared up in the luxurious bed. Clammy sweat clung to his naked skin. He flung off the linen sheet. Leaning elbows on his knees, he rubbed his scalp.

*The same dream again. How many times?*

He climbed out of bed and moved restlessly across the spacious chamber. Furnished with Persian rugs and Phoenician tapestries, it was the most opulent bedroom he had ever occupied. Life as a houseguest of Ambassador Manolis certainly provided its comforts. Korax leaned against a pillar at the edge of his balcony, looking out over the palace gardens to the sea.

On the surface, everything in his life seemed perfect. His love for Kalyssa blazed as brightly as ever. Now that he lived in the same residence, they enjoyed frequent opportunities to be together.

Korax was continuing his magical studies. He planned the rite of the Second Tower for the next winter solstice, since the book required an interval of at least one year. The magic gained from the First Tower had dwindled over the months, but that was expected. The power took time to consolidate in the magician's being, to settle as it were, leaving room for the next infusion. Along with his magic work, he found time to read in the great Library, to enjoy recitals and plays. Thanks to Kalyssa, he had plenty of money. Besides, as a houseguest, most of his needs were supplied in any case.

From all angles his life appeared ideal—except for this troubling dream. Always it was the same, groping blindly in the labyrinth, running out of time.

Korax made up his mind. He marched across the chamber and opened a wicker basket set against the wall. Searching below his clean garments and other belongings, he uncovered the wax figure of Thoth. The statuette was a bit battered, the image faded. It had been a long time since Korax summoned his ally.

Thoth-Hermes had seemed wary of Korax's studying the *Book of Nectanebo*—though he had certainly not forbidden it, nor even advised against it really. Still, since beginning the work, Korax had felt rather sheepish about conjuring the god.

He set the figure on the basket, lit a candle and a pinch of incense. He sat down on the rug and slowed his breathing.

"Hermes, swift-traveler, I call you to me now."

He waited. No response came.

"Thoth-Hermes, god of magicians, I bid you now appear."

"I answer." The voice sounded muffled and distant. In character it was solemn, more the ancient Thoth than the youthful, carefree Hermes.

"I seek the meaning of this dream."

Silence. Korax stared at the waxen god, the rising smoke.

Finally: "Your dream is a warning. You pursue the study of magic with too much haste."

The answer made no sense. "But in the dream there is great urgency. I am running out of time."

"Because in your hurry you have chosen the wrong path. You try to retrace your steps, but you are lost."

Did this describe the current state of his magical progress? Korax did not want to believe it. "What do you advise me to do?"

"If you would heed your dream, postpone your preparations for the Second Tower."

"For how long?"

"Until you are truly ready."

"But how will I know that? I feel ready now."

"If you were, your dreams would not be turning on you. These rites are designed to take many years, even for a mature and accomplished practitioner. Why are you in so much hurry?"

"Why so forlorn this morning, my love?"

Kalyssa reclined before a table laden with grapes, bread, and honey. Her black hair tumbled unbound over a silk camisia. The trilling of songbirds and the sweet scent of oleander drifted from the garden.

Korax sat down on the opposite couch. "I seem to have lost my way."

Kalyssa sat upright, her dainty feet hovering over the sea-blue tiles. She listened with strained brow as Korax told her about his recurring dream and his talk with Thoth-Hermes.

"I understand your distress," she said. "If you feel you must delay the Second Tower, then I think you should."

Did he hear an edge of disappointment in her voice, a veiled fear that his magic might fail her?

"I don't feel that way," he insisted. "But Thoth certainly was warning me. And Miriam—she finally concluded this path was unwise."

Kalyssa's face paled. "I miss Miriam too. I regret that she broke her bond with us. But I know in my heart her decision was not caused by your magic. She could no longer bear the strain of living in our world and her father's, so she had to choose."

Korax believed it was the truth. Still, Miriam's absence hurt, and the loss of her support added to the doubts dragging down his confidence.

Kalyssa moved around the table. She sat close and laid a hand on his shoulder.

"Listen, my love. How quickly you proceed is a decision only you can make. But I am sure this path is right for you. I have felt your rising power—with my spirit and my body. I believe it is not only wise but wondrous. I understand your uncertainty. But doubts and fears must be expected as part of the path. How could they not be, when the changes are so great? You must ask yourself: Are they enough to turn you back?"

Apprehending the fierce light in her eyes, Korax could not consider turning back. "Of course not."

Kalyssa twined her finger in his. "As for the dream, maybe I can help. I could do a working to send it away—with your permission, of course."

Korax squeezed her small, soft hand. "Very well. Why not?"

"Listen, here is some good news: Manolis told me this morning that Ptolemy is taking a voyage up the Nile next month. He is inviting a select group of his friends, and Manolis is included. I will stay behind in Alexandria, to watch the court and correspond with Carthage."

Kalyssa brushed herself against his elbow. "You see what this means? You and I shall have the residence to ourselves for three months. Imagine how pleasant that will be."

Her bare toes caressed his shin. Off in the branches, sparrows were chirping.

Nine brass birds perched at the top of the ornate water clock, a huge contraption of jars, conduits, and metal chambers installed on one wall of the throne room. When Ptolemy pulled a lever, a brass cat popped up and the birds whistled, each emitting a different note. Normally the display occurred to mark each hour. But to please the king the inventor Ctesibius had added the lever, so Ptolemy could make the birds sing at will.

"Really, brother. Could you play with that toy later? We have appointments to prepare for."

"Oh, very well." Ptolemy closed the lever, shutting off the flow of air.

Arsinoe seemed particularly impatient this morning. But then, she never had shared the king's fascination with mechanical contrivances. Ptolemy strolled across the throne room with its giant murals and gilded cornices. The magnificent chamber stood empty except for the dais, where the queen sat enthroned amid a coterie of ministers and scribes.

"But I still say Ctesibius is a wonder. We must find a way to properly reward that man."

"And we shall, husband," Arsinoe answered. "We shall lavish even greater riches on him than we have already, if you wish. But for now other matters press."

Ptolemy slouched on his rosewood throne. "I am all attention, dear queen. Pray proceed."

Arsinoe gestured toward the royal secretary. "Didymus was reviewing our audiences for today. Our first is with the ambassador from Macedonia, Miltiades. He awaits our answer on the offer from King Antigonus to recruit mercenaries for our service."

"Hmm. The Celts you mean." Ptolemy viewed with suspicion any overture from Antigonus Gonatas. "And you still think this is a sound idea?"

"I do," Arsinoe replied. "It is a chance to immediately augment our armies with 4,000 spearmen. Gonatas would no doubt employ them himself if he could afford to pay them."

"I know. He has far too many Celts settled inside his borders. He sees obvious advantage in exporting as many as possible."

"True," the queen said. "But we should not ignore a favorable opportunity just because it offers some help to a rival. The Celts are redoubtable fighters. Gonatas is using them in Greece, and there are reports that Antiochus has begun hiring warriors from the tribes in Anatolia."

Ptolemy rubbed his chin. Manolis had mentioned that Carthage too employed Celts in their armies. The barbarians were renowned for their toughness and ferocity.

"Drakas, what is your opinion?"

The marshal's good eye blinked. "I have some concerns about their discipline, majesty. And of course, we don't know how well trained they are. But I agree with the queen: we do need the men. I would suggest we take all 4,000, but divide them up among existing regiments."

"Very well." Ptolemy had tired of the subject. "I agree. What other audiences are on the schedule?"

Didymus referred to his papyrus. "City officials and envoys from the governors of Egypt will attend your majesties this afternoon, to present their preparations for the king's excursion up the Nile."

Ptolemy shifted in his seat. "Actually, Arsinoe, I wanted to speak with you about this. I understand the necessity of sailing down into Egypt and playing pharaoh from time to time. But I really believe it would be better for both of us to go. We are co-pharaohs, after all."

The queen's pale forehead wrinkled. "Darling, we've discussed this already."

"I know. But I am reopening the subject."

Arsinoe leaned toward him and spoke in quiet, urgent tones. "If trouble arises, one of us must be in Alexandria—not a month's distance away. I would go instead, if you preferred, but you know the natives would never be satisfied to see a female pharaoh without her lord."

That was true enough. Ptolemy cast a fretful eye on his advisors. No help there. Drakas, Didymus, Eupolis—all would concur with the queen on this. Still, it made him greatly uncomfortable to leave Arsinoe alone in Alexandria for three months. For one thing, he would miss her. He had come to rely on his shrewd, efficient older sister for all the important decisions. At the same time, he distrusted her. The thought that she might grow accustomed to ruling without him made his stomach queasy.

"Don't worry, dear husband," she purred, as if reading his mind. "You can trust me and Drakas to safeguard your throne."

*Well* ... He could probably trust Drakas at least.

"Cheer up," Arsinoe laughed. "Think of all the gifts the natives will lavish on you, the parades and banquets. Not to mention the chance to collect new specimens for your Garden."

Ptolemy smiled wanly. That part did sound agreeable.

Across the chamber on the waterclock, the brass cat suddenly reared, marking the hour. The mechanical birds tweeted in sequential alarm.

# Chapter Nineteen

**M**ost authorities on the subject agreed that King Ptolemy's pleasure barge was the largest ship ever built. Her benches sat three thousand oarsmen, while her vast sail and yardarm would have spanned the mouths of many harbors.

Launching the barge from the Royal Harbor would have been impossible in any case. The craft was not built for the open sea. Instead, the barge was moored south of the city on Lake Mareotis, near the canal that connected Alexandria to the Nile. The canal had been dredged and widened especially to allow the huge craft's passage.

On a glorious day in late summer, the canal docks swarmed with activity. Hundreds of slaves carried parcels and bales up a half-dozen gangplanks. On deck, an orchestra of flutes, harps and drums played stately melodies. Near the bow of the gorgeous barge, a stream of litters and carriages stopped to deposit their passengers: a small army of priests, courtiers, scholars and diplomats who would accompany the king on his voyage.

Manolis and Kalyssa disembarked from their carriage and said their farewells beneath the brightly-painted rails.

"Remember to use my seal on all letters, and to trust only our own men as couriers," Manolis advised in suppressed tones.

"I will remember," Kalyssa said.

"And keep me informed of any news. But write discreetly. I'm not confident our letters will go unopened."

"I will be discreet," Kalyssa promised. "And rest assured, if the queen makes any significant moves, I will learn of them."

"I believe you will," Manolis admitted. Over recent months, his wife's abilities had gained his grudging respect.

"Hello, Ambassador, Kalyssa!"

Bilistiche descended from a sumptuous litter, her sandals treading on a silk-covered stool hastily set down by a slave. Behind the litter, a train of porters carried an inordinate amount of baggage. Dressed for travel and breathless with excitement, Bilistiche approached the Carthaginians.

"A splendid day for sailing. But I did not know you two were on the guest list. How charming!"

Manolis showed a frozen smile.

"Actually, only my husband will be attending the king," Kalyssa explained. "I was forced to decline the invitation, due to my religious obligations."

"Oh, yes. I had forgotten you are a priestess. Such a talented girl!" Bilistiche took hold of Manolis' arm. "Well, don't worry, my dear. I will do everything possible to ameliorate your husband's loneliness on the voyage."

For Korax, the following months were the happiest times he could remember. With Manolis gone from the city, Kalyssa relaxed her inhibitions and secrecy about their love affair. The couple attended plays and recitals together and openly shared the same couch at banquets. At night, they slept together in Kalyssa's bed.

Whatever working Kalyssa performed on Korax's dreams had proved effective. His nightmare of wandering lost in the labyrinth disappeared. Now, he woke in the night only to the peaceful sound of her breathing and the softness of her hair on the pillow.

Each day, the lovers strolled together in the gardens. Sometimes, they would idle away an hour beneath an arbor or beside a fountain, Kalyssa hugging her knees and listening dreamily while Korax played his lyre and sang love songs.

Most of his time alone Korax worked on his magic, writing and rehearsing his formulas for the Second Tower. He no longer attended Krateros' study group nor even the monthly meetings of the Society, but he did often travel to the Paneum. There he would read in the library and discuss his progress with Krateros. The high priest of Pan maintained his keen interest in Korax's work, as he did in all magical studies.

Some evenings, Korax and Kalyssa would ride in a carriage out to Peristeria's vine-covered house in Eleusis. There, they would drink the Nectar of Astarte and pass the night with music, dancing, and the voices of the spirits. In the morning, they would rise from the same couch and take long walks on the beach.

But the wheel of the year continued to turn. Almost before Korax knew it, summer had turned to late autumn. One day, all too soon, word arrived that the king's royal barge had been sighted approaching the city.

The afternoon of his arrival, Manolis conferred with his wife in the garden. The tall statue of Hermes loomed over the fountain above, while the roaring waterfall muffled their voices in case anyone should have tried to overhear.

"Essentially, I found Egypt a disappointment," the ambassador commented "The temples are monstrous and gaudy, the towns primitive and foul. Of course, I made a detailed survey of the cities, caravan routes, and fortifications. All is written down and ready to send to Carthage."

"What about the king?"

"That is most disappointing of all. Ptolemy remains annoyingly cordial—constantly besieging me with prattle about his hobbies. But he consistently sidesteps any mention of alliance." Manolis shook his head ruefully. "I fear your soothsayer may be wrong after all. I don't see Ptolemy ever committing to a treaty without the instigation of the queen."

Kalyssa nodded, her complexion colorless. Her husband's return was hardly welcome. His gloomy, agitated demeanor made her tense. But it was more than that.

Lately a new vision had haunted her meditations, an appalling picture of Carthage sacked by the Romans and burning. The vision prodded her with new urgency. Any chance of altering that terrible future might be slipping away.

From the bench beside her, Kalyssa picked up a faience jar. She held the lid in place as she shook the jar in her hand. Then she spilled out the contents: seeds and grains collected from many lands.

She studied the pattern, a clear image of impasse. Perhaps Manolis was right after all. Somehow, they needed to win over the queen.

A breeze stirred, blowing away some seeds, moving others. Kalyssa waited for the breeze to die then scrutinized the new arrangement.

"Well?" Manolis demanded at last.

Kalyssa had grown paler still. "A new path will open in the coming year. It will require that we risk everything. But I think we must seize the chance. Our time is running out."

The queen's private bathroom was walled with dark green marble from Thessaly. Gold statues of Nereids riding dolphins poured streams into three spacious pools: hot, cold, and tepid. At the moment, Arsinoe relaxed in the hot pool, her hair pinned up and steamy water lapping around her neck. A dark-skinned girl from India knelt in the water and diligently massaged the queen's left foot.

Distant bronze doors swung open, and a serving maid hurried down the carpeted corridor. She prostrated herself at the edge of the bath.

"Majesty, your friend from the king's barge reports as instructed and begs audience."

"Oh, yes." Arsinoe opened her large blue eyes, instantly alert. "Send her in. Everyone else leave us."

Maids and bath attendants walked briskly up the corridor. Only the Indian girl remained, impassively continuing the massage. The girl understood no Greek, and certainly not the Macedonian dialect still used in private conversations by members of the inner court.

At the far doorway, the departing women stepped aside to allow the queen's friend to pass. A statuesque young woman strode down the carpet as the bronze doors shut behind her.

"Bilistiche," the queen smiled. "Join me, my dear."

"Thank you, my queen." Bilistiche sat on a marble bench and began unstrapping her sandals.

"How was your voyage?" Arsinoe had shut her eyes again.

It was an open secret of the court that Arsinoe hand picked—or at least approved—all of the king's mistresses and concubines. That many of them also served the queen as informers was somewhat less well known.

"Tiresome for the most part," Bilistiche replied. "A few nice parties, especially in Thebes. The chef at the Temple of Amum prepared a delicious duckling with a syrup of pears and cherries."

Discarding her bronze girdle, Bilistiche lifted the long gown over her head. The queen appraised the younger woman's nude body as she stepped gingerly down the pool steps. Bilistiche looked as firm and desirable as ever.

"Well, I see you didn't let it go to your waist." The queen's voice might have carried a note of jealousy.

"Oh, I am careful as ever, majesty." Bilistiche settled into the hot water opposite the queen.

"And how is my brother?"

"Fine. I think the king enjoyed himself for the most part. Especially with a certain doe-eyed Nabataean girl he was given in Hermopolis."

"Indeed? I will have to meet her."

Bilistiche rinsed her forehead with a sponge. "Oh, he's lost interest already. You know how he is. Once we got to the south, he only had eyes for hyenas and ostriches."

The two women shared a droll laugh. The queen shifted and gave her right foot to the Indian girl.

"So nothing of political consequence occurred?"

Bilistiche searched her memory. "Not really. The high priests made their usual complaints about taxes. But mostly it was pompous processions and ceremonies. Oh, Ambassador Manolis did try to engage the king a few times."

"His alliance again. How did my brother respond?"

"Same as usual, with firm equivocation."

The queen smiled. "He's rather good at that."

"Manolis keeps trying though—a very determined man. He's not the hapless fop he pretends to be. There's much that bubbles under the surface with those two—he and his wife I mean. You know, she stayed in Alexandria."

"Kalyssa, yes. To keep her eye on me, no doubt. She allowed herself to be seen in society on occasion, usually in the company of her Greek paramour."

Bilistiche opened her large eyes. "Ah, Astrametheus—there's another mystery. I vow, he's a magician or soothsayer or something."

The queen frowned. "My dear, there is nothing mysterious about magicians and soothsayers. They are as common as crows. I've never found one worth the table scraps it takes to keep them. Ahh!"—She moaned as the masseuse found a tender spot on her sole. "You are correct about Kalyssa though. She is certainly not the naïve waif she appears. She watches everything under those fluttering eyelashes. I judge her to be intelligent and ruthless, like most Phoenician women. No doubt, she uses her charms to manipulate the men around her into doing exactly what she wishes."

The queen fixed Bilistiche with an artful look. "In other words, she is rather like you and I, my dear."

Bilistiche lowered her eyes, blushing. "Your majesty flatters me over much."

# Chapter Twenty

From the rooftop, Korax watched the red sun settle into the sea. He wore a white tunic with a yellow sash and clutched his falcon staff. His stomach contracted and ached sharply. He had fasted for five days, taking nothing but water.

He had judged it prudent to find a more private place than the Paneum for performing the Second Tower. At Kalyssa's request, Peristeria had generously offered her villa. Korax arranged a chamber below for receiving the god. He made his high place on a corner of the roof facing the sea.

As the sun disappeared, he set a torch to a tripod brazier. The oiled charcoal took the fire, and the flames crackled and danced. Mouthing incantations, Korax fed in the prescribed herbs, which he and Kalyssa had collected and dried over the year: chrysanthemum, myrtle, rose leaves, heliotrope, rue.

In the drifting smoke, Korax raised his arms and chanted a long, convoluted formula to summon the god. Nearby, on the wrought-iron table where he had made his altar, a starling fluttered and cheeped in a straw cage. Beside the cage lay a decanter of red Egyptian glass, an alabaster bowl, and a copper knife with a crescent blade.

Korax finished the invocation and lowered his arms. In the writhing firelight, he stepped before the altar. He prayed over the alabaster bowl then filled it from the decanter—water from the Nile tinged with the drug of the blue lotus. He pulled the starling from its cage and pressed its squirming body against the tabletop. With grim purpose he sliced off the bird's head and poured its blood into the bowl. Impassively, he cut his wrist and added his own blood to the mixture. Uttering words of power, he stirred the liquid with the knife, then brought the bowl to his lips and drank it down.

He grimaced, his stomach cramping.

Woozy, he sat down on a rug beside the brazier and folded his legs. He tied a band of black silk over his eyes. Calling to mind the image of the inner sun, he settled down to begin the nightlong vigil.

Soon the cramping subsided. Tranquility entered his soul. The ineffable sun pulsed within his heart, cool and white as a star. Korax fixed his mind on its soothing light, returning there whenever his thoughts wandered.

By this process, he began to comprehend that all of his thoughts were merely reflections of that pure, internal light. Over time, he realized with certainty that all the world, all that filled his senses, people and events, even daemons and gods—all were simply emanations of the one divine light. Contemplation of this mystery absorbed him, extinguishing all other thoughts.

Abruptly, he opened his eyes and tore off the blindfold. The night had passed; daylight was rising. He struggled to his feet, his legs weak and throbbing. He added charcoal to the brazier and blew on the fire. Flames spurted to life.

Korax burned incense and sang a hymn of thanks to the rising sun. He lifted the falcon staff and repeated his formula, summoning Helios. As he chanted, the sun came up and a glittering light appeared on the sea. The light rushed into his body, touching the inner sun that still pulsed in his breast. As he finished the chant, the inner and outer suns fused.

*He and Helios were one.* The great sun of creation now blazed in his very heart.

After a time, he wandered downstairs to the lower chamber. The room was spacious and airy, flushed with a shimmering radiance. It was prepared for receiving the god, but the god had already arrived.

He lit the twelve white candles on the altar and watched them slowly burn.

Eventually, he noticed the table laid out with the sacred meal. He sat down and placidly consumed the cakes and wine. Light quivered and flowed all around him. Somewhere, birds were singing.

"Korax? It is noon."

The voice brushed his heart like the sweet, high tune of a flute. He turned to the speaker, Kalyssa.

Could it be noon already? It seemed impossible. He gazed at Kalyssa, standing in the doorway. An aura of many colors shimmered around her. Her lovely face wore an expression of concern. Her dangling earrings gleamed.

"Are you well?"

*Was he well?* Korax mentally scanned himself. The divine vitality of Helios suffused every nerve and fiber.

"Oh, I am very well. More than I can say."

He crossed the chamber, took her in his arms, kissed her.

"Hmm." She whispered: "There is a working we must do together—now, while the power is strongest in you. Will you help me, my love?"

*Love.* Love for the entire Universe filled his heart, his heart which was the sun.

But he loved Kalyssa most of all.

"For you, I will do anything."

Smiling radiantly, she took his hand. She led him down steps and along a corridor. They entered the rectangular hall with the open roof—the meeting place of Peristeria's circle. It stood empty now, dim and cool. The statue of the three goddesses hovered at the center of the room, candles burning at their feet. A brazier emitted pink, perfumed clouds.

Kalyssa positioned Korax on a cushion at the edge of the sunken floor. "Watch the smoke," she said. "And listen."

She unfastened her girdle, removed her slippers, pulled the silk gown over her head. She stood naked except for her bracelets, earrings, and rings. She pulled the pins from her hair and let it tumble down her back.

"Watch the smoke," she chided, smiling.

Dreamily, Korax obeyed.

Kalyssa picked up a black tambourine and slapped it with her open hand. She walked sinuously toward the altar, then began to dance. Her hands twirled in the air and her hips rolled. She sang in the Phoenician tongue, a weird, keening chant. Her voice and the tambourine sound shivered in the air, vibrating in Korax's brain like flashes of light.

Above the brazier, the pink cloud moved in time to Kalyssa's dancing. As Korax watched, a figure coalesced in the smoke, a veiled goddess with black hair and robes of gold. She peered out into the chamber, and her eyes locked with his. Her arms came up, reaching toward him in supplication.

Kalyssa slipped down beside him, warm and perspiring. "Do you see her, Korax?"

"Of course."

Kalyssa gripped his hand with the firmness of a soldier. "She is Tanit, the Lady of Carthage. We must help her."

"How?"

"By sending her power, all the power we can raise. She strives to protect my city. She needs all the strength we can give her."

"I will."

Korax rose easily and braced his feet apart. He opened his heart and let the light of Helios beam forth. A pure white ray lanced across the open space and touched the heart of the goddess. Her mouth opened wide. She lifted her face in exaltation.

Korax heard Kalyssa panting beside him. His own breathing quickened. Gradually, he became aware of a dull pain in his chest. He cringed and started to shut down the ray.

"Not yet!" Kalyssa pleaded. "She needs more."

Korax steeled himself and let the power flow out of his heart. The pain grew sharper.

"Not yet," Kalyssa cried. "Please, not yet."

Korax's vision wavered. The smoke had vanished, and Tanit floated in the air, solid and shining with life. Korax could not draw breath. He willed the channel of light to close, but his will no longer controlled it. He choked, watching the life-force stream out of his body.

Suddenly his spine went rigid, and he pitched forward like a felled tree.

Somewhere an owl was crooning. Korax followed its call, clambering up a dark, treacherous slope.

He opened his eyes. Lamplight flickered. A mild breeze blew from a balcony. He lay in a bed, Kalyssa leaning over him, strained and worried.

"How do you feel?"

He tried to rise, winced. "Dizzy."

"Drink this." She pressed a shallow cup to his lips—a tepid concoction of wine and herbs. "Peristeria's own mixture." Kalyssa stroked his hair. "Guaranteed to restore."

He swallowed it down, rested on the pillow. Memories rolled in. "What did you do?"

"Do you not remember?"

"Oh, I remember you dancing, raising power ... and giving it to your goddess. But why?"

She turned her face away. "I needed to do something. Manolis has made no real progress with the king. I called down Tanit, and she asked for this working."

"But I told you this effort to win over the king would take years." A bit of his strength had returned and with it, a simmering anger. "What are you so impatient?"

"Because my visions tell me we are running out of time!"

Korax glared at her. His chest felt bruised inside, and it hurt to breathe. "Why didn't you at least tell me?"

"I know I should have. But you had so much to prepare. I did not want to distract you."

*Or feared that I might not agree.* Korax realized, with an inner chill, that Kalyssa had used him, taken advantage of his vulnerable state to draw out the power of Helios. And it was so unnecessary. Hadn't he pledged all his power to her service?

"I might have been killed, you know."

"No! I would never have allowed—I did not think it would be so dangerous!" She gripped his forearm with both hands. "You must believe me. I would never harm you. Never! I love you, more than I've ever loved anyone."

She laid her forehead near his pillow. Her shoulders quaked, and he realized she was weeping. Korax caressed her hair. His anger and suspicion melted in the warmth of his love.

"It's all right. I am fine."

"I was so frightened that I might have lost you."

Korax gripped her arms and pulled her down beside him. He kissed away the tears, then kissed her mouth. Despite the soreness, arousal surged in him. Fasting was not the only abstinence that the ritual had required.

"No. You must rest."

"My recovery is complete! Peristeria's drink is a marvel."

Kalyssa giggled as his hand snaked up her thigh. She whimpered and clung to him.

But even as their coupling commenced, Korax wondered if a portion of his heart had not closed to her—perhaps never to reopen.

# Chapter Twenty-One

After their lovemaking, Korax fell into a deep sleep. He was wrong in thinking that he had so quickly and completely recovered. A measure of his life-force had been drained by the working, and for several months he was listless and weak. Severe headaches plagued him at times, often preceded by a strange, shimmering disturbance of his eyesight.

He continued to do magic with Kalyssa. He meditated with her often, and they raised power to further her cause. Yet Korax had lost some of his enthusiasm for the work. Her mission no longer appeared quite so noble, her motives so pure. He did not like to think about it. He loved her too much to contemplate where those thoughts might lead.

Instead, Korax willfully distracted himself with the many diversions available in Alexandria. The sparkling intellectual life of the city continued apace, as unconcerned with the plots of courtiers and magicians as it was aloof from the common crowd.

At the Museum that winter, the revered mathematician Euclid lectured on books 11 through 13 of his monumental work, *The Elements*. Across the courtyard in the Library, the young astronomer Aristarchus taught his revolutionary thesis that the Sun, not the Earth, was the center of the Cosmos. Ctesibius the master engineer continued his inventive experiments in mechanics and hydraulics. This year, it was said his workshop had attracted a new student of genius, an eighteen-year-old prodigy from Syracuse named Archimedes.

Less tasteful research was underway across town in the fortified prison at Rhakotis. Under the king's patronage, the physician Herophilus was documenting the knowledge he gained from dissecting condemned criminals—some of them still alive.

JACK MASSA

In the arts, the Athenian sculptor Polyeuktos won the competition to create the statue of Arsinoe for her new temple. The temple itself was still at least two years from completion, construction slowed by inconsistent shipments of marble from Attica and Crete.

Of course, the most celebrated achievements were those of the poets. New mimes by Theocritus and the young Herodas drew considerable acclaim. A satyr play by Asclepiades pleased a broad audience, though Callimachus dubbed the work venal and gross. Asclepiades responded with a scathing invective in which he likened Callimachus to a posturing sponge. Callimachus continued the feud in his next poem, calling Asclepiades an odious dwarf.

But by far the most tumultuous event on the literary scene arrived in early spring. Word reached Alexandria that Apollonius was returning from exile.

His tale was well known in learned circles. Korax had heard it often from Asclepiades, who delighted in retelling the story. Apollonius was a brilliant young poet, raised in Alexandria, a former pupil of Callimachus. But the two men's aesthetic value systems had clashed. Callimachus favored epigrams and concise idylls; Apollonius longed for the grandeur of the epic. When still in his early twenties, Apollonius composed an epic about the voyage of Jason and the Argonauts. When he dared to perform it in public, Callimachus savaged him in verse and in the back rooms of the Museum. His reputation in tatters, Apollonius fled the city, sailing for Rhodes.

That was six years ago. But young Apollonius did not give up on his vision. Instead he revised and polished his work. In the past year, his *Voyage of Argo* had won prizes at Athens, Megara, and Delphi. Antigonus Gonatas declared the poem a masterpiece and granted the poet lifelong citizenship at his capital of Pella. Now, calling himself Apollonius of Rhodes in honor of his adopted home, the poet was staging a triumphant return to Alexandria.

His prizes and newly-won fame guaranteed a distinguished audience. By order of the king, the Salon of Calliope would host the first public performance. Four successive nights were scheduled, for the four books of the epic. The Royal Quarter bubbled with anticipation.

After much cajoling and many cups of wine, Korax managed to wangle an invitation through Asclepiades. The bleary-eyed poet warned that no seats would be available—Korax would have to stand with the crowd at the back of the hall. The king and queen planned to attend all four nights. Every banquet couch would be taken by Museum faculty and members of the court.

Korax did not care. He arrived early and squeezed into the pillared gallery with students and musicians, many of whom he knew. The salon convened in the same painted hall where he had first laid eyes on Kalyssa. Manolis and Kalyssa strolled in some time later, part of the royal entourage.

After the king and queen were seated, Callimachus poured the libation. He spoke graciously in his introduction, praising Apollonius as a stupendous talent and favorite son of Alexandria—much to the disappointment of those in the audience who had expected some subtle swipe.

Apollonius made a point of bowing to his former teacher as he stepped onto the dais. He was a handsome man with aristocratic features and curly, light-brown hair. He wore a simple, sleeved chiton, dyed pale blue and cinched with a yellow cord. Affecting the appearance of an antique bard, he even carried a herald's wand and had allowed his beard to grow. He played no instrument, but instead was accompanied by a pair of musicians who alternated on lyre, flute, and drum for different passages. The poem was impressive in its scope and contained lines of true eloquence.

Korax thought Book One admirable in its story-telling, if somewhat overwrought.

As Asclepiades quipped afterward at the reception: "Well, he is no Homer. But on the positive side of the ledger, he is also no Callimachus!"

Korax wished for an opportunity to speak with the poet, but the mob of admirers surrounding Apollonius made that impossible.

By the third night, the crowd at the reception had thinned. Korax waited until all other well-wishers had made their comments and stepped away. Then he approached Apollonius, who stood by a staircase leading down into the garden.

"My name is Astrametheus, a student and player." He introduced himself with a bow. "I want to add my voice to the chorus of acclaim for your accomplishment."

Apollonius nodded blandly. "Thank you, my friend."

Korax's voice dropped to a lower tone. "I also wanted to ask you about your time in sun-blessed Rhodes. How does the city fare?"

"Oh, are you familiar with Rhodos? It is a genial town, truly." The poet's manner became more intimate. "Let us stretch our legs in the garden, for I weary of standing here."

He set down his cup, and they descended the steps together.

"Many were the happy days I spent in Rhodos, composing my verses by the pool of the great Colossus. But to be honest, my friend, I fear the island of Rhodes is in decline."

The remark struck Korax with irrational dread. "What? How do you mean, sir?"

They paused before a lighted fountain with a sculptural group of Apollo and the Nine Muses. "The city's fortunes are not what they once were. Her mercantile fleet has suffered from weather and piracy. Just last summer, part of her navy was lost in an engagement with the brigands of Crete. But it goes beyond that.

The mood of the city is gray and dismal. The sparkle of optimism has somehow fled—as though Fate has turned away her smile."

Korax contemplated these words with alarm. He was about to probe deeper when another voice interrupted.

"Apollonius! There's the poetical genius!"

King Ptolemy and a small entourage were parading down the steps. Korax and Apollonius both bowed low as the party approached on the white-pebble path.

"I wanted to compliment you on your characterization of the sorceress Medea," Ptolemy said. "I was enthralled. Callimachus thought the portrayal slightly flawed—and far be it from me to question his literary judgment. Still, I found it scintillating. I don't care what he says!"

"Your majesty is too generous," the poet murmured.

Ptolemy cast an inquiring eye on Korax. "Who is your companion? Have we met, young sir?"

"No, your majesty." Korax repeated his bow. "I am Astrametheus, merely a humble student."

"Astrametheus, I thought that was you!" Lady Bilistiche spoke from behind the king's shoulder. "Are you still serving as language tutor to Manolis and his dear wife, Kalyssa?"

Korax swallowed and nodded his head.

"Oh, really?" Ptolemy brightened. "Manolis is a good friend of mine, a wonderfully cultured man. And I must say, he speaks very well. You have tutored him admirably."

"Thank you, majesty. He is intelligent and learns quickly."

Bilistiche sidled around the king. "Kalyssa also speaks Greek adroitly. No doubt you have found her a quick-learner as well. But then, Astrametheus is rumored to have exceptional talents. He is a skilled soothsayer, I understand."

"Indeed?" The king's interest was piqued.

Korax laughed uneasily, filled with a new worry. "Idle rumors ..."

"Oh, no. You are too modest." Bilistiche pressed relentlessly. "I myself have known this young man to pick seven winners out of nine at the racetrack."

"Really?" Ptolemy asked. "I must say I am intrigued by occult philosophy. I sponsor a society for its study. Krateros is my man in charge of that group. Do you know Krateros?"

Korax could see no point in denying it. "I have studied with him, majesty."

"Excellent. You know, I am always entertained by a spot of prophecy after dinner. You must come and do your soothsaying for me some time."

"Oh, that would be marvelous," Bilistiche gushed. "Please, my lord, make it an evening when I am invited."

The prospect of scrying for the king was frightening—yet oddly tempting. In any case, Korax saw no alternative but to bow yet again. "My humble talents are at the king's command."

Beside him, the great poet Apollonius watched it all with a visage of bafflement.

"What do you think has happened?" Manolis stormed into Kalyssa's herbal room. "The king has discovered Astrametheus. He chided me today for not introducing my *soothsayer* to him!"

Kalyssa looked up from the cutting board, where she was chopping euphorbia root with a copper knife. Jars, phials, and pots stood arranged on shelves behind her. Bunches of fragrant herbs hung drying from the low ceiling.

She set down her knife. "How did this happen?"

The agitated ambassador threw up an arm. "They met at the poetry salon. The king plans to invite him to entertain after dinner some night."

"Entertain? You mean--"

"Yes! Soothsay, prophesy, do magic tricks!"

Kalyssa stared vacantly out the open doorway at her sun-dabbled garden. She had not foreseen this. Yet now the promise of it was easily grasped.

"Korax will become a soothsayer to the king. Think about that, Manolis. This is not a disaster, but a boon."

Manolis crossed his arms. "I see only hazard. A careless word in that company and our use of him will be exposed. All our hopes could be shattered."

"Korax will not be careless. He is far too clever, and flawlessly discreet. And a careful word, here and there, delivered as prophecy—that might sway the king."

Manolis frowned, skeptical. "Will he do that for us?"

"No." Korax spoke from the doorway. "He will not."

# Chapter Twenty-Two

Korax had walked through the garden, looking for Kalyssa, had overheard his name spoken, and then the rest of the conversation.

Kalyssa and Manolis gaped at him. He stared back, angry and defiant.

"Leave us, Manolis," Kalyssa murmured. "Let me speak with him in private."

The ambassador shrugged. He brushed past Korax at the door.

Korax fixed his glance on Kalyssa, trying to measure her motives. Had she manipulated him all along? Were all her professions of love merely lies? In a corner, she had erected a small altar with a statue of Tanit and a chased silver wand. For some reason, it reminded Korax of Circe's wand in Homer's epic—Circe the witch who turned men into beasts. Supposedly, she dwelled on an island not far from Carthage ...

"I would not ask you to do anything you found objectionable," Kalyssa said.

"That is good." He paced toward her. "Because I have no intention of giving false prophecies."

She stiffened, as if injured by the remark. "I would never ask that. I only meant that ... the *way* a reading is delivered, how the words are chosen, can have influence. And you are so artful with language."

"It's a moot question. Of course, I will go if Ptolemy summons me, but I don't intend to become a regular entertainment at his parties. I am planning to leave Alexandria."

"What? But why?"

He leaned on the doorjamb, turning his face from her, peering at the sunlight and shadow on the garden path. "Impressions I got from speaking with Apollonius. The times are ill in Rhodes. I ought to go home, back to my family. I don't even know if my parents still live. Besides, I never meant to stay in Alexandria forever."

Kalyssa gripped the edge of the table, dazed.

"I was coming here to ask if you would go with me," Korax muttered. She had hidden things from him, perhaps even used magic to ensnare him. He did not care. He wanted her still.

Her pretty mouth fell open. She paced over to him, gripped his arm. Her voice was choked with emotion. "Darling, you know that is not possible."

"*Why* is it not possible?"

"Because of my duty. You know how important my work for Carthage is to me."

"More important than I am, obviously."

She held his face, tears shining in her eyes. "Do not ask me to choose. Please. I cannot!"

Korax hugged her fiercely. Her perfume assailed his senses, sweeter than the flowered air of the garden. His love for her lifted his troubled heart. He recalled the pledge he had made in exchange for that love, to put all his magic, all that he was, at her command.

"Listen to me, please." She clung to him, her head on his shoulder. "Help me for one more year. Tanit has seen that in another year the alliance can be forged. After that is done, if you still want me, I will go with you—to Rhodes or anywhere."

One more year? Perhaps she had manipulated him, lied to him. He could not be sure. But from the depths of his soul, he could not deny her.

"One more year," he murmured, stroking her hair. "So be it."

The Temple of Astarte was a pink stucco hall of moderate size, with doors of beaten bronze set behind painted cedar columns. The shrine stood in the district of Eleusis, one of the many temples that served the foreign communities.

This afternoon the entry court was lined with worshippers practicing for the spring procession. Marching to the slow music of flutes and cymbals, they filed up the steps: little girls decked in garlands and bearing trays of offerings, boys in armor of stiffened linen, acolyte priestesses in sparkling veils and bracelets.

"No, no. Stop!" Peristeria lurched from her stool in the shade of the portico. She waved her arms in disgust as she ambled down the steps.

"Remember, my dears," she admonished the girls, "you are conveying gifts to the Queen of Heaven, not carrying slop to the pigs. Hold those trays steady and keep your heads up! And you, young men, you are supposed to be warriors of the Lady of Battles. Walk proudly and keep those spear tips high!

"Everyone back! Let's start again from the beginning."

With sighs and muttering, the whole procession dutifully turned and headed back toward the temple gates. But when Peristeria returned to the porch, a young woman confronted her, a bent figure wrapped in a turquoise himation.

"Kalyssa."

"High priestess, I know you are very busy. But when you have a few moments, I must speak with you."

Peristeria cringed at the young woman's haggard face, the sore redness in her eyes. She answered gently: "Go inside." She walked to the top step and shouted across the courtyard. "Everyone rest. We will resume in a little while."

She followed Kalyssa into the cool of the temple. Clerestory windows along the roof illuminated rows of squat pillars. A curtain sewn with stars hung across the sanctuary, veiling the Great

Goddess. In Phoenicia she was called Astarte, in Carthage Tanit, elsewhere by other names. To all her people she bore two aspects: goddess of love and fertility, goddess of war and death.

"What troubles you, my daughter?" Peristeria asked.

"My heart is tearing. I feel Korax slipping away."

Peristeria intuitively recognized the cause. "He feels betrayed because you are using him. I warned you this might happen."

"Yes. But I never used magic on him—I mean, perfume and dancing, of course, after I fell in love. But I never bound him with a spell. Only now, I fear I may have to."

Peristeria winced with empathy. "We've spoken of this before. You cannot make the wind blow in two directions. You cannot turn a man into your slave and still honor him with your love."

"I know!" Kalyssa's voice cracked with anguish. "That is why my heart is breaking."

Peristeria reached out with her feelings, seeking to encompass her friend's dilemma so she could offer her best wisdom.

They belonged to the same race, but their nations differed so. Kalyssa's ancestors had colonized the west, founded great cities, Carthage the greatest of all. Grown rich and mighty, they had never known defeat. Now they lived in constant dread that the time of their preeminence might pass. Peristeria's people, in contrast, still dwelled in the Phoenician homeland. Their cities had been conquered repeatedly in the ebb and flow of empires. Centuries of subjugation had taught them a fatalistic detachment.

"Kalyssa, why must you view it as your obligation to make this alliance for Carthage?"

"Because it is possible. And I am obliged to do whatever is possible to protect my city's future. I would not have chosen this, high priestess. But I cannot avoid it."

Peristeria sighed. Love and Strife, they moved all things—so some Greek sage had written. But only a woman could appreciate all the suffering involved.

"Plainly, then, you must choose."

Kalyssa reflected stonily. "I have no choice. In Carthage, at times of crisis, we still observe the ancient rites of Bel. At his high place, we cast an infant into the fire. It is considered a deification of the babe, a great honor for the family. When I entered the temple as priestess, I swore I would throw *myself* into the fire if it served Carthage. How then can I refuse to sacrifice my love?"

While she spoke her back had straightened, was no longer bent. Her eyes, dull and cold, glanced at the shrouded sanctuary. "I was hoping, if it came to this, that you might help me weave the spell."

"Oh, no," Peristeria demurred. "That is for you alone, daughter. You are perfectly capable, if that is what you must do." She clasped Kalyssa's hand. "But I will go with you now and part the veil. We will make sacrifice to the Lady of Heaven, and I will pray for you—that she may bless your heart with peace."

# Chapter Twenty-Three

Late one afternoon, without warning, Korax was summoned to attend the king and queen at dinner. A herald appeared at the ambassador's residence. The man waited outside the door while Korax put on his best chiton and gray, star-bordered chlamys, and packed his lyre into its drawstring bag.

Though Korax had known this summons might come, it incited a keen anxiety. He was accustomed to some stage fright whenever he performed, but this anticipation cut much deeper. Tonight he must play the part of soothsayer to the most powerful king on earth. The royal party would expect entertainment, but also convincing readings of their characters, forecasts of their fates. Korax would need not only inspiration, but also cleverness and caution.

Instinctively, he knew that if he failed, if he displeased the monarchs, it could jeopardize all of Kalyssa's hopes. From the time he began weaving magic for his love, Korax had sensed that he was the fulcrum that could eventually shift the king in favor of Carthage. Tonight, that delicate point of balance was at risk.

The royal party was dining on the pleasure island of Antirrhodos. The islet lay in a corner of the bay near the palace complex, forming a boundary between Ptolemy's royal harbor and the commercial Great Harbor. A natural sandbar, the islet had been reinforced with boulders, topped with a layer of soil, planted with lawns, groves, and gardens.

By the time Korax and the herald reached the water's edge, the sun had settled behind the Lochias promontory. They walked along a granite dock lined with white sphinxes. Down a flight of stone steps, they boarded a waiting skiff with whimsical dolphins carved on stern and bow. They sat behind two oarsmen, while a third boatman held the tiller.

In the twilight, Antirrhodos floated toward them across the silvery water. Cressets flamed on the sandy beach and colored lanterns were strung in the branches of the groves. The skiff coasted to a limestone landing crowded with pleasure boats.

Disembarking, Korax followed the herald up a path of stepping stones that crossed the beach and curled through the trees. Bronzes of fauns and dryads peered from the shadows though painted, lifelike eyes. The two men passed a round pavilion and approached a pillared hall set at the crest of the islet. Spearmen stood guard on the steps, interspersed with fiery braziers. From inside the hall came riotous laughter.

Korax waited in the vestibule while the herald approached the king. The man would not speak until given leave, so Korax had ample time to survey the banquet and absorb impressions. A score of feasters reposed on couches set amid a throng of attendants and slaves. Korax spotted Ptolemy at the center, with Bilistiche on his left hand and Arsinoe on his right. He also recognized Chancellor Eupolis and Marshal Drakas, for once not wearing his armor. The old warrior occupied a couch to the side, clad in a gray chiton. He sat with eyes shut while a tall, black-haired slave kneaded the muscles on his shoulders.

Dinner had finished some time ago, and the party had progressed far toward emptying a huge gold krater. At the moment, they were playing the ancient game of *kottabos*, flicking dregs from their emptied cups at a target. In this case, the target consisted of lily pads floating in a shallow pool at the center of the floor. Whenever a pad accumulated enough weight to be sunk, the feasters celebrated with a roar.

Men and women both competed in the sport. Arsinoe seemed particularly skillful and zealous. Across the chamber, Korax read in the queen an almost fevered desire to win.

But the more wine was consumed, the less accurate grew the players' tosses. Presently, the king grew bored and called a halt. He then noticed the herald attending patiently by the foot of his couch.

"Majesties, the soothsayer Astrametheus of Hermopolis awaits your command."

"Oh, yes." Ptolemy brightened. "Bring him in at once!"

The herald faced the door and signaled with his wand. Lyre in hand, Korax marched into the hall. He bowed to the three sides of the chamber, saving his deepest obeisance for the king and queen.

Ptolemy leaned on an elbow and regarded him with a besotted expression. "My young friend, I'm so glad you could attend us on such short notice. Bilistiche tells us you are an ingenious soothsayer. We are all anxious to hear what you predict."

Striving to hide his nervousness, Korax plucked a note. "Prophecy, O King, is simply the art of listening to the voices of the gods within. I make no claim to unique powers, nor that all I speak will prove true. Only the gods who hold the open sky know the fates of all with certitude."

"Hah," Arsinoe scoffed. "He temporizes well. His speech would better suit a lawyer than a seer."

"Come, Astrametheus," Bilistiche cried amid the laughter. "I know you have abilities. You cannot deny what people say."

Korax played three rapid notes. "People say many things. As a truth-sayer, I can attest that many of those many things are false."

"An able riposte!" Ptolemy chuckled. "But surely we did not summon you to our little island for no reason. What talent you have, you must share with our company."

"As your majesty commands." Korax scanned the courtiers' faces. "I will read the soul and fate of anyone who wishes, and speak whatever words the gods put in my mouth. Perhaps, Lady Bilistiche would care to go first."

She sat up straight. "I am all eagerness."

Korax fixed her with a piercing stare. Presently, he played and recited:

Diomedes reborn as woman,
She is named Bilistiche.
Tamer of horses, swift and wild,
Tamer of men's passions too.
One day her team might win at Olympia.
Still would she seek prizes more grand.

The lyre's sound faded, and the hall stood hushed. Bilistiche raked a hand through her disheveled hair, red-faced, as if her inner being had been laid naked. Everyone else waited for the king or queen to judge.

"I think you perceive Bilistiche quite clearly," Arsinoe declared at last. "Do you dare to read my soul, young man?"

Korax replied amid strokes of the lyre. "The queen gives little credence to soothsayers. In another, this very skepticism might make a barrier. But the queen's soul is so strong, it is as plain to read as a stele in daylight."

A murmur of anticipation crept across the audience. There was much Korax could discern in Arsinoe, even more he could not see. While speaking only the truth, he carefully avoided delving into the dark places.

The queen is like unto Sekhet,
The Lioness of Egypt,
Ferocious and brilliant as the Sun.
Of all the Arsinoes history will know,
She will have the highest renown.

A chattering of approval and a round of applause greeted this recital. Arsinoe was a common name among the Macedonian nobility and history already knew several famous women of that name. The queen stared at Korax with a severe, measuring look, but a half-smile bending her lips.

"I must be next," Ptolemy said. "Read my inner being, young man."

Korax nodded. Ptolemy was easy to peruse. If the queen's soul was a deep amphora of unmixed wine, the king's was a shallow bowl. Happily, his fate appeared most fortunate. The lyre sang high and exalted notes.

> The king is a man of many thoughts,
> Of many gifts, by Zeus bestowed.
> His reign is favored with prospects bright.
> The rule of his issue over Egypt
> Even the Nile in length exceeds.

Applause and loud shouts of approbation echoed under the roof. Korax relaxed, knowing he now had the audience well in hand.

"I call that excellent prophecy!" Ptolemy declared smugly. "And you play the lyre skillfully too."

"Your majesty is most kind."

Other nobles now begged to have their readings sung. Korax obliged them, observing what he could of each person's character and destiny. While scrupulously avoiding any untruths, he deliberately stressed the favorable aspects for each subject. After all, his role was chiefly to amuse. And, as Kalyssa had said, he could be most artful with language.

"This was enjoyable," Ptolemy remarked, when all who wished a reading had been satisfied. "You must come back and soothsay for us often."

At the king's word, a steward presented Korax with a tumbler of wine and a small bag of coins.

Later, back in his room, Korax spilled out the bag on a bedside table—and discovered with amazement that the coins were not silver but gold. Counting quickly, he realized he had been given enough money to buy a fair-sized house in Rhodos.

# Chapter Twenty-Four

In the chilly dawn, Arsinoe hurried along an enormous portico. A gaggle of maidservants hastened with her, straining to smooth the queen's garments and finish arranging her hair. Arsinoe paid them no heed. A military courier had appeared at the gate of her apartments, bringing dire news.

Cold light slanted into the council hall as she arrived. Drakas waited, crisp and erect in his armor. He conferred at the edge of the mosaic floor with officers from the field—weary soldiers, their boots and cloaks mud-stained from the road. They had traveled by boat from upriver, then raced on horseback from Canopus.

Everyone bowed when Arsinoe appeared. She sank onto her throne. "Where is my brother?"

"On his way, majesty," Drakas answered. "Eupolis and the others too."

"Tell me what is known. I've only heard there's been a mutiny."

"Celts," Drakas said. "The encampment at Athribis."

"How many?"

"A few hundred to start. But more joined them from the garrison at Leontopolis. Now there are 2500, perhaps more." Drakas sat down in the front row of benches. He allowed the couriers to answer the queen's subsequent questions.

Brisk and efficient, Arsinoe elicited the essentials of the disaster. The Celts had been trainees, newly arrived in Egypt. The uprising started in the night, without warning. After burning the camp, they'd marched north, sacking villages along the way. The Macedonian governors had called up their retainers, and the nearby cities had shut their gates. At last word, the Celts were still moving north, into the central Delta.

Ptolemy and more of his councilors filtered in during the questioning. They listened with an air of shock and foreboding.

"What are they after?" Ptolemy demanded. "Can anyone guess their plan?"

In his petulance, he reminded Arsinoe of the brother she had known in childhood—an oversensitive and easily frightened child. Vaguely, she wished maturity had brought him better nerves.

"By nature they are raiders," Drakas replied to the king. "When the Celts sacked Delphi, they took the treasure from the sacred site and simply tried to carry it home."

"They can't maraud over the Delta on foot," the queen observed. "Especially with the river rising. And they'll never be able to commandeer enough boats to keep their horde intact. No, they will have to besiege one of the cities, or else turn south again."

"Our commanders at Heliopolis and Memphis can be counted on to contain them from the south," Ptolemy said. "We should send transports to reinforce the Delta cities. With any luck, the brigands will be driven into the swamps, and the river will finish them."

"No," the queen answered sharply. "They must be hunted down to the last man. An example must be made."

In the next hours, plans were drawn to send warships down the Nile and reinforce the walled cities. Dispatches were drafted to the governors of the district capitals, to coordinate the movement of troops. By noon, the situation seemed better in hand, and the king ordered a meal brought in for the council.

While they paused to eat, Ptolemy brooded over his platter. "This should never have been allowed to happen. I thought we agreed the Celts would be broken up among many different regiments."

"They have been, once deployed," Drakas answered. "But these men were in training. It was thought less trouble to train them as a lot."

"Less trouble indeed. I do not recall approving that decision."

"I approved it," Arsinoe told him flatly. "Obviously, a misjudgment."

"Obviously," Ptolemy retorted. "In the future, dear queen, I think it best if we review all military decisions in concert. This, I believe, was our original agreement."

*He dares say this to me*, Arsinoe thought in fury. For years her brother had cast more and more of the burden of rule onto her shoulders, while he toyed with his mistresses and hobbies. Now, at her first misstep, he had the gall to humiliate her in front of the council.

She forced a soothing reply. "Of course, dear king, if that is your wish."

The council resumed, discussing alternative plans, the details of terrain, troop dispositions. Arsinoe followed the arguments and commented when necessary, but part of her attention was now withdrawn.

From the beginning, she had known the time might come when her control of her brother would slip. Her aging body could no longer captivate him quite so well in bed. Now, he was beginning to dispute her decisions.

Suddenly the omens seemed stark. The day was coming when only one of them could sit on the throne of Egypt.

The officer of the Royal Bank finished counting the gold coins from Korax's purse. "Eight hundred drachmas." He recorded the sum on papyrus. "Exactly the same deposit as the last three times—and almost no withdrawals. Your account is becoming formidable. What business did you say you were in, young sir?"

"Perfumes," Korax answered, straight-faced. "I supply tinctures and sweet-smelling airs to the court."

"Oh, yes. I can see how that would pay very well." The banker affixed his signature and seal to the document. "Your funds are of course guaranteed by the crown. However, given the growth of your account, you might want to consider more lucrative investments. Naturally, your principal could not be guaranteed, but the interest rates are much more favorable. If you wish, I know several prominent brokers who would be most happy to advise you."

"Thank you, but no," Korax replied merrily. "I am quite content with the modest rates offered by the king."

He took the sheet from the disappointed banker's hand, rolled it tight, and stashed it in his satchel. In a cheerful humor, he left the fortified treasury building and strolled onto the Canopic Way.

The summer sun rode high, and the sky was a brilliant blue. Chariots and fine carriages traveled the broad avenue, while handsomely-dressed citizens roamed the steps and stoas.

Korax browsed through a row of import shops, which carried prime merchandise from the East. He purchased some Indian incense and a filigreed oil flask. Impulsively, he bought an expensive Bactrian rug as a gift for Kalyssa. She favored the rich colors and intricate weave of that particular style, and this thick rug would be perfect for lying together on the terrace under the stars.

After arranging for delivery of his purchases, Korax ambled back into the sunshine. His next stop was Philopixea's barbershop, an establishment frequented by poets and intellectuals. The shop occupied several rooms of an emporium across from the Library. As usual, the porch was crowded with idlers and customers awaiting service. Men young and old lounged on benches in the shade. A clusters of players crouched over a game of knucklebones. The rest of the mob read or conversed and argued, filling the stoa with a continuous babble. Korax paused at the fountain to splash cool water on his face.

"Well, is it a shade from Hades' realm? No, he yet breathes and walks among the living!" Asclepiades sat down on the fountain's rim.

Korax grinned. "How are you, my friend?"

"Oh, odious and dwarfish as ever. But you! I hear astonishing gossip about Astrametheus. Is it true you are now a fortune-teller for the king?"

"Well." Korax tilted a shoulder. "It pays better than the chorus."

"So I see." The poet rubbed the fabric of Korax's chlamys between his stubby fingers. "Persian wool, is it? And look at that headband set with lapis! You must still be living with Ambassador Manolis; his sartorial style is rubbing off."

Korax laughed good-naturedly. "Not so bad as that I hope. At least I still shave my chin every day—unlike you. I did not know you ever visited the barber."

"Only for the cheap wine." Asclepiades winked and raised his tumbler.

But after a long swallow, his mood suddenly turned pensive. "What a year it has been, my boy. First Apollonius stages his rebellion, then the Celts have theirs. I swear, the world is moving under our feet."

Korax took a cup of chilled wine from the tray of a serving boy, replacing it with a copper coin. "Well, the barbarians were crushed, at least."

By all accounts, the Celtic uprising had lasted just over a month. The rebels had been driven onto a neck of land in the

Delta, then left to starve when the rising flood turned the ground into an island. A few had drowned trying to swim the river. The rest had committed ritual suicide.

"Poor savages," Asclepiades commented morosely. "They are fodder for the sculptors and dramatists now. And Apollonius may yet share their dismal fate—figuratively speaking."

"Why? I thought his epic was well-received."

"Exactly. Too well-received. There was immediate talk of an appointment to the faculty. This raised Callimachus' snakelike envy to perilous heights. Now he slithers around the palace, poisoning everyone against Apollonius with his subtle venom." Asclepiades shook his head. "The intrigue and backstabbing in the Museum are beyond belief. I swear, no royal court has ever known the like."

# Chapter Twenty-Five

The shrine of Isis by the Sea stood at the midway point of the Lochias promontory, a modest temple in the old Egyptian style. The original inhabitants of Rhakotis had erected the shrine long before Alexander. In planning their enormous palace, the Ptolemies had wisely left the sacred site undisturbed.

Accompanied by a royal herald, Kalyssa approached the painted pylons. A narrow parasol shaded her face from the fierce afternoon sun. She had crossed the gardens and courts of the palace in a welter of excitement and apprehension. Yesterday, a courier had arrived at her door, bearing a letter from the queen. It said simply: "Please attend me at the shrine of Isis by the Sea, tomorrow at the ninth hour." It was signed 'Arsinoe' and bore her royal seal.

Beyond the pylons, two sentries stood watch in the small courtyard. The herald conducted Kalyssa as far as the porch of blue lotus columns. He bowed and signed with his wand for her to proceed.

Kalyssa set down her parasol and marched through the portal. She entered a shadowy hypostyle hall. At the front, the doors of the small sacristy stood open. A life-size statue of Isis looked down, merciful and serene. The queen stood facing the statue, wrapped in a sea-blue himation that covered her head like a veil. Kalyssa tread quietly toward Arsinoe, uncertain how near to approach or if she should somehow signal her arrival.

Without turning, the queen said, "Do you know Isis?"

"Yes, your majesty, of course."

Arsinoe beckoned. "Come stand beside me."

Kalyssa stepped closer. The queen finally turned to look at her. She stood taller than Kalyssa by more than half a head.

"You know, I am identified with Isis and also Aphrodite." She peered into Kalyssa's eyes. "Do you believe I am immortal?"

In all her time in Alexandria, Kalyssa had never considered herself out of her depth. Now she felt like one tripping along a precipice at midnight.

"Of course, your majesty. Everyone is aware of your deification."

"That's not what I mean. You, Kalyssa, who are a priestess: Do you really believe I am a goddess?"

Kalyssa quailed inwardly. The usual facile lies would not serve here. "It is a complicated question."

"And you are just a simple young woman, is that it?" Arsinoe's voice dripped with impatience and scorn. "Tell me the truth."

Pushed to the edge of the precipice, Kalyssa summoned her own inner strength. "The truth is that the Goddess is one, though she has many names. She dwells in all women and expresses her divinity in varied ways. In your majesty's case, she has bestowed gifts in great measure: beauty, cunning, and a ferocious will."

Arsinoe smiled with half of her mouth. "A shrewd and insightful answer. You are not so simple after all."

Kalyssa stared back in silence.

"Come with me," said the queen.

She led the way past the statue and through the sacristy. She opened a secret door, revealing a spiral stair. Kalyssa followed her down the narrow steps and out into the daylight.

They stood outside the temple walls. From here the Lochias stretched a quarter-mile, a narrow headland curving out to sea to form one arm of the Great Harbor. The Ptolemies had fortified the promontory with a long parapet, inaccessible to anyone except by royal permission. Apart from a few sentries, the rampart stood deserted.

"Let's walk to the end," Arsinoe said. "I think you will appreciate the view."

Kalyssa covered her head with the himation, wishing she had brought her parasol. Arsinoe seemed not to notice the implacable sun.

They walked a little way in silence. Then suddenly the queen took a whole new tack: "You have no children. Do you plan on children in the future?"

"I do not know, majesty. I doubt it."

"You drink a preventative, I am sure. Phoenician women are clever with such things. But that never would have been an option for me. I was raised to bear royal children." Arsinoe reflected quietly for a few steps. "All of them are dead now, of course."

Kalyssa said nothing. If the queen was baiting her, she thought it best to lie low and wait.

She knew Arsinoe's story perfectly well. Raised at her father's court in Alexandria, the queen had been married off at fifteen to Lysimachus, then the regent of Macedonia. He was a much older man, one of Alexander's marshals. Arsinoe had borne him three sons and a daughter.

But Lysimachus had another son, Agathocles, a popular soldier and the old man's heir. Arsinoe was in her thirties when the trouble started. She accused Agathocles of plotting treason. She convinced Lysimachus to have his son executed, to make her own eldest son heir to the throne. That arrangement lasted only a year. Arsinoe's half-brother, the violent and unpredictable Ptolemy Keraunos, defeated Lysimachus in battle and staked his own claim to the throne. To add legitimacy, he offered Arsinoe marriage. She accepted, on the condition that the wedding take place before the assembled Macedonian army. But even that precaution proved inadequate. At the wedding feast, Keraunos had Arsinoe's children stabbed to death. She herself only barely escaped—Kalyssa was not sure how. Arsinoe took refuge on Samothrace for two years, before accomplishing her return to Alexandria and marriage to her brother.

"My children were murdered before my eyes, you know."

"Yes. How horrible."

"More than you can imagine. Some people thought I deserved it, because I betrayed Agathocles. But he really was plotting against his father. Once on the throne, he would have murdered my sons, for certain. I knew him only too well—you see, Agathocles was my lover." She glanced sideways at Kalyssa. "Does that shock you?"

"No. I am only surprised that you mention it to me."

"You wonder why I make such confessions? Naturally, it is to test your reactions."

"And how well am I standing the test?"

"About as I expected."

They approached the end of the rampart, a round bastion overlooking the sea. Recognizing the queen, the lone sentry withdrew, well out of earshot.

Arsinoe leaned her back to the wall, facing across the harbor to the splendid city. "Your husband continues to approach us about forming an alliance against the Romans."

*At last we come to the heart of things*, Kalyssa thought.

"You want this badly, I believe," Arsinoe said.

"My husband deems it crucial for Carthage."

"Oh, please. You can stop pretending, Kalyssa. There are no men here, only two women talking. *You* want this badly, don't you?"

"Yes."

The queen paused, her himation fluttering in the steady sea-wind. "I learned long ago that great things are accomplished by those who take great risks. What are you willing to risk?"

"Anything—but not for just the alliance. Alliances are broken as often as forged. You must send your fleet to Syracuse. Hieron would welcome the support of Egypt, would readily become your client. Then, with Syracuse, Carthage, and Egypt united, we can crush Rome."

Arsinoe tilted her head, impressed. "An ambitious project."

"But not beyond your majesty's abilities."

The queen's sober visage expressed satisfaction. "I knew you were a woman I could deal with. What I say now must remain secret—whether you choose to accept my offer or not. If you were to betray me, I would of course deny it. You would be arrested and tortured to death. The same would happen to Manolis and your lover, Korax—Oh, yes, I know his real name."

Kalyssa's nerve faltered. "Believe me, I will not betray your confidence."

"I believe it. Here is my dilemma: I am nearing the point where I must dispose of my brother—before he decides to dispose of me. Arranging his death would not be overly difficult; there are a variety of ways. The aftermath is the problem. I must have soldiers to support my hold on the throne. Unfortunately, the Royal Guard is tight in the claws of old Drakas, and his loyalty to my brother is unshakeable. There are a few generals in the regular army who will support me, but they could never march on Alexandria by surprise. That leaves only one option: I must land foreign troops in the city. I have a long-standing pledge from my half-brother Magas to place the army of Cyrenaica at my disposal. But Magas lacks a fleet and by treaty cannot build one. That is where Carthage is needed."

"You need our warships. How many?"

"Only a squadron or two, as escort. Troop transports are the main thing: enough to carry 10,000 spearmen."

Kalyssa gripped the rough stone of the parapet as though it were the rail of a lurching ship. "You do ask us to take a great risk. If we failed, your brother might make war on Carthage in reprisal."

"True. But I offer much in return. Once my hold on Egypt is firm, I will send my Aegean fleet to Syracuse. To assure this, I am prepared to make any pledges you require—gold, hostages, what you will."

"I'm not sure what pledge is precious enough to bind your majesty," Kalyssa said frankly.

Arsinoe took no offense. "My sons, my daughter, even they."

"They are adopted children."

In the pitiless sun, the queen suddenly looked old and bitter. "They are the only children I have left, and they are precious to me. Does my proposal interest you or not?"

Kalyssa swallowed, a thousand thoughts and feelings whirling in her. "When would you need the ships to arrive?"

"Early next summer, during the Synod. My brother will be distracted then, and Drakas' eye will be on the Egyptian clerics. This gives your city plenty of time to decide and make arrangements."

Kalyssa peered across the water at the crowded docks, the gleaming halls and temples. How beautiful Alexandria looked under the summer sky, how much like Carthage.

"I will speak to my husband. I believe I can convince him the risk is worth taking. And if he goes to Carthage in person to make the case, well, that would carry great weight with our council."

# Chapter Twenty-Six

W hat is your verdict?" Manolis inquired, peering over Kalyssa's shoulder.

In the twilight of the garden, she studied the arrangement of seeds and grains on the marble rim of the fountain. The waterfall roared steadily a few yards away.

"The queen is certainly in earnest. From the indications, she would keep her pledge to us."

"But what are her chances of success?"

Kalyssa hesitated. "The spread looks favorable, but the matter is complex. These branching lines at the top imply that events could go many different ways."

Manolis grunted. "Perhaps we should ask Korax to prognosticate."

"No!" The abruptness of her response surprised them both. "He does not know. He *must* not know about this. His sense of honor might compel him to reveal it to the king."

She stared at the oracle once more. Korax might well be a deciding factor, for good or ill. He had become so powerful.

"Then perhaps it is time to end your involvement with him," Manolis suggested. "I do not think you can hide something this important."

"I can hide whatever I need to," Kalyssa insisted. Intuition told her Korax must remain involved and on their side. She was convinced that it was his power, working through the goddess, that had made this opportunity manifest.

Manolis appeared skeptical. "I will leave the sorcery to you, my wife. But you must promise this: If you begin to suspect, even in the slightest, that Korax is a danger to us, then he must be removed—by any means necessary."

Inwardly, she cringed. But her shoulders stayed level, and eyes grew cold as iron. "I agree. Is it your judgment then that this risk is worth taking?"

Manolis gave a fatalistic shrug. "I have felt all along that we must appeal to the queen. Now she has come to us. Naturally, I will want to meet with her in person, and Ambassador Prodotus too, to make sure we all concur on the details of the scheme."

"She anticipated as much. Of course she insists on absolute secrecy. She suggests a meeting here, late at night."

"Perfect." Manolis stretched, yawning. "I've long desired the honor of a royal visit to our home."

At the next dark moon, Kalyssa rose from her bed in the middle of the night. Wearing a light camisia, she walked barefoot down the unlit corridors and stairs. On the lower floor, she moved noiselessly past the slaves' quarters and through the kitchen. She lit a candle from the embers of the cooking fire and carried the light into her herbal room.

She dragged the square table that she used as an altar to the middle of the floor. From a hidden cupboard, she produced a small doll, a man woven of straw. She placed this on the altar in front of the statue of Tanit. She brought out a black, three-legged cauldron the size of a human head. She filled the cauldron with crumpled herbs from various jars.

She raised the camisia over her head and discarded it. With a pungent black ointment, she drew designs on her forehead and torso. Then she set fire to the contents of the cauldron.

As the smoke rose, she prayed to Tanit in her aspect as Queen of the Dead—for in that guise she was also the Great Deceiver, the

Mistress of Secrets. Breathing in the fumes, Kalyssa raised her silver wand and called the goddess into her body.

She began to dance, stepping and gliding around the altar. In a soft and forceful voice, she chanted over and over:

Hide from his eyes, O Lady,
All that I must conceal

Impelled by her circling motion, the cauldron smoke spiraled inward under the low ceiling. Thickening, it soon obscured the statue of Tanit and the little man of straw.

Korax hurried down the high-roofed corridor, struggling to stay on the heels of the royal herald. The fellow strode with crisp alacrity, as if it were morning rather than the dead of night.

The herald had appeared at the ambassador's residence some time after midnight. He roused the household slaves and demanded that they waken Astrametheus. The king wanted to see him at once. Numbly, Korax pulled on his clothes and grabbed his lyre. The king had summoned him without warning before, but always in daytime.

They approached massive doors embossed with gold images of Isis and Serapis—the gates to the royal apartments. In front of the sentries stood another man in armor. Korax recognized him with a twinge of alarm: Drakas.

"I will conduct him from here." The marshal dismissed the herald.

He turned grimly and led the way through the doors. Korax noticed the hint of a limp in the old soldier's stride.

"The king is not unwell, I hope," Korax ventured, falling into step.

Drakas' ruined eye was toward him, so he could discern no reaction. "He had a troubling dream. He wants your opinion."

They crossed a giant reception hall and then a banquet room. Only a few lamps burned in niches, revealing little of the palace's grandeur. Past two more sentries, they entered a corridor, long and straight, with rose-colored tiles and statues set on pedestals. Korax had not been this way before, and he scrutinized the marble sculptures in the dim light. Most he recognized readily, gods and heroes: Ptolemy the First, Heracles, Apollo, Alexander. The corridor smelled of polish and fine wood.

They turned onto a shorter hallway with candlelight shining at the far end. As they approached the bright chamber, Drakas thrust out an arm.

"A word with you, before we enter."

Korax looked up into the marshal's face, and his tension heightened.

"I do not trust soothsayers," Drakas said. "I have never met one who was not a fraud. In your case, that does not concern me. But soothsayers who ply their trade in royal courts are often spies as well as charlatans."

"I am neither," Korax interrupted. "Only an honest man commanded by the king to tell what he sees."

"Indeed?" Drakas' face was a baleful mask. "An honest man does not forge his identity. Did you think no one would check the letters of introduction you presented at the Museum?"

Korax flinched, now truly frightened. Drakas commonly tortured men he even suspected of crimes against the crown.

"Very well," he admitted. "Astrametheus is a fiction. But I am no spy."

"Really? You live with a foreign ambassador. His wife is your lover."

"And I have never asked the king or queen to favor them in the slightest way." Korax forced himself to show an attitude of strength. "Nor have I advised on any political matter—except when directly asked. Even then, I insisted that what I saw might not prove true."

"I will give you all that," Drakas replied. "But you are not here tonight for entertainment. You are sailing into deep waters now. Be advised: I show no mercy to anyone who betrays the king. Your death would not be swift or pleasant. Now come, his majesty awaits. By the way, I do not think you will need the lyre."

"That's just as well. I am decidedly not in a musical mood."

Scores of white tapers illuminated the royal bedroom. Exquisite furnishings and a legion of attendants crowded the chamber. Ptolemy lay in a vast gilded bed, looking frail and careworn amid the coverlets and pillows.

"Ah, Astrametheus, good of you to come." The king patted the bed. "Sit down, my friend. Everyone else leave us."

In silence, the attendants moved toward the door. Only Drakas remained, sturdy arms folded over his chest. Ptolemy addressed Korax in a hushed voice.

"I had a dream tonight, very disturbing. Normally I pay scant attention to dreams, but this one frightened me. It felt very real, like a warning of danger."

"I understand, your majesty. I will interpret as best I can."

"I was a child," Ptolemy recounted, "very young. I was playing in my mother's garden. Arsinoe was there. I was three or four, so she must have been nine or ten. Both of us were naked. We were running along the edge of a fountain, chasing each other, laughing as children do. My mother cried out for us to stop, afraid we would fall. But even as I heard her voice, I slipped. I dashed my head on the fountain's edge. Then I woke, full of terror."

The king's trepidation was palpable in the air. The room seemed gloomy despite the many candles.

"If I may have a bowl of water," Korax said.

"There." Ptolemy pointed at a nearby table.

Korax filled a bowl with clear water from a silver ewer. He added a few drops of wine for color and stirred the mixture with his finger. He carried the bowl back to the bed and gazed into the swirling liquid.

For some reason, the mystery was hard to penetrate.

"The dream reveals your majesty's inner fears," Korax said at last. "You have misgivings about the queen."

"Yes, exactly." Ptolemy cast a meaningful look at Drakas. He continued in a tense, confiding tone: "My relations with Arsinoe have felt strained of late. She appears the same as ever, yet when she is near my stomach recoils. And there was an unverified report of a secret courier leaving her apartments late at night."

He gripped Korax's arm. "I'm afraid she is plotting against me. Can you tell me if she is?"

His anguish swarmed over Korax's senses like a rough wave at sea. Korax clenched his lips and gazed into the scrying bowl. Images flickered through his mind, but they were vague and fractured.

"I cannot say for certain. The queen has a deep and formidable soul. What she chooses to hide may be more than I can pierce."

Ptolemy's hold tightened on his arm. "Do not be afraid of her vengeance. I promise, Drakas and I will protect you. Look again. I must know the answer."

Korax re-stirred the bowl. He watched for some time, straining for clarity. But it almost seemed that an unknown force deliberately obscured his vision.

"I am sorry, majesty," he confessed at last. "I can only say that it is possible. Nothing more."

"Agh! What good are you?" Ptolemy fretted. "Go away. Drakas, send him back to his quarters. And bring my retinue in again. I shall sleep no more tonight."

Korax bowed and gratefully retreated. As he neared the door, he heard the king call out to Drakas.

"Send for Bilistiche. She will soothe my nerves."

# Chapter Twenty-Seven

Korax tried repeatedly with the scrying bowl, but he never could reveal a clear answer to the king's query. He was greatly relieved that Ptolemy did not summon him again in the ensuing months, even to provide after-dinner entertainment. Astrametheus the soothsayer had acquired a reputation and now had other wealthy clients. Korax was quite happy to steer clear of the treacherous politics of the court.

Besides, the year was growing old, and he needed to concentrate on getting ready for the next ritual. The Third Tower of Nectanebo demanded preparations even more stringent and difficult than the previous workings.

Luckily, he had Kalyssa to help with the herbs—in that lore, she was an expert. Various plants had to be harvested with precise art, at certain times of day, under certain phases of the moon. Korax was able to leave those labors to Kalyssa, while he focused on the interior spiritual work and on writing his formulas.

Much of this work he did at the Temple of Pan. He meditated in the sacred groves and used the library for his studies. One day, just over a month before the solstice, he was deeply immersed in a text when a female voice startled him.

"Krateros said I would find you here. I've been hoping for a chance to speak with you."

Korax stood in surprise. "Miriam. It is good to see you."

Almost a year-and-a-half had passed since they had last spoken. Korax had seen her only a few times, at the Society's monthly meetings, and then from a distance. She seemed taller, perhaps more slender in her loose robes. Her eyes were solemn and piercing as ever.

"You look well," she commented, sliding onto a bench across the table. "I hear you are growing rich telling fortunes."

He did not want to discuss that with her. "How are you? I have missed you."

A shade of discomfort passed over her features. "I am well. I am going to be married, you know. Next year, in the spring."

"No, I had not heard." He found the news stunning—and oddly painful. "Is it courteous in your culture to congratulate a bride?"

She smiled, the old warmth resurfacing. "I would be happy to have your good wishes."

"You do, of course. I am just so surprised. Who is the man?"

"No one you know, a young man of my tribe—so my father approves. He is a jeweler; he makes beautiful things." She drew back her sleeve, showing him a gold-wire bracelet, a work of delicate craftsmanship.

"It is beautiful," Korax agreed. "He is not in the Society then?"

"Oh, no. He is not a magician. But it does not bother him that I am. I think he finds it exciting." Her eyes shone with a distant tenderness. "He is very fond of me."

"You deserve nothing less," Korax said softly. "I wish you every happiness."

"Thank you." She reached into an inner pocket. "I've brought you something."

She showed him a silver medallion, the size of a drachma, affixed to a slim cord. "I hope you will not find this presumptuous. My angels told me to make this for you—a protective amulet."

"But it is I who should be giving you a gift."

"I want you to have it," she said earnestly. "My betrothed made it in his shop, from my design. Then I did workings over it. You see: it has the sigil of Maat on one side and that of Thoth on the other. I don't know why I received such strong guidance about this. Perhaps it is not important at all."

"I will wear it from now on." He placed the cord over his neck. "And I will buy a gift for your wedding—something equally beautiful." His thumb caressed the sigil of Thoth. "I will let you in on a secret, Miriam. When I summoned a magical ally in Memphis, Thoth was the one who answered ..."

"You have told me that before."

"I know. But the secret is that I have lost him. I stopped following his advice. Now when I call him, he does not come."

Miriam sucked in her breath. "That is troubling, Korax. Thoth is not a god that a magician should be estranged from."

"Indeed," Korax nodded, gloomy and bewildered. "I promised to serve the gods—that used to be my guiding principle. But here in Alexandria, I have learned it is not so simple. Different gods have different ideas. Thoth counsels one thing; Tanit demands another."

"Is it Tanit who makes the demands, or Kalyssa?"

He tensed at the question. "What do you mean to say?"

"I've said more than I meant to. Forgive me." She started to rise.

"Wait. We are friends, Miriam. You can say anything to me. Please."

She settled back on the bench, her eyes downcast. "It's only that, after I broke my connection with you and Kalyssa, I came to believe ... to feel ... that Kalyssa had not truly been my friend. Not in the same way I was hers. I felt that she used me, first to get close to Peristeria's circle, then later to get close to you. I feel she is using you now."

Korax stared into her eyes. "Sometimes I feel the same way. But she is not like you and I. She places her duty above her feelings, even above friendship and love. In a way, I admire her for it."

"You see all this, but your heart is not changed?"

The question made his flinch inside. He still loved Kalyssa, but he was forced to acknowledge that his deepest feelings had faded over time, slowly and imperceptibly. Her husband had sailed to Carthage for the winter, and Korax had hoped that Manolis' absence would allow them to re-forge the deep connection of their hearts. So far it had not happened.

"To be honest, it is not the same. I do not know why. I suppose it is as the philosophers say: Perfect happiness never lasts in this world. It is not in the nature of things." After a moment, he shook himself. "Listen to me. Fine words to speak to a future bride! Forgive me."

"You don't need to apologize," Miriam said. "I have no illusions about permanent happiness. In this world, all conditions pass away. On that point, I believe the sages of all nations must agree."

Three chests stuffed with clothing: chitons, cloaks, linens, belts, boots, sandals. Toiletries: flasks of oil and perfume, ointments, a strigil, combs, a mirror, a razor. Weapons, candles, incense, magical implements, the lyre in its drawstring bag. A large basket full of papyrus rolls.

*How on earth had he accumulated so much baggage?*

Korax shook his head in bafflement and resumed packing. Porters would arrive soon to carry his belongings down to the carriage. Less than a month remained before the winter solstice, and he was moving to Peristeria's house to complete his preparations.

"Are you nearly ready?"

Kalyssa stepped into his room, wearing a white gown and lapis necklace. She seemed almost anxious for him to go.

"I do wish you were coming with me."

She petted his shoulder. "I know, my love. I will come to Eleusis as often as possible, I promise."

Frowning, Korax returned his attention to the packing. Kalyssa had insisted she must stay in Alexandria. To Korax, it made no sense. With Manolis gone for the winter, Kalyssa attended very few diplomatic functions. Besides, Peristeria's villa was only a carriage-ride away. When pressed on the subject, Kalyssa offered vague excuses about needing to stay in contact with the court. Korax sensed she was hiding something, perhaps many things. He did not like to think about it. That line of thought confronted him with his growing estrangement from her—and from his own inner feelings.

"What is this?" Kalyssa fingered the amulet on his chest.

"A gift," he said, "from Miriam."

He had not worn it since the day he received it. It never seemed to suit his outfit or his mood. He had found it this morning, while going through his things, and placed it over his neck on a whim.

"When did you see Miriam? You never told me."

"Some time ago." Korax fixed the latches on the chest. "At the Paneum. She is getting married, you know."

"Yes. I heard that from Peristeria. Why did she give you the necklace?"

"For protection." Korax shrugged. "Perhaps it was her way of purging her feelings for me."

"That might be." Kalyssa peered suspiciously at the amulet. "Have you considered it might be unwise to wear it? Its influence could be unbalancing, going into your ritual."

"That's ridiculous." Korax slipped the amulet under his chiton. "It's a simple protection." Kalyssa's remark had angered him. Perversely, he added, "I intend to wear it from now on."

Kalyssa looked stricken. "Let us not quarrel, my dear." She stepped close and hugged him tenderly. Her voice was a fervent whisper. "We must hold on to our love for each other and to our purpose. After you've done the ritual and had a chance for the power to settle in you, we will do our workings for Carthage. By next summer it will come to fruition. Then we will be free, to do whatever you wish, together. Everything will be all right then, I know it will."

# Chapter Twenty-Eight

The sun set, a liquid red orb into a silvery sea. Korax waited till the last drop of red had vanished, then began the rite of the Third Tower.

Standing on Peristeria's rooftop, he set a torch to a brazier full of charcoal and dried herbs. Amid the smoke, he held out his arms, the blazing torch in one hand, the falcon staff in the other. As the night came on he sang his invocation to Helios.

The chant complete, he extinguished the torch. He sat down cross-legged and fixed the black cloth over his eyes. He slowed his breathing and brought to mind the inner sun.

In the vigil of the First Tower, he had visualized the sun at the center of his spine, in the Second Tower at his heart. The discipline of the third rite called the radiance higher, into his throat.

But this night steady vision did not come. Anguished doubts distracted his thoughts. There was too much he had failed to see— or willfully ignored. Kalyssa's scheming: what was she hiding and why? Arsinoe the queen, was she plotting against her brother? Why had he not been able to pierce that veil? Perhaps, as a seer, he had a duty to uncover the truth, a duty he had shirked.

The hours of the night dragged by. Korax's stomach, empty from fasting, burned with smoldering fear. For the first time, the rites of Nectanebo seemed beyond his ability. What foolish arrogance had convinced him to tread this path, to ignore the words of Amasis, even the warnings of Hermes?

Daunted, his mind told him to turn back, to flee from this rooftop now. The only thing that stopped him was the dreadful suspicion that to break off the rite in the middle could invite an even greater risk of insanity. Korax rocked back and forth as if comforting a mewling infant. Repeatedly, he pulled the blindfold from his eyes and scanned the eastern sky.

Finally, as if in answer to his woeful prayers, a silvery sheen lit the horizon. He staggered numbly to his feet and made his way downstairs. The next part of the rite had to be performed in the lower chamber, as the sun was rising.

In the center of the room stood an altar covered with a scarlet cloth. Korax lit twelve white candles in holders of gold. On the altar stood a vat filled with white liquid, the milk of a black cow mixed with honey. Beside it lay a gray and dusty thing of resin and bandages—the mummy of a young falcon.

Korax sliced his wrist with a crescent blade and dripped blood into the milk. Uttering a prayer, he submerged the mummy in the vat. He held it down until it was well-soaked, then placed it on a stand of juniper wood in the midst of the candles. He lifted the vat to his lips and drank all that it contained.

In a shaky voice, he prayed to the god.

I summon you God, Helios,
Lord of the Sun,
All-seeing and all-knowing One,
You who are young in the morning
And old in the evening.

I am he you have blessed
With your knowledge,
With your might.
I am your son, O Mightly God,
Fill me with your power.
Abaoth Bakre Bakrabbe!

Daylight shone at the open balcony. Milk dripped from the drenched mummy and stained the scarlet cloth. Korax waited, nauseated and dizzy.

Out of the silence, he heard a distant, rumbling voice. "I cannot come to you, my son, unless you are willing to see."

Agony pierced his soul. "I am willing. I must!"

"Then shut your eyes."

As his eyelids closed a burning hand gripped his forehead. Blinding whiteness burst inside his skull. A jolt of power thrust him off his heels. He landed hard, the back of his head slamming the floor.

Visions streamed into his brain—undeniably, unbearably true. Kalyssa had bewitched him—not from the start, but as soon as she needed to keep him under control. And the queen, yes, she was plotting to murder her brother. Worse still, Kalyssa had a hand in the plot.

Korax rolled onto his side, clutching his cramped belly, groaning in torment both physical and mental. He desperately wished the visions to stop, but he could not look away. He saw King Ptolemy, lying still and wild-eyed, poison shining on his lips. He saw a hundred ships brimming with spears sail into the Great Harbor, a wave of war ravaging the beautiful city.

He twisted on the floor, opened his eyes, but the visions would not vanish. Mindless armies streamed across the earth like crawling ants. Cities were razed, their people put to the sword or burned alive in their houses. The acrid stink of burning timber and flesh choked him. Thunder cracked, and fleets of ships drowned in monstrous storms. An earthquake devastated his beloved Rhodos, the great Colossus tumbling into ruins.

The whole pageant of history rolled through his mind, a hideous parade of misery and death. The Universe no longer appeared a bright continuous series of divine emanations as he once believed, but an unending nightmare of futility and chaos.

"Korax. Korax!"

Amid the scattered visions he glimpsed Kalyssa's frightened face. She shook him by the arms.

"My love, come back to me."

"No!" He thrust her away savagely, a visceral reaction of disgust. Screaming with horror, he stumbled to his feet.

"Korax. What is it?"

He staggered against the altar. The whole thing toppled over. Candleholders clanged on the floor and pottery shattered.

"Stay away from me." Korax warned, as Kalyssa took a step toward him.

"What has happened?" she cried, aghast.

He gazed at her wildly. "Do you want to see? I will show you, Kalyssa."

Before she could react, he seized her forearm.

"You're hurting me."

"Not yet."

Filled with pure hatred, he opened his mind and let the visions pour out. Her eyes widened with panic. She whimpered, squealed, struggled to pull free. But he held her slim forearm tight in his fist. Torturing her somehow soothed his suffering.

Suddenly he let go, loathing himself for hurting her. Kalyssa collapsed on the floor, whining in pain.

Korax observed her for several moments. He had to get away from here, away from her. Otherwise, he might kill them both.

He donned a cloak and straightened it on his shoulders. He picked up the falcon staff and strode from the room. In the hallway, he brushed past two maidservants who had come in response to the terrible commotion.

Kalyssa focused her eyes, her brain reeling. Her whole body ached, but the smarting pain on her arm was the worst.

"There's my child. Back to us at last." Peristeria wiped her forehead with a wet cloth.

Kalyssa lay in a bed. She strained to remember ...

"O Goddess! Korax!"

"Gone these three hours."

"Where?" Kalyssa shifted as if to rise.

Peristeria held her down firmly. "Last seen walking toward the city. Nevermind him. You must lie still."

Kalyssa examined her forearm, shiny with ointment. The skin was bruised where Korax had gripped, blistered where his fingertips had touched.

"He has done you violence," Peristeria murmured. "And not just your arm."

"No, it is my fault. What I did to him ... the *despair*. I must find him."

She tried again to sit up. Vicious pain at the base of her skull forced her back onto the pillow.

"Lie still," Peristeria said. "I don't know what passed between you. But I do know spiritual injury when I see it. Your nerves have been scorched by too much power. You need time and rest to recover."

"Please, priestess. He must be found. He will harm himself, I know it."

"Peace, daughter." Peristeria dabbed the wet cloth on the young woman's forehead. "I will make you a bargain. I'll mix a potion to make you sleep. After you have drunk it, I will go myself and look for Korax."

# Chapter Twenty-Nine

Late in the day, Peristeria's mule-drawn carriage rolled to a stop at the gates of the Paneum. The priestess of Tyre instructed her driver to wait nearby, then ambled through the open gates. She had searched the length of the Canopic Way from Eleusis and had stopped to inquire at the residence of Ambassador Manolis. But she had suspected all along that Korax had most likely gone to the Temple of Pan.

She strode over the lawn with sober determination. When she turned her intuition on Korax, the impressions returned strong and disturbing—spiritual agony, fabulous power out-of-control. The high priestess had long worried about the course that Kalyssa and Korax were pursuing. But young people had to make their own mistakes, especially young people of such strong will. Now the whole shaky edifice had come crashing down on them.

Peristeria crossed the pavilion of Pan and unlocked the secret door. She hastened down the passageway and entered the vast interior. A young initiate stood at the center of the floor, his head tilted upward. Following his gaze, Peristeria spotted a figure seated dangerously on the railing of the highest gallery. Her heart sank.

"Korax?" She didn't really need to ask.

The young magician, one of Krateros' students, gave a quick bow. "Yes, priestess. I fear he has gone mad."

"Where is Krateros?"

"In his study. Working a spell to balance the madman."

Peristeria marched across the empty floor. She met Krateros as he emerged from the gray-lit corridor. Before she could question him they both froze, startled by a hideous scream that sounded near the ceiling and echoed through the enormous hollow space.

As the echo faded, Krateros eyed her gravely. "He's been up there for hours. Mostly, he sits quietly, but every so often he screams—like Prometheus with the eagles chewing out his liver. He vows he will jump if anyone comes near. I've done a working to try to restore his sanity. But his mind is very far away."

"Miriam," Peristeria said.

"Yes. I thought of her too. I sent a messenger."

Miriam and Zakur arrived a short time later. The messenger had told them only that Krateros needed them to come to the Paneum at once, that a member of the Society was in trouble. Miriam had surmised it must be Korax. She hurried ahead of her father and emerged from the passageway first. She spotted Peristeria and Krateros and ran to them.

"Is it Korax?" she demanded. "Where is he?"

For answer, they inclined their heads toward the roof.

"Oh, no," Miriam moaned.

"Daughter, wait!" Zakur called.

Miriam was already running toward the ramp. The three elders looked at one another, then hastened after her.

"Be careful," Krateros warned. "He said he will jump if anyone goes near."

Miriam took the fastest way up, a zigzag path that climbed each ramp then doubled back along the gallery to the foot of the next. By the time she reached the seventh gallery, she was breathless.

Deliberately, she slowed her steps. She edged along the curving wall to the place where Korax sat, his legs tucked beneath him, his face to the void.

"Go back, Miriam." He spoke without turning around. "You should not have come. It's better you do not see this."

Miriam swallowed her fear. "I won't go back until you come with me."

"Why? I am only doing what you taught me," he replied with a morbid calm. "Seeking balance. I am very much out-of-balance right now."

Suddenly he moved, pressing down on his hands, slipping his feet under him. Miriam gasped as he stood up on the rail. He pivoted toward her, his face gaunt and ashen.

"I have so much power now, Miriam. I really believe I could jump off and fly if I willed it." He lifted a foot.

"Don't!" she screamed.

"Ah, but there is a problem." Korax set the foot down again. "The will must be directed from the soul. And my soul is so full of self-loathing, it might possibly deceive my mind and make me fall." He seemed to ponder the idea. "That would be the end of me, of course ... Such a relief that would be."

"Listen," she said firmly. "If you are my friend, you will come down from there now."

He spread his arms wide. "I think I am your friend. But how can I know? I can see so much. Why is it impossible to see the truth of myself?"

"You said you would give me a wedding gift." Miriam's voice trembled. "This is the only gift I desire: your life. I could not bear it if you died."

"Oh, such a paltry gift. You deserve much better."

But he stepped forward and dropped to the gallery floor. Miriam rushed over and embraced him.

"Oh, thank you," she sobbed with relief.

"Dear Miriam," he muttered. "What I have seen—it is beyond bearing. You were wrong about all conditions passing away. Misery and grief and horror, *they* are eternal."

She wept in his arms, and her weeping seemed to open his heart. His face contorted and he wailed, a soul in torment. He crumbled to his knees, clinging to Miriam, whimpering piteously.

The elders came and gently lifted them. Krateros and Zakur supported Korax's arms over their shoulders. They half-carried him, faint and sobbing, down the ramps to the lowest level.

They brought him into a small room with a star-shaped window and laid him down on a couch. Miriam sat beside him. Korax clutched both her hands.

"I will stay till you are well," she promised.

"Daughter," Zakur said. "That could take days."

"I will stay with him, father," she answered resolutely. "He is my friend."

The elder heaved a dispirited sigh. "Very well. Then I will stay also."

Zakur brought a stool from another room and sat with his back to the wall. After a while, Peristeria appeared with a potion in a silver chalice. Korax drank it obediently. His forehead now burned with fever, and his will was exhausted.

Soon his eyelids closed, and he drifted off to sleep, still holding Miriam's hands.

Korax dreamed many things that night.

He walked in darkness, along the shore of a river. He gazed at the tossing waters, shiny with a luminescence like moonlight that seemed to have no source. All of life, he thought, was this restless tossing of waters—trickles, streams, torrents. What mortals thought of as themselves was simply their awareness of the changing surfaces. Which philosopher was it who had said, you cannot stand twice in the same river?

With a spasm of fear, he realized where he was, the shore of the River Styx, where the shades of the dead pass over. *He had been here once before.*

In one of his last memories of Rhodes, he had conjured the god Dionysus to help him win a singing contest. And he had used the god's power to mock and humiliate his enemies, bullies from his school who tormented him. The next morning, those young men had cornered him on the street and taken their revenge, beating him, smashing his head against the cobblestones. He had died, or nearly died, before his mother found him and ...

*Was this dream a memory of that time? Or was he about to die again, to truly cross over?*

He recalled his mother's face under the gray sky, staring down at him. Her voice sounded hollow and deep in his brain. "I will bring him back."

*She had changed the flow of events*, he realized. *She had channeled her own life force to restore him.*

Even as these thoughts appeared, the dream changed.

He found himself on the citadel of Lindos, one of the old cities on Rhodes. He had visited the town once as a child. The acropolis stood on a cliff, five hundred feet over the sea. Temples to Zeus and Poseidon were built there, and a small Temple of Athene on an outcropping at the edge. Korax sat on a low wall behind that temple, his legs dangling over the precipice. He gazed down on the foaming sea, thinking how easily he could slip off and fall. *How tempting to end all the torment.*

"Why do you despair, my son?"

He turned his head and saw his mother, treading down the temple steps. With her dark red hair flowing loose, Anticleia looked young and beautiful, full of magic.

He went to meet her, dropped to a knee. "Oh, mother. I have done such stupid things—foolish, arrogant things. I have seen too much. It is all hopeless."

"You have lost your way."

"Utterly."

"You allowed yourself to be blinded, because you loved so much. That was an error, but not a crime."

Her kind words brought tears to his eyes. "I have wasted the talent I was given."

"Yes. It is time to stop wasting your gifts." She held out her hand. "Come, she is waiting for you."

Bewildered, Korax grasped her hand. They walked together up the temple steps. Passing into the shade of the porch, he glimpsed a figure of ivory and gold shining within the cella—the Goddess Athene.

He woke.

Gray light illuminated the star-shaped window on the wall above. Miriam was asleep, slumped on the floor, her arms and head resting heavily on the couch. One of his hands held her wrist, the other clutched the medallion on his chest—the amulet she had given him.

He had worn it constantly for over a month, even during the ritual. Perhaps it had protected him after all. He turned it in his fingers: Thoth on one side, Maat on the other. The old question ran through his mind.

*Are you willing to serve the gods?*

Miriam lifted her head. "Korax?"

He smiled and brushed the hair from her eyes. "I am all right, Miriam. You have saved me."

She blinked sleepily. "Are you certain?"

"Yes. I know now what I must do."

# Chapter Thirty

In the cool winter morning, Korax marched through the streets of Alexandria. The babble of traffic assaulted his senses, noises and smells gnawing at his nerves. In each passing face he recognized simmering emotions—anger, pain, frustration, grief. The unending sorrows of the world pressed on his heart.

Doggedly, he placed one foot in front of the other. At least now he had a direction, a purpose.

He bathed at the gymnasium, scraping with a strigil, scrubbing himself thoroughly in hot water, then applying fresh oil to his skin. Next, he went to the Royal Bank and emptied his account. Clutching two sacks full of silver, he slunk warily into the marketplace. He purchased a strong satchel to hide his money and a sword with a baldric. He bought other gear for traveling: a spare chiton, boots, a wide-brimmed hat. From the food stalls he picked up bread, dried fruit, a water skin.

By the fourth hour he was making his way down the Street of the Soma toward the south. He passed through the city gates and scouted along the canal docks. He found a barge being loaded with jars of wine and oil, imports headed downriver. He bought passage from the captain and found an empty space on deck to stow his gear.

The barge departed the next morning, under oars. For three days the craft labored along the broad canal. At points, the crewmen were able to raise sail, but mostly the brisk wind blew too close to the bow and they were reduced to rowing. Korax kept to himself, pacing the broad deck or sitting wrapped in his cloak, staring blankly under the brim of his hat. At night he slept under the stars, the heavy satchel for a pillow.

On the fourth day the barge reached the end of the canal. The craft turned downstream onto the Nile, and the weary crewmen hoisted sail. Two days later, they docked at Naukratis.

Beyond the limestone quays rose a walled town with five gates facing the river. Established as a trading post by Dorian mariners centuries ago, Naukratis had lost none of its Greek character. Korax knew the town well, having lived here for three months after his escape from Memphis.

He entered through one of the river gates and climbed the gently rising streets, past the marketplace, guild halls, and houses. He approached the acropolis, a low hill configured with public halls and temples.

Inquiring at the office of the city magistrates, Korax was directed to the home of the current high priest of Athene. He called at the man's residence and made an offering of a hundred drachmas to pay for sacrifices at the next festival. Overwhelmed by the stranger's generosity, the priest readily agreed to allow him to sleep in the temple cella.

Korax returned to the marketplace, bought food and wine, incense and an oil lamp. The day had grown late by the time he approached the house of Athene. The winter sun was settling over the desert to the west, and a rich gold light clung to the roofs and pillared halls. The steps to the temple were littered with votive offerings, black stelae etched with writing, pottery jars of oil and wine.

Korax stopped at the base of the steps and put down his gear. He poured a libation from his wineskin then held up his palms. He prayed to the goddess, using her ancient epithets:

"Glorious Athene, bright-eyed maiden, daughter of the Thunderer, wise in counsel, protector of cities, steadfast in heart, mighty in valor. I, Korax of Rhodes, invoke your blessings. Accept the gifts of a humble wanderer, and honor me with your wise counsel. I vow to stay within your sacred hall until you bless me with guidance."

Gathering his gear, he trudged up the steps and passed through the tall wooden doors. Inside was a pillared cella with a bare stone floor. The only sculpture was the painted statue of the goddess at the front of the hall, twice the height of a man. It was fashioned in imitation of the famous Pallas Athene in Athens, outfitted with helmet and spear. A round shield leaned against her thigh, embossed with the terrible face of the Gorgon, its hair a mass of writing snakes.

Korax dropped his bundles against the rear wall. He sat down facing the statue and began his vigil.

The goddess came to him that night. He had entered a state of trance and never knew if her manifestation was dream or waking vision. He simply lifted his head and she was there, a strong and lovely maiden, shining with an aura of divinity. Her face, serene and proud, was familiar from countless portraits. Her gray eyes gleamed, just as described in Homer's epics.

"Arise, Korax son of Leontes."

Korax struggled to his feet and bowed, trembling. "Blessed goddess, I was directed by my mother to seek your counsel."

"I have been waiting for you." She evinced a solemn sympathy. "First, I must give you painful news. Your mother has passed from this life. She died on the very day you left Rhodes."

Korax brought his fist to his mouth, gnawed the meat of his hand with grief. Yet even amid the shock, he recalled his realization from the dream—that Anticleia had channeled her own life-energy to restore him.

"She died because she brought me back from death."

"It was the choice she made, from her great love for you."

The familiar self-loathing stirred in his soul. "And I have wasted her sacrifice."

"No," Athene said. "By her death, Anticleia opened a new road for you. That road has many twists and turns, but your journey is far from over."

Korax stared at her bleakly. He felt only misery and despair.

The goddess set a hand firmly on his shoulder. Her voice, strong and profound, yet carried a teasing note. "Korax of Rhodes, will you wallow in self-pity like your friend Asclepiades? Or will you rise from your grief like a hero and serve the gods?"

Her touch renewed his fortitude. "I am scarcely a hero," he answered hoarsely. "But I will serve the gods."

Her silvery eyes beamed with satisfaction. "You are courageous and wily. Of such wool, heroes can be woven. Perhaps in time you will surprise yourself."

"Great goddess, what must I do?"

"Go home to Rhodos. Your father still lives, and he needs you. More, your city needs you. When you were struck down, and Anticleia sacrificed her life, it began a chain of events that has brought misfortune to Rhodes. In the old times, priests would have recognized the omens. They would have known that the city was polluted by an undiscovered crime. They would have said the Furies were wreaking vengeance, until atonement was made." The goddess leaned her head with irony. "Unfortunately, these days there are few with the vision to read the signs, and most people wouldn't believe them anyway. But I am the protector of free cities. And free cities will not perish so long as they have citizens of wisdom and valor."

"Your words inspire me," Korax said. "And my heart longs to go home to Rhodos. But what of Alexandria? I fear that city too is threatened—and that I bear a portion of the blame."

"True. Your magic has contributed to the stirring up of trouble," Athene remarked. "I concur: Before you return to Rhodes, duty obliges you to set things right in Ptolemy's city."

"Well ... But how?" Korax imagined the vast, inexorable forces converging on the city. "I am vowed to serve the gods. But I think it will take more than my skills to fix things in Alexandria."

Athene smiled with the confidence only an immortal can possess. "Do not be concerned. I will guide you."

Nebrus the slave-seller stood at the entrance to his establishment and hawked his wares to the townsfolk passing on the dusty street.

"Step inside, my friends. Excellent merchandise within. No charge for looking. You, dear lady. You need a strong young girl to carry water and do your washing at the river .... Oh, esteemed dock master! An important official needs a stout bodyguard in these dangerous times. I have just the man. Wait! His price is extremely low ...."

Disconsolately, Nebrus sank onto a stool under his awning. Winter was normally a busy season, but this year sales had been miserable. Customers seemed to be hoarding their money, perhaps still insecure because of the military uprising. But that ended seven months ago. People ought to have forgotten by now...

Nebrus stood, leaning on his walking stick. A young man was approaching, a wealthy Greek by the look of him. He had the aspect of a buyer, and his satchel looked heavy.

"A thousand greetings, good sir." Nebrus smiled ingratiatingly. "The worthiest slaves on the Delta await your pleasure within. Please, come and browse."

Korax stared blankly. He remembered this place all too well—the smells of iron, unwashed bodies, rancid oil. In the years since Korax was a slave here, Nebrus had only grown more crooked and leathery.

It made no sense that Athene had insisted Korax return to the city of Zau. It took half a month's journey, first down and then up another branch of the river. The goddess said he must recruit a warrior to help him. "You have the cunning of Odysseus, but lack his brawn." True enough. But there were slave markets in Naukratis and Alexandria, not to mention plenty of free mercenaries he might have hired.

"Nacht! Come here!" Nebrus shouted for his clerk. "We have a Greek customer. I need you to translate."

"No, no." Korax held up his hand. "I speak Egyptian."

"Oh, forgive me. Of course, an educated gentleman such as yourself, I should have known."

"I wish to purchase a bodyguard."

Nebrus dropped his jaw with excitement. "Excellent, excellent. I have just the man."

He ushered Korax through the dim entryway and into the courtyard. Nacht the clerk appeared and followed them dutifully, wax tablet in hand.

"This man is a veritable giant," Nebrus continued, "like your Greek hero—what's his name?—Heracles!"

"Sounds promising," Korax admitted. "Is he skilled at arms?"

"Yes, yes. Trained for the army." A frown swept over the slave-seller's face. "I must tell you frankly though, he is one of those wild men from the north."

Korax halted stiffly. "You mean from the mutiny? Oh, I don't like the sound of that."

"But he is reformed, I assure you." Nebrus gestured frantically. "He's been gentle as a kitten since we got him. He's given us no trouble whatsoever, has he Nacht?"

"No, master," Nacht answered quickly.

"His only complaint has been being locked in a cell," Nebrus went on. "He longs for a fair and kind master that he can serve and protect. Oh, and he speaks Greek fluently, and has even begun to learn Egyptian—a clever, intelligent man!"

"I shall examine him," Korax agreed reluctantly. He had no wish to acquire a savage likely to murder him at the first opportunity.

When they reached the cell, the sight of the Celt did nothing to alleviate his doubts. Nebrus had not exaggerated the man's size. Even slouching against the iron grate, the captive stood taller than Korax by head and shoulders. He had a broad chest and long, clean-muscled arms. His skin was the milky white of his race, his hair and wild beard a reddish color. He wore a torc of twisted bronze around his neck, over a filthy gray chiton. He stared through the slats with bright, sorrowful blue eyes.

"How did you acquire him?" Korax asked. He had understood that none of the mutineers survived.

"From a captain of militia," Nebrus confided. "This man escaped from the island where the rebels were trapped. He swam the Nile at its crest—a testament to his astonishing physical prowess! Most who tried the swim drowned. The few who reached the banks were hunted down by patrols. But instead of spearing him, this particular captain decided to turn a profit on the man, so he sold him to me."

"Are you going to buy me, master?" The Celt spoke in koine, from a raspy throat. "I promise to serve you well."

Korax heard guile hidden in the plea. "I think not."

But as he turned away, Athene whispered in his ear. "He is the one I found for you."

Korax winced, thinking: *This man will cut my throat while I sleep.*

"He only wants his freedom," Athene said. "Something *you* can surely understand. Offer him a bargain. You asked for my guidance, son of Leontes. Are you now unwilling to trust me?"

Korax slumped his shoulders and pondered. Suddenly, he showed a forced smile to Nebrus. "May I speak with him in private?"

"Of course." The slave-seller grabbed his clerk by the sleeve, and they both scurried away.

Korax fixed his eyes on the Celt, who stared back warily. The man knew it was in his best interest to humble himself, but had too much pride to bring it off.

"What is your name?" Korax asked him.

"Leukon, sir, son of Balaudos of the Trocmi people."

"The Egyptian tells me you are a soldier. I need an able warrior to protect my life. You are skilled at arms?"

Leukon dropped his hands from the grill and straightened, his chest swelling. "Of course. I am deadly with spear, sword, and dagger."

"Deadly? Have you killed many men?"

"Hundreds—in Macedonia, Greece, and Egypt."

Korax smiled skeptically. "I've heard it said your race is prone to exaggeration."

Leukon replied with a short, barking laugh. "Your race just fails to appreciate our manner of speaking. Well then, to *your* way of speaking, I have killed four men in war that I know of."

Korax considered. "I think you might be suitable. Only I am concerned about your loyalty. You don't seem like a man who would readily accept the life of a slave."

Leukon spread his arms woefully. "Anything would be better than this cell."

"I know that is the truth," Korax said. "I was a slave myself, sold from this very yard. Eventually, my fortunes turned and I won my freedom. I will offer you the same chance. If you will vow to serve me for one year, then I will buy you from this Egyptian buzzard. When the year is over, assuming we both still live, I will make you a free man."

"Tell me your name," Leukon growled eagerly, "so I can swear a binding oath."

"It is Korax of Rhodes."

"Korax?" The Celt reared back in surprise. "Doesn't that word mean 'crow' in your tongue?"

"Crow or blackbird, yes."

"Then this is fate! Crow is sacred to my tribe." He thrust his hand through the grill and clutched Korax's forearm. "Korax of Rhodes, Leukon son of Balaudos swears on his sacred honor to serve you in peace and war for the length of a year and a day!"

# Chapter Thirty-One

After coming to terms with Nebrus, Korax decided the most pressing need was to have his new bodyguard washed and deloused. The tall Celt followed him from the slave-seller's yard and down the thoroughfare. His long legs easily kept up with Korax's impatient stride.

The public baths in Zau were primitive by Greek standards— little more than a series of stone pools in a walled courtyard beside the river. Korax arranged for the Celt to have a thorough scrubbing with natron, followed by a shave and haircut. At the same time, he had the man's chiton laundered. Leukon emerged looking significantly more civilized, though he had refused to allow the barber to remove his mustache. Well enough, Korax thought. The barbaric lip-hair only made his bodyguard look more menacing.

Next, they visited the docks and Korax inquired after boats heading downstream. He wanted a freighter that would take them along the coast to Alexandria, or at least as far as Canopus. He found a weather-beaten coaster scheduled to depart in two days.

Korax rented a room at an inn near the river. It was a squalid, two-story structure of brick and peeling plaster, a square of rooms and stables built around a sandy courtyard. The inn lacked a dining room, so Korax purchased supper at an open-air food shop nearby. They served plain Egyptian fare: lentils cooked with onions, flatbread, and beer. The shop had no tables, so the two men sat on the ground beneath an awning facing the street.

Leukon wolfed down three portions, belched expressively, then offered his appraisal of the meal. "The beer is bitter and delicious, but this food is sorry indeed. I don't mean to insult your hospitality, Blackbird, but in my land we'd only feed slaves and pigs on such porridge."

Korax suppressed the impulse to mention that he himself had just dined on the same fare and that, besides, Leukon *was* a slave. "No insult taken. I'm sure it's better than what you ate at the slave-seller's yard."

"That's true enough. The quality and quantity both are superior." The Celt shrugged philosophically. "Among my people, a chieftain is obliged by honor to feast his retainers on the best meat and drink he can provide. But I know you folk of the south have different customs. To you, it's more important to hoard your money."

Korax laughed derisively at the man's impudence. "We use our money to trade and build. We men of the south have created a civilization of wonders. It's ludicrous to boast of your culture in comparison to ours."

Leukon arched his back, his face a comical portrait of disdain. "Oh, really? Well, I would pit the lore and poetry of my race against that of you Greeks any day of the year. And while it's true we are not great builders, what does that gain you in the end? All your stone temples and fine towns will be dust one day, exactly the same as our wood houses and forts."

Korax stared pensively at the ground. He could not dispute the barbarian's words. In his inner soul, he had already seen them come true.

With twilight coming on, they repaired to the inn. Leukon stretched out on one of the mattresses, grunted happily, and was soon snoring. Korax sought to quiet his emotions through meditation.

He slept fitfully, and woke in the middle of the night, aching with nameless fear. The spiritual agony brought on by the disastrous Third Tower rite had lessened but not disappeared. Korax still carried in his heart a boundless disquiet, which broke into his awareness at odd times of the day and disturbed his dreams at night.

To regain his balance, he had resumed practice of the spiritual exercises he learned in Memphis. Now he rose in the dark and stood in the center of the tiny room. He steadied his breathing and envisioned interior light. Straight and still, he focused the light at the various centers along his spine, then moved it in a current through his body.

On completing the regimen, he opened his eyes to find the Celt awake, watching impassively from his bed.

"You did not tell me you were a wizard," Leukon remarked.

Korax mirrored his steady gaze. "Does it change our agreement?"

"Of course not. I gave my oath. Besides, I guessed it at once. With 'Crow' for a name, what else could you be?"

A twelve-day voyage brought them to Alexandria. The coaster sailed into the Port of Eunostos, on the opposite side of the causeway from the Great Harbor. After disembarking, Korax rented rooms at a large inn near the docks. Travelers from many lands frequented the waterfront, so he hoped he and Leukon would attract no attention. Wisdom urged that he keep his return to the city as inconspicuous as possible.

Still, his talks with Athene and his inner sense made it clear he would not be staying long. And there were a few things he was not willing to leave behind.

So, the day after his arrival, Korax hired a carriage. Accompanied by Leukon, he rode on the Canopic Way through the Gate of the Sun and out to Eleusis. The carriage rolled to a stop in front of Peristeria's villa.

The priestess of Tyre received him in her entry hall. She greeted him warmly, yet with a slightly guarded demeanor. Korax himself was taciturn, reluctant to say anything about his plans. He had left most of his belongings at her house and had come to retrieve them—particularly his books, lyre, and magical tools.

"What shall I tell Kalyssa?" Peristeria asked, as servants loaded his gear into the carriage. "I am sure she will want to see you."

"No doubt I will see her soon," Korax answered, intentionally vague. He thanked the priestess for all her kindnesses and took his leave.

On the way back through the city, Korax ordered the carriage to halt and wait outside the Great Emporium. He bought a serviceable cloak for Leukon and ordered three spare chitons to be made. The tailor informed him with feigned regret that he would have to charge twice the usual price, since the Celt's broad back and shoulders required twice the normal amount of material. Luckily, Leukon still had his soldier's boots, Korax reflected. No telling what a pair of shoes might cost for the feet of Heracles.

Next, they shopped for weapons. Leukon picked out a long, brutal dagger at the first armory they visited. But though they examined swords of many types, he could not find one long enough to suit him. After trying numerous arms dealers and blacksmiths, Korax concluded the quest was hopeless.

But as they passed the stall of a fine imports dealer, the Celt suddenly brightened.

"*There* is a proper blade!"

He pointed to a Celtic long sword, hung as a wall ornament amid silk tapestries and marble statuettes. He dashed to the front of the shop and pulled the sword from its bracket.

"You there! Stop!"

The portly merchant hastened from behind the counter. But the man went rigid as Leukon drew the sword and swung it in the air with violent expertise.

"Try not to be so conspicuous," Korax admonished.

"Crafted by the Tectosages tribe," Leukon answered joyously. "See the horned stag here on the sheath? I shall have it!"

"How much?" Korax asked the merchant.

"Oh, a rare item, sir. Eighty drachmas."

"For one sword?" Korax exclaimed. "Ridiculous."

"Not a mere sword, a barbarian artifact." The merchant sniffed. "Extremely desirable in today's market. Very much in demand—especially since the insurrection." He tried in vain to wrest the bronze and leather sheath from Leukon's massive hand.

"This man is a thief," Leukon said bluntly. "Why don't you bind him with a charm, Blackbird? Or should I break his nose with my fist?"

The merchant stepped back, appalled. "What? You threaten me in front of my own establishment? This is monstrous!"

"Twenty drachmas," Korax said, opening his purse.

"Impossible! I will summon the city watch."

"Thirty."

The merchant held out his palm. "Sixty, and not one obol less."

Korax glowered and counted out coins. "Fifty."

"Done. But only because you threaten me with injury." The merchant closed his fist and pressed the money to his chest. "Take it and begone! And in the future, my shop is closed to you." He waddled back behind the counter, still muttering. "Savages roaming the Emporium, threatening honest dealers ..."

"Well done, Blackbird," Leukon grinned. "You made a shrewd bargain."

"Put that thing in its sheath," Korax said, "and let's get away from here."

With an air of urgency, Ambassador Manolis marched into his wife's herbal room. Kalyssa sat at the long table, crumbling leaves of aromatic rue into an alabaster jar. Her face was haggard and her eyes dull—lingering effects of her illness. Manolis had noted no change in her listless condition since his return last month.

"There is news," he said. "A man resembling Korax was spotted at the Great Emporium yesterday. It's possible he has returned to Alexandria."

"He has," Kalyssa answered. "Peristeria sent me word. She saw him yesterday."

Manolis placed hands on his hips. "Really? And were you planning to inform me at any time?"

"Of course I was. I only learned of it this morning."

Manolis fingered his beard. "He has not tried to contact you, so we must assume his affections are still estranged. And from what you've told me of the events at midwinter, we must suppose that he knows something of Arsinoe's plot—or, at the very least, that he is unstable and might make accusations."

Kalyssa knew what was coming, but did not wish to face it. "What do you propose, husband?"

"Above all, the queen must not learn of this little indiscretion. She would lose all confidence in us at once. No, our own agents and those of Cyrenaica must be employed. They must find Korax and silence him—as unobtrusively as possible."

A thought occurred to Manolis. "Can you use your arts to locate him?"

Kalyssa eyed him hollowly. "I don't know ..."

"Are you unable or unwilling?"

She stood, evincing a torpid anger—the strongest emotion she seemed able to muster. "You understand nothing of my arts, Manolis."

"Then enlighten me, dear wife. Are you too feeble to work sorcery against Korax now? Or are you still in love with him?"

She dropped her gaze, the apathy returning. She almost wished ... but it was far too late for that. She had chosen Carthage over her love, and the choice was irrevocable. No point in regretting it now.

"I told you, that is over. But Korax is very powerful, and he will no longer trust me. If he chooses to conceal himself, I don't know if my arts can find him."

Manolis glared. "I suggest you try, Kalyssa. We are at war, remember. Carthage is assembling her ships, and Cyrenaica massing her armies. The next few months will be very dangerous for us. We cannot afford the luxury of weakness."

# Chapter Thirty-Two

Queen Arsinoe slept in her gilded bed, the posts carved with winged figures of Eros, the headboard painted with a luxuriant nude Aphrodite. As she reposed, a stray breeze from the portico shifted the bed curtains. A footstep brushed over the carpet. The queen opened her eyes, instantly alert and terrified. Gasping, she sat up and glared at the intruder.

She did not shout for the guards. The fact that the cloaked prowler had penetrated to her bedchamber told her instantly the sentries had been eliminated or, more likely, had allowed the man to pass.

"Did my brother send you to murder me? Or was it someone else?"

The hooded man stepped closer, gliding like a shade. "I am not here to harm you, only warn you."

Recognizing him, the queen regained some of her nerve. "Soothsayer ... Korax—Isn't that your name? I underestimated you. I took you for the glib and harmless charlatan you portrayed, not an assassin."

"I know about your plan," Korax said.

Cautiously, Arsinoe slid from the bed, gained her feet. She equaled him in height. "A ruler has many plans," she answered airily.

"I mean the one that involves murdering your brother. And ten thousand spears from Cyrene arriving on ships from Carthage."

A brief grimace played on her lips. "I fear my friend Kalyssa has been talking over her pillow."

"How I know does not matter. I am giving you the chance to annul the plot. Notify the ambassadors. Have their cities cancel the orders."

She turned and paced slowly away. "And if I don't, you will do what? Inform my brother? Why should Ptolemy believe some soothsayer over his own sister?"

"He suspects you already," Korax said. "It will not be hard to convince him."

The queen paused, placed fingers to her lips. Perhaps she heard a note of forced confidence in the man's voice. Still, his statement was quite possibly true. She could not afford the risk.

She smiled and walked toward him, a graceful roll in her hips. "You didn't risk your life to come here out of loyalty to my brother. What do you really want? Gold? A place at court? I can give you all that and more."

"Your majesty does not understand me."

"No? Explain yourself then. Why would you choose sides against your own Kalyssa? There can only be one reason. I know how love can tarnish over time." She traced a finger over his chest. "But there are many beautiful women in Alexandria. For a man of your abilities and daring, the opportunities would be endless— especially with my patronage. You might have any woman at all ..."

Korax gripped her wrist firmly and pushed it away. "Please. Call off your plot."

"How dare you lay hands on me?" the queen flared. But when he did not flinch, she composed herself, spoke quietly. "Perhaps it is you who do not understand me, my friend. I have not survived this long by shrinking from bold deeds when boldness was required." She paced idly as she talked, moving surreptitiously toward the door. "If I fail to depose my brother, then sooner or later he will depose me. He will have me assassinated or worse, divorced and sent into exile. I could never accept such a fate."

Suddenly she darted into the vestibule and opened the door by its heavy bronze ring. Two sentries stood outside.

"An assassin within," she cried. "Hurry! Strike him down. Kill him."

The spearmen rushed past her into the chamber. Arsinoe followed close behind.

*But the intruder had disappeared.*

She sat up in bed, rigid, gasping. The room stood silent and empty.

*A dream ... only a dream.* She hugged a pillow to her stomach, aching with fright. It felt more real than any dream.

Between the Museum grounds and the palace complex a vast garden spread over seven tiers. An artificial stream descended through the garden, forming pools and waterfalls. Late in the night, Korax waited beside the stream. He had a second warning to deliver.

A dim slice of moon rose in the east. Along with the perpetually-burning lamps of the palace grounds, it lent the scene a vivid, unreal light. Wrapped in a hooded cloak, Korax leaned on his falcon staff, dazed and tense. The power that raged in his blood was so strong, so difficult to control.

Still, the spell to send himself to Arsinoe in a dream had worked flawlessly. Perhaps he should have used that same formula again. But that would not have satisfied his heart. He needed to meet Kalyssa in the world of touch and sense.

Suddenly, he heard a footfall. He watched her approach, past cypress trees and a massive bronze of a wounded centaur. She wore a white mantle, the hood pulled over her hair. She stopped on the other side of the stream. For some time, they faced each other across the rushing water—two powers, aligned in opposition.

"Your call was very plain." Kalyssa broke the quiet at last. "I wondered if you would meet with me."

"I had to, one last time."

"To know that it is really over," she agreed.

Korax felt a twinge at how frail she sounded. "I regret that I injured you. I despise myself for it."

"We hurt each other. It cannot be undone. The question is, what happens next?"

"I have come to warn you. I tried to convince the queen to call off her plot. But in her heart she sees no other option. So, I must expose her plans to Drakas and the king. You and Manolis will likely be arrested and questioned. As I foresee it, you will be exiled; your status as diplomats will spare you any harm. Still, I could be wrong. I will give you time to leave Alexandria, if that is what you choose."

"Why are you doing this?" Her voice cracked. "Is it only to punish me, because I hurt you?"

"Of course not."

"Then why? Arsinoe has as much right to the throne as Ptolemy. You must see that she is the stronger and more able ruler. And she has promised to help Carthage."

"My duty is to Rhodes not Carthage," Korax answered without pity. "Ptolemy is ally to Rhodes, and in his reign our freedom has flourished. Besides, I have been a guest and seer in his banquet hall. For that, I owe him the truth, on my honor."

Across the stream, Kalyssa flinched at the bitterness in his voice. Korax continued, unrelenting.

"Here is a third reason and the most compelling: you drew the power of Helios from me and used it to change the stream of events. I see now how that upset the balance of Maat. That balance is sacred. Ptolemy is meant to rule, not Arsinoe. I must forestall the queen's plot to restore the balance—that is what my heart and the Goddess both tell me."

A deep breath brought Kalyssa back her composure. "You have strong reasons then, Korax. But so do I. As a soldier of Carthage, I can regret nothing that I have done. And I will do whatever I must to stop you."

Her flinty look made him shiver inwardly. Her appearance of frailty had dropped away like a heavy cloak. He did not want a contest of magic, not with her. She knew his soul so well. In her, even a little strength might be enough to destroy him.

"I beg you, Kalyssa, leave Alexandria."

Kalyssa watched him mutely, unreadable emotion smoldering in her dark eyes. Without warning, she turned and walked back the way she had come.

# Chapter Thirty-Three

With his long, deft fingers Korax stacked silver coins on the tabletop. "Twelve drachmas. The other half to be paid when we arrive in Rhodes."

The ship's captain picked up one of the coins and tested it with his front teeth. They stood over a gnarled table bolted to the floor of the cramped deckhouse. The ship rocked gently under their feet, and a clay lamp emitted flickering light.

"Very well, sir." The captain scooped up the rest of the coins. "And when will you be coming onboard?"

Korax gestured at Leukon, who stood with shoulders hunched under the low ceiling. "My man will come aboard tomorrow with our gear. I will arrive late tomorrow night, or early the next morning."

The captain grunted. "Remember, we leave at dawn, day after tomorrow. If you're not onboard, we must sail without you."

"I understand," Korax answered. "I will be here. If I am not, then you will take my man to Rhodes with my belongings. On arrival, he will pay you the balance of the fee."

Leukon scowled with surprise at this disclosure. But he made no comment until after he and Korax had left the ship.

They marched swiftly along the quay of the Great Harbor, all but deserted at this late hour. Ship's lanterns and streetlamps glimmered in the misty darkness.

"And what would I be doing going to Rhodes without you?" the Celt demanded.

"I meant to explain that tomorrow," Korax said. "In the event that I do not return to the ship, I'm counting on you to bring my belongings to my family. There will also be some letters, including one that sets you free once you have completed this errand.

There'll be some money for you too, enough to buy passage wherever you wish."

"Very generous," Leukon remarked. "So you are going on another raid tomorrow night, and not taking me along?"

"In a manner of speaking, yes. It is the same as the other night: I must move about unnoticed. With you, that would be impossible."

"Fair enough." The Celt sighed with resignation. But after a few more steps, he grumbled: "Still, I am beginning to wonder why you need a warrior in your service. So far, it seems a porter would have served you better."

"Perhaps you are right," Korax responded dryly. "At least, it would cost much less to feed him."

"Hah!" Leukon laughed harshly. But he made no other rejoinder.

They crossed the open square where the causeway to Pharos Island met the Street of the Soma. Beyond the square, they descended into narrow streets and twisting lanes. Here, on lower ground, the harbor mist settled into veils of fog that floated over the damp, grimy pavement.

As they approached their inn, Korax noticed a carriage with a team of mules. It waited in the darkness, midway between two streetlamps. Someone approached from that direction, a bulky man wrapped in a cloak.

"Pardon, sirs. Is one of you Korax of Rhodes?"

Leukon's hand settled on his hilt, but Korax gestured to stay him.

"Who inquires?"

"Just a poor messenger, sir, sent by Zakur the Jew—Or, actually, his daughter Miriam sent me, with her father's consent of course."

"I am Korax. What message?"

"Oh, the lady herself will deliver it, sir. She awaits you in the carriage."

Korax hesitated. It seemed strange that Miriam would come in a carriage in the middle of the night.

"Miriam says it's most urgent she speak with you, sir. 'Pressing' is the word she used."

It must be pressing indeed for Miriam to come so late, Korax thought. "Wait here," he ordered Leukon.

He hurried toward the carriage, the cloaked messenger a step behind. He wondered anxiously if Miriam was in trouble, or if she meant to warn him of some danger. As he neared the mules, he heard a shout that seemed far away.

"Turn, Blackbird. He has a knife!"

Korax whirled and glimpsed a sparkle of steel in the messenger's hand. Instinctively, he flung himself backward. The point flashed past his torso, stabbing empty air.

Korax staggered two steps, regained his footing. His attacker crouched, thrown off-balance. Leukon howled as he rushed at the man, his long sword lifted high. Armed men were spilling out of the carriage. Korax threw off his cloak and drew his sword.

The first assassin started to flee as the Celt reached him. The man partly turned before the long sword swooped down with the force of an axe and split his skull to the ear. Leukon roared and wrenched the blade free. The assassin crumbled dead onto the street.

Three swordsmen stalked forward to confront the Celt, while a fourth man charged at Korax. Korax gave ground, dazed by the onslaught, parrying desperately. The killer wielded a curved sword with a fine point, equally deadly at cutting and thrusting. It swooped in the air, then plunged past Korax's guard. By reflex, Korax blocked with his free arm. The edge raked his flesh, drawing a spray of blood.

Leukon drew his dagger and circled, waving both blades at his three foes, taunting them and boasting. The assassins moved to surround him, needing only to keep him occupied while the fourth man finished Korax. But Leukon charged into their midst, wheeling and dodging, attacking with such ferocity and speed that the three men could only duck and parry.

Korax meantime had regained his wits. Setting his back to a wall, he jabbed and hacked violently, keeping the assassin at bay. The killer was a professional, but he had not expected much fight. Hearing the Celt's rampage behind him, he felt pressured to finish quickly.

Poking the blade at Korax's face, the man bent to pull a dagger from his boot. Korax seized the chance. He smashed the curved blade aside and lunged, piercing the killer's shoulder. The man groaned and slipped to a knee, dropping his sword. Korax stepped in for leverage and stabbed upward, deep into the belly. The man gasped and sank onto the sword, wild-eyed. Korax wrenched his blade free, and the man fell over dead.

One of Leukon's three opponents was down in a puddle of blood. Seeing Korax approach, the two remaining assassins bolted. They abandoned the carriage and fled on foot.

"Come back, cowards!" Leukon shouted. "I'm not finished with you yet."

He moved to chase them, but Korax gripped his arm. "No. We must get inside. If the watch comes, we'll be arrested."

The Celt frowned in disappointment. "Can't we at least despoil the dead?"

"No! Come on."

"Wait, you are cut," Leukon noticed. "Let me see." He twisted Korax's forearm and prodded the wound. "Not bad. A tight bandage will fix this."

Reluctantly, the Celt followed Korax toward the inn. "That was exhilarating, wasn't it? I won't say again that you might not need a warrior. But you should never have told me to wait behind. Lucky for you, I didn't obey."

"Yes." Korax reviewed the moments leading up to the ambush. He had acted with an odd lack of caution. Somehow, hearing Miriam's name made him drop his guard.

Suddenly, he knew. Kalyssa had tricked him with a charm. She would have known that mention of Miriam would tap feelings of warmth and trust in him. Rousing those feelings had been enough to make him vulnerable.

Inside the inn, they crossed the common room and went into the kitchen. Leukon washed Korax's cut with wine and applied a smear of honey to prevent infection. The Celt proved as skillful at dressing wounds as he was at inflicting them.

"You fought astonishingly well," Korax congratulated him. "I will never again complain that it costs too much to feed you."

"Ha! I should hope not," Leukon answered, pleased. "Those men were no amateurs. They fought with skill. Are you sure you won't bring me on your raid tomorrow?"

The shock and exhilaration of the attack was draining away, leaving Korax numbed and appalled. He had fought for his life against assassins. He had killed a man.

"At this moment, I am sure of nothing."

They retired upstairs to their rooms. Korax bolted his door and lit several candles. From one of his chests he removed a statuette he had bought, a figure of Athene made of shiny electrum. He set this on top of the chest between two candles. He fired a lump of incense, then sat down cross-legged.

He had intended to do a working tonight, to help assure his success. Now new doubts nipped at his confidence. He felt the need of counsel. He shut his eyes and entered trance. After a time, the goddess came to him.

"You fought with valor tonight, man of Rhodes. Well done."

"I have survived tonight, thanks to you and the warrior you found for me," Korax said. "Now, it is tomorrow that concerns me."

"You feel the vulnerability of a wounded man. That is natural. But I am with you still."

Korax mused. "I believe I can get myself in front of the king. But, although I boasted otherwise to Arsinoe, I'm not so confident I can convince him. I can only say what I've seen in visions. I have no proof of the queen's treachery."

The bright-eyed goddess smiled. "You forget, you have the all-piercing sight of Helios at your command. Use that to find the proof you need."

# Chapter Thirty-Four

Perfumed oil burned in delicate lamps, illuminating an elegant writing table. A manicured hand wrote with a silver filigreed pen on a sheet of fine papyrus. It was said that the great Callimachus wrote his best verse late at night.

"A word, if you please, master poet."

Callimachus shot up from his stool and whirled in fright. "Who are you? How did you get in here?"

Korax lifted his shoulders under the gray cloak. "Let's just say I have mastered the art of coming and going."

"How dare you disturb my solitude? What do you want?"

"Your assistance for an hour or two, in service to the king."

The poet's gray eyebrows merged in a frown. "What do you mean? Speak plainly."

"My apologies." Korax chuckled ironically. "I would hate to annoy you with obscure and impenetrable language. To be blunt then: for some years you have secretly conveyed letters between the government of Cyrenaica and the queen."

Callimachus blanched. "You speak absurdity. Get out, or I will call for sentries to oust you."

"I do not think you will do that."

Korax raised the falcon staff and whispered a charm. Callimachus stared, distracted by the hovering image. Korax peered into the poet's eyes. He had perceived that an incriminating letter could be found in this chamber, but where? He hoped to read Callimachus' mind to discover the hiding place.

Callimachus sensed the mental intrusion. His eyes grew wild as he strained to conceal his inner thoughts. The two men stood, tense, struggling in silence. Callimachus displayed a stubborn will. Korax probed harder, spurred by desperation.

Suddenly Callimachus sat down, whining, clutching his skull. With his inner eye, Korax glimpsed this same writing table ... and a switch.

"Get out. I'll call the guard," Callimachus grunted feebly.

Korax sidled past him, keeping the falcon staff leveled at the man's face. With his free hand, Korax searched the underside of the table.

"Ah, yes." He flipped a bronze lever and a slim panel at the back of the table sprang open. Before Callimachus could react, Korax's hand darted into the compartment and snatched out a rolled papyrus.

"Why, here is a letter in a secret hiding place. And look, it bears the royal seal of Cyrenaica."

Callimachus leaped up, his slim body rigid. "I advise you to put that back and forget that you know of it. It concerns secret matters at the highest levels of government."

"Of that I have no doubt. Matters so secret that the king himself knows nothing of them. I am sure his majesty will find this letter extremely enlightening."

The poet made a move to snatch the papyrus. Korax's staff pressed firmly into the man's chest, holding him at bay.

Defeated, Callimachus sank onto his stool. "I know nothing of the contents, I've never opened any of the letters."

Korax nodded. "Yes, I believe you. That is the one thing that will probably save you from the executioner."

The poet cringed. "What? But I am just a courier. I take no part in politics. I have no interest ..."

"I understand. Your only interest is in the favors you have gained from the queen in exchange for your services. But you can no longer remain aloof. Now you must choose sides."

"What do you mean?"

"Before morning, this letter will be in Ptolemy's hands. I can give it to him and say where I found it. Or you can come with me and explain your part in the plot."

Callimachus looked aghast. "I can't. He will blame me."

"He will blame you either way. I am giving you the chance to mitigate the blame by telling all you know. You are the master of subtle language. I am sure you can relate the story in a way that best suggests your innocence."

Korax tilted his head toward the door. "I am leaving now. Come with me or not as you wish."

A flurry of blatant emotions passed over the poet's countenance. He half-rose from the seat, collapsed again. Korax was nearly out the door when he cried out.

"Wait! I am coming with you."

Side-by-side with Callimachus, Korax ascended through the garden of the seven tiers. Neither man spoke, so the only noise was the murmur of the artificial stream and the crunch of their footsteps on the pebbles. Ahead, multitudes of lamps and cressets illuminated the palace. Grand colonnades and roofs climbed in a splendid array to the heights of the Lochias.

Sentries confronted them at the high bronze gates. The spearmen recognized Callimachus as a member of the inner court. Still, with the hour so late, they halted the two men and questioned them.

"We have urgent news for King Ptolemy," Korax said. "Go and rouse Marshal Drakas from his bed. Tell him that Callimachus the poet and Astrametheus the soothsayer have uncovered a plot to murder the king."

One of the sentries ran to deliver the report. Two others conducted Korax and Callimachus to a guardhouse just inside the wall. A short time later a captain of the royal guard appeared to interrogate them. It took a half-hour to convince the man to summon Drakas, another half-hour for Drakas to arrive.

Straight from his bed, the old marshal appeared in a rumpled robe and sandals. He scrutinized the oddly-matched companions through his single eye.

"What is this about?"

Callimachus shrank from the marshal's inspection. Korax stood up and answered.

"You remember months ago, when the king summoned me at a late hour? He wanted to know if a certain person might be plotting against his throne. We have brought you evidence that it is so." He produced the letter from inside his cloak. "Notice the seal."

Drakas grabbed and examined the papyrus. "Magas of Cyrenaica." He broke the seal and unrolled the document. He read for several moments, his head swiveling back and forth.

"Where did you get this?"

Korax glanced at Callimachus. "We will tell that to the king. I think he will want to be informed at once, don't you?"

Drakas pivoted. "Come."

The marshal paused outside the guardhouse. He sent a runner ahead with orders to wake the king. He dispatched another man to the barracks to turn out a hundred of the royal guard.

Korax and Callimachus then followed Drakas through the halls and courtyards of the palace. The marshal walked with vigor, no trace of any limp.

A sleepy Ptolemy received them in the banquet hall of his apartments. A small coterie of attendants surrounded his gold-covered couch. A lovely slave-girl massaged the king's neck. Extra guardsmen in armor had already filed in to stand at the edges of the hall.

"Drakas, what news my friend?" The king blinked, spotting the other two men. "Callimachus, Astrametheus ... strange company indeed."

"It concerns the queen," Drakas said. "Evidence of a conspiracy."

Ptolemy stood, no longer sleepy. "Speak. Tell me everything."

Drakas waved a hand at Korax and Callimachus.

"Majesty," Korax said. "You asked once if the queen might be plotting against you. At that time, my vision was obscured. But in recent days, the veils have lifted. I have seen that Arsinoe plans to murder you at midsummer, during the Synod. To support her claim to the throne, an army from Cyrenaica will land in Alexandria, ferried by ships from Carthage. Some portion of the plot is intimated in the letter I gave the marshal."

Drakas handed the document to the king. "It is addressed to the queen and speaks of troop landings and supplies. It also mentions a Carthaginian flotilla. It certainly supports the soothsayer's story."

Ptolemy scanned the document hastily. "Where did you get it?"

Korax backed a step, referring the question to Callimachus with a movement of his head.

"I-I had it, majesty," the poet stammered.

Ptolemy stared, then leaned back in amazement. "What? Callimachus, my own friend, *you* are part of this treachery?"

"No!" The poet threw himself on the steps of the dais in supplication. "I only conveyed letters for the queen. I had no idea she was plotting against you. It never occurred to me that such a thing was even possible. I wrote the hymns of your joint deification, songs in celebration of your love match. The very notion of disharmony between you and Arsinoe was beyond my ken."

"Come, Callimachus," Drakas sneered. "You carry secret letters from an enemy king, but claim you know nothing of their meaning? You cannot be so naïve."

"Yes, I can. I am," the poet insisted. "I had no wish to dabble in politics. The queen forced me. She threatened me with the loss of her favor unless I carried an occasional letter for her. But I never read them, never suspected what they might contain." He crawled over the dais and clasped Ptolemy's shins. "My lord, I was raised as one of your companions. I would never betray you, never! You must believe me."

"Get off me," Ptolemy commanded with scorn. "We will decide about you later."

The king turned to Drakas: "Have the queen brought here at once, under guard. We will see what protestations she can offer. And arrest Prodotus and Manolis. We will bring them all before us and see how they explain themselves. Now, Astrametheus, you must tell us everything you—Where is Astrametheus!?"

Heads swung in all directions. Drakas sent guards running to the veranda. Other men searched the corridors and outer chambers.

But the man called Astrametheus was nowhere to be found.

Miriam opened her eyes in the dark. The gray cat meowed on the coverlet beside her, its round eyes reflecting dim light from the window casement.

"Oh," the girl exclaimed.

She climbed out of bed. Feeling in the dark, she found slippers and pulled a woolen robe over her nightdress. She lifted the latch noiselessly and swung the door open.

A few stars shone amid low clouds. Outside the walls of her father's house, streetlamps added to the faint light. Miriam hurried along the peristyle and down the steps to the courtyard. Her father's watchdog stood before the closed gate, wagging his tail, not barking.

Miriam did not bother with the peephole. She already knew who waited outside. She slid the heavy bolt. The door creaked faintly on its hinges.

"What are you doing here?" she whispered. "Are you in trouble?"

Korax slipped through the opening. "Not any longer." He bent to pet the dog, which quietly licked his hand. "I apologize for calling so late."

Miriam spied the bandage on his forearm. "You are hurt!"

"Just a cut. It is healing already."

Miriam touched the bandage gently. "Honey mixed with ground acacia leaf. And change the dressing every day."

Korax smiled fondly. "I will take care of it, I promise. I'm sorry if I frightened you. I had to see you, to say goodbye. My ship leaves at dawn."

Miriam leaned back, a twinge crossing her features. "But you've only just come back. Where are you going?"

"Home to Rhodes. My family needs me."

"I see."

"I'm afraid I will miss your wedding. But I brought you a gift, as I promised."

From inside his cloak he took an amulet of carved rosewood. Its hinged compartment contained a tiny roll of papyrus with a handwritten spell.

"It is for your marriage, a charm for felicity. I searched through the library looking for the best spell, but finally decided I must compose my own. I wrote it from my heart."

Miriam held the amulet to her breast. "Thank you for your blessing, my dear friend."

"It is I who must thank you. Your spirit brought me back when I was lost. I will never forget it."

Miriam clutched his fingers. "I will miss you, Korax. I wish ... Well, perhaps we will meet again."

"I hope we will." Korax lifted her hand to his lips.

He squeezed her fingers a moment longer, then reluctantly let go. He turned and slipped through the opening. After a few steps, he heard the gate creaking shut.

He hastened through the streets of the Jewish Quarter. Reaching the Canopic Way, he broke into a trot. He ran through dim islands of light cast by the streetlamps, past the theater, the Museum, the great Library. Then he turned, traversing the dark lanes and deserted stoas of the Emporium. Light was just rising in the east when he reached the docks.

# Chapter Thirty-Five

Arsinoe paced along the terrace, her white himation and loose red hair lifted by a stiff sea breeze. Pairs of sentries, posted at either end of the tiled veranda, watched her warily.

For over a month she had been a prisoner in her own apartments, confined to a few rooms and this one terrace. By Ptolemy's order, all her faithful retinue had been dismissed, replaced by a handful of suspicious servants. Royal guards followed her everywhere, even to her bath. Always they watched with furtive anxiety, as if she might turn into a dragon and devour them.

If only she were able.

The queen paused at the rail to gaze out over the Great Harbor. Ships with billowing sails glided through the blue water, coming and going in the port.

In just two months, according to her plan, one hundred ships from Carthage would have swooped into the harbor like gulls, harbingers of her great destiny.

Now that day would never come.

Arsinoe faced the sea unblinking, the salt wind stinging her eyes. Her memories flowed back to the night it had all come undone.

Called from her bed by royal guards, she had suspected at once that her plot had been discovered. Her dread was confirmed when she entered the king's banquet hall and saw Drakas, Callimachus, and a company of spearmen. Confronted with the letter, she had protested her innocence, calling it a trick, a plot to impugn her. But when Prodotus and Manolis skulked into the hall, she knew their nerve would never hold. Interrogated in separate chambers, under the threat of torture, they had soon confessed. Of course the cowards blamed everything on her, claiming she forced their connivance with threats of war against their cities.

Faced with their betrayal, the queen had fallen to her knees. Tearfully, she claimed she had been driven mad by fear her brother no longer loved her. She begged for his forgiveness, swore that she loved him desperately. Ptolemy had met that gambit with an icy stare and sent her back to her apartments under guard.

Since that night her mind had worked ceaselessly, hunting any chance to escape from the trap. She had tried every lure and entreaty imaginable to get her brother to come and see her. But all her letters had gone unanswered, her messengers sent back unheard. Nor had he allowed any friends or even their children to see her. Arsinoe missed the children most of all. She supposed her brother feared she would attempt to poison them against him. Perhaps he had good reason.

She stared at the long rampart that ran along the Lochias. How pleasant it would be to walk to the bastion on such a windy day. Of course, Ptolemy had refused permission. Perhaps he feared she would throw herself off the parapet onto the rocks.

If so, he still did not know her at all.

The sentries snapped to attention. Arsinoe swung around and saw Marshal Drakas walking toward her. She looked into his ruined face and saw her death.

She responded with an inner rage and refused to flinch. She thrust back her shoulders and lifted her chin.

"What have you come to say to me, Drakas?"

"If you would, majesty, please come inside."

She followed him into her audience hall, an opulent chamber furnished with silk hangings and fine rugs. She halted just inside.

All the servants and guards had been sent away. Other than Drakas, the only person in sight was an old woman in a black robe, a black veil covering her face. A priestess of Hecate, she was pouring a bone-colored powder into a shallow cup of wine.

Fearing her legs would give out, Arsinoe went to the nearest chair and sat down on the edge. Holding her spine erect, she eyed Drakas in silence.

The old marshal set his feet wide apart and placed his hands behind his back. He waited till the priestess finished stirring the poison, then ordered her out with a movement of his head. He took the gold cup and set it down near the queen.

"Your majesty, I must inform you that the king has judged you guilty of treason. The royal retainers have concurred in this judgment and sentenced you to death. I have been appointed to carry out the sentence."

Arsinoe stared dully at the goblet. "What is it?"

"Aconite."

Painless, at least, and quicker than hemlock. The queen knew her poisons.

"And if I refuse to drink it?"

"It would be better if you do not refuse."

Arsinoe's thoughts raced in desperation. Her life could not end like this, on a lovely spring morning with a strong wind blowing from the sea. There had to be a way out.

"Does my little brother not grieve to condemn me?"

"He does. I have never seen him so lost and bereft. He begs me to tell you that he wishes this had not happened, that he would never have turned on you if you had not betrayed him."

Arsinoe grimaced. If that were really true, how cruel of Fate ... No, she refused to believe it. She could never have trusted it.

She answered with scorn. "But he will not come himself to say this to me? Even now, he lacks the courage to face me?"

The marshal bowed his head. "He lacks the courage."

She sensed a faint hope. "Drakas, it is not too late to change your allegiance. You loved my father, I know you did. You must see that I am stronger and more cunning than my brother, more fit to rule. I have more of my father's spirit in me than he does."

The old warrior clenched his mouth. "All that is true. But it makes no difference."

"Why? Because I am a woman?"

"Because the old king bequeathed the throne to your brother. That was his will. I am nothing but the instrument of his will."

She glared at him for several seconds. Then her eyelids fell, and her shoulders dropped.

"There are letters, in the gold box on my dressing table, one to each of my children and one to my brother. I would count it a kindness ..."

"I will deliver them myself," Drakas promised.

"In the letter to the king, I request that he finish my temple, that my cult be maintained as long as the House of Ptolemy endures." A tone of defiance entered her voice. "It is the least he can do for me, after all I've done for his kingdom."

Drakas grunted to clear his throat. "The king has every intention of completing your temple and servicing your cult. I will use what influence I have to make sure he does not waver from that resolve. If nothing else, I can promise you this: So long as I live, I myself will burn offerings on your altar."

The queen gazed with surprise and a bleak appreciation. "I thank you for that, good Drakas. If only I had had a strong and loyal man like you for a husband. Together we could have won an empire greater even than Alexander's."

She picked up the cup, her hand trembling only a little. "Now it is time for me to truly become a goddess. I want you to watch and report to my brother. I want you to tell him how bravely Arsinoe died."

The queen brought the poison to her lips and gulped it down. She set the cup back carefully on the table. Folding hands in her lap, she gazed straight ahead and waited.

Under a cloudy sky, a lone, small figure trudged up the monumental steps of the Museum. With tangled hair and wine-stained chiton, Asclepiades moved like a man recently wakened from a drunken sleep—which, in fact, he was.

"Well, here's a famous poet who looks like he slept in the gutter."

Asclepiades squinted at the man descending toward him, a brown-haired young scholar, handsomely draped. "Herodas, good morning."

"Good afternoon, you mean," Herodas retorted. "Aren't you late for your seminar?"

"Oh, I am always late for that one. The students expect it. They'd be very upset if I showed up on time."

Herodas leaned close and spoke confidingly. "Have you heard the news? The queen is dead."

"No!" Asclepiades' look of shock twisted into a desolate grimace. He sat down heavily on the steps, a man overcome by the sorrows of the world.

"A sudden seizure, they say," Herodas muttered.

Asclepiades snorted. "Oh, I'm sure. A seizure brought on by Drakas' knife under her breastbone."

The younger man glanced around to make sure no one was close enough to overhear. "You think the king had her killed then?"

"Naturally. He could not let her live."

"So you believe the talk about her plotting to depose him?"

Asclepiades sighed morosely. "My dear Herodas, they reigned together nine years without a single conspiracy between them. It was long overdue."

Herodas shook his head. "I still say it's all speculation. They ruled together as equals and everything was glorious. Why should they disrupt the situation?"

"My naïve friend, your rustic background on Cos simply did not prepare you for the world. They plotted against each other because that is the nature of monarchs. They could hardly do otherwise. If you doubt the truth of it, how do you explain the sudden exile of the ambassadors from Cyrenaica and Carthage? Not to mention the disappearance of Astrametheus."

"Oh yes, the shadowy soothsayer. Wasn't he a friend of yours at one time?"

"Yes, the poor young fool. Up to his neck in the conspiracy, I'm certain. He was in love with Kalyssa, the wife of Manolis. And he vanished at the very time the plot came unhinged. Tortured to death by Drakas, I have no doubt."

"Not so loud." Herodas peered about furtively. "So then, do you also believe the claims that Callimachus played a role?"

"Him? Hard to say. At first glance it would seem out-of-character, but then Callimachus always was a deceptive reptile. If he was implicated, he somehow escaped the calamity unscathed."

"Well, perhaps not unscathed. He still has his post, but he has lost the king's favor."

"Bah! Wishful thinking on the part of his rivals."

"Oh, no. You have not heard the other news. The king appointed Apollonius to the faculty, over all Callimachus' objections. And the proclamation names Apollonius the next chief librarian, after Zenodotus retires."

"Really?" Asclepiades gaped in amazement. The post of chief librarian was the most prestigious of all. It had long been assumed

Callimachus would have that honor. "Perhaps some twisted justice has come from these shameful events after all."

"Well." Herodas rolled his eyes. "I suppose we'll never know the truth of it. But one thing is clear: I'm more convinced than ever that the only sane course in Alexandria is to steer clear of politics all together."

Asclepiades groaned with disgust. "A cowardly attitude, but one we all share. We make no difference in the world, Herodas. All our art and study amount to a grand triviality. The great men of former days would hold us in scorn. We are exactly as that man Timon described us: 'Fatted fowls squabbling in the chicken coop of the Muses.'"

The two poets regarded each other glumly for several quiet moments. Finally, Asclepiades roused himself.

"Help me up, will you my friend?" He grunted as Herodas assisted him to stand. "I mustn't be *too* late for that seminar."

With a heavy heart, Herodas watched as the elder poet climbed the steps of the renowned institution and disappeared within the portico.

In the cool hour before sunrise, Korax stood on the rear deck and gazed at the dim, silvery sea. Low hills loomed, rough and black in the distance. The ship had anchored for the night off the southern coast of Anatolia. Overhead, the last stars were fading.

For 42 days the freighter had made a slow voyage along the coasts of Egypt and Syria, stopping to deliver goods at Sidon and Tyre, waiting a week for a whole new cargo at the port of Berytus. Ten or 15 days more would bring them to Rhodes.

Since that night in Naukratis when he first spoke with Athene, memories of his last days in Rhodos had come to Korax—long-repressed fragments rising to the surface like drowned corpses. He recalled lying in bed after his grievous injury, his mother healing him, pouring her very life-force into his body. When he was only partially recovered, his father had placed him on a ship bound for Thrace, to stay with his mother's people. That ship, he believed, had been taken by pirates, and subsequently he had been sold as a slave. Many points remained unclear, the memories dim or nonexistent—many questions he hoped to answer in Rhodes.

The sun peeked over the horizon, spilling orange light on the water. Sailors were moving about on the deck now, preparing to get underway.

"There you are, Blackbird." Leukon approached, carrying a wax tablet that looked tiny in his large hand. "It's light enough, and I am ready to resume my lessons." During the voyage, Korax had been teaching the Celt to read and write in Greek. The man's intelligence and nimble mind were impressive.

"I will be down shortly," he said.

With a twitch of his mustache, Leukon glanced at the sunrise, then scanned the horizons all around, as if wondering what Korax could possibly find more interesting than instructing him. "Very well," he answered with a shrug.

Korax watched as the man loped down the steps to the main deck. He felt lucky to have the Celt, both as bodyguard and companion. Not much else remained from his time in Alexandria—garments and trinkets, some scrolls, a sword, a lyre. Little enough to show for three years of his life. He had lost Kalyssa, his great love, left Miriam and his other friends behind.

But at least he had set things right in the kingdom, saved Ptolemy from Arsinoe's plot, re-established the course of Maat. Amasis, his Egyptian master, would be pleased.

Sunlight glittered now on the water. Sailors called out and heaved to raise the anchor.

In his folly, he had lost Hermes as his magical ally. But he had found Athene to guide him, and the power of Helios still burned in his blood.

Korax resolved to make offerings to all three deities, at their temples in Rhodos.

# Afterword

Alexandria in the 3rd Century BCE was a crossroads of learning and culture, a cosmopolitan center such as the world had not seen before. While this is a work of fiction, the story takes place against a backdrop of real people and events.

The political balance of power that Ptolemy reflects upon in Chapter Ten is accurate as of 271 BCE. In the west, the rivalry between Carthage and Rome as presented by Manolis in Chapter Fourteen is also historically correct. The First Punic War would begin in 264 BCE, with Carthage utterly destroyed a century later.

The Alexandrian poets, scholars, engineers, and scientists are represented according to surviving evidence. The rivalry between Callimachus and Apollonius is based on an account in scholar Peter Green's monumental and very entertaining book, *Alexander to Actium*.

The importing of Celtic mercenaries into Egypt and their subsequent mutiny is also based on history, although the likely date of the events has been altered for the purposes of this fiction.

Arsinoe's fascinating story as related in Chapter Twenty-Five is also mostly true. She married her brother Ptolemy II and reigned with him as co-pharaoh for a number of years. Arsinoe died between 270 and 268 BCE. Her temple in Alexandria was completed, and her cult flourished thereafter. The notion of her being executed for plotting to assassinate her brother is pure invention.

§

*The Lights of Alexandria* is the second book of the *Conjurer of Rhodes* series. As of this writing, the titles are:

Book 1- *The Mazes of Magic*

Book 2 - *The Lights of Alexandria*

Book 3 - *The Treasure of the Sun God*

I am very grateful to my beta readers, John W. Kelly, Richard Fisher, Scott Corwin, David Wilson, and Marilyn Massa. Thanks also to my erudite editor Jaime Henriquez, and talented cover designer, Mirna Gilman of BooksGoSocial.

If you enjoyed this story, please consider leaving a rating and review on Amazon, as well as other sites. The algorithms of the publishing business make this extremely important to a book's success.

I love hearing from readers. You can connect with me at:

Web: triskelionbooks.com or jackmassa.com

Facebook: www.facebook.com/AuthorJackMassa/

X/Twitter: @JackMassa2

www.ingramcontent.com/pod-product-compliance
Lightning Source LLC
Chambersburg PA
CBHW020619260626
47157CB00003B/1082